KING'S CAPTIVE

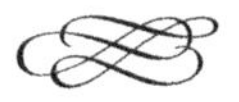

PIPER STONE

Published by Stormy Night Publications and Design, LLC.
www.StormyNightPublications.com

Stone, Piper
King's Captive

Cover Design by Korey Mae Johnson
Images by Depositphotos/Tverdohlib.com, Depositphotos/Vecster, and Shutterstock/Sean Pavone

This book is intended for *adults only*. Spanking and other sexual activities represented in this book are fantasies only, intended for adults.

CHAPTER 1

ristiano

"Revenge is an act of passion; vengeance of justice."

Samuel Johnson

Vengeance.

I wasn't a just man. In fact, the majority of those who knew me considered me evil, a monster, commanding the streets of New Orleans with an iron fist. I controlled by ensuring an understanding of my family's power, using threats to handle business so violence was rarely needed.

Unfortunately, there were those who'd crossed a line, something that could no longer be tolerated.

I took a deep breath, enjoying the unexpected freedom, prepared to retake my command of the King fortune.

However, there were actions that required consequences, and I would provide them. I dragged my tongue across my lips, hungry to move forward, the future brighter than ever.

Even if blood flowed in the streets.

Power was something that I excelled in creating for my family, even though the way we'd garnered such significant influence was considered… controversial. I laughed at the notion. The King family reeked of power as well as wealth, our kingdom built decades before.

However, our gilded crowns had become tarnished. That would no longer be tolerated.

I was heir to a throne, first-born son of Sylvester King, a man feared by every person living within the city of New Orleans as well as beyond. Considered one of the most notorious crime syndicates in the United States, our kingdom had allowed us good fortune over our decades of maintaining tight reins.

There were some who said that wealth had a requirement of hard work. With regard to our family, the reality was a product of certain unsavory practices, ones considered monstrous by most people. Building an empire was something else entirely.

That had taken stamina and fortitude, often paying a hefty price for living behind a steel-plated shield.

I'd allowed a crack in the armor, and paid the price, but at least I'd protected my family.

Now there would be hell to pay for my penance.

The humidity was thick, enough so that even taking a deep breath felt suffocating, yet a smirk crossed my face as I adjusted the cuffs on my sleeves. I continued to stare into the sky, enjoying the string of vibrant colors dancing across the horizon. A storm was brewing, the tumultuous clouds creating an ominous setting over the dilapidated parking lot, the brisk breeze shifting the stench of garbage over the parade of reporters who'd ventured all the way to the Louisiana State Penitentiary.

I chuckled as several of them coughed, still pressing closer in order to obtain the perfect picture, perhaps a caption on the nightly news.

"Mr. King. What's it like to be out of prison?"

"Mr. King. What are your plans now that you're released?"

"Mr. King. What do you have to say to the family of the man you murdered in cold blood?"

"Cristiano. What do you have to say regarding the accusations that your early release was due to money exchanging hands? Given there was a mistrial, do you expect to be tried again?" The male reporter had a smirk on his face, the familial name meant to goad me into doing something stupid.

I walked close enough that I was able to look him directly in the eyes, remaining unblinking.

"*Ubiraysya proch' prisoski,*" Dimitri growled, my Capo shifting into his protective mode. He issued a series of actual barks after tossing out the nasty sentiment. Then he lurched in front of me, flexing his muscles, his six foot four inch two hundred plus pound frame terrifying at least half the crowd.

Three of the reporters glared at the oppressive, dangerous-looking tattooed blond with fear in their eyes; however, the asshole male wasn't one of them. I'd be curious to find out his name.

I pushed Dimitri back casually, giving him a heated look, keeping my voice low. "While I want the freaking lot of them to get the fuck away as well, I don't think calling them cocksuckers will help in that endeavor."

"Yeah? Well, the motherfuckers deserve worse. We need to get you the fuck out of here," Dimitri growled, his gruff voice exactly as I'd remembered. He knew better than to attempt to maneuver me in any manner, his years of training in handling my mood swings allowing him a position of authority.

And tonight, I was pissed as fuck.

I shot a cold stare to the closest female reporter, allowing her to catch the stark look of rage only shown in my eyes. She seemed startled, her hands shaking and her lovely mouth twisting. When she slowly lowered her microphone, taking a step back, I resisted the urge to smile.

Toying with them wasn't in my best interest, but I'd never been a man to follow anyone's rules, including the staunch requirements laid out by my father years before. After all, I was a brutal man, a ruthless killer, at least according to the very reporters standing in front of me like lambs awaiting their slaughter.

I gave the reporter a lust-filled look, allowing my gaze to travel all the way down to her patent leather pumps, chuckling under my breath as I dragged my tongue across my lips. The ragged breath escaping her mouth was a delicious reward, although only slightly enticing the hunger that had been placed on lockdown for far too long.

"Yeah. I'm ready for a stiff drink and a hot shower." I was sure my father wouldn't be impressed with the photographs that would appear on the front page of the local news.

"Don't blame you. Shithole of a place."

My Capo had been incarcerated in his native homeland for three years, the time spent doing hard labor. While the penitentiary I'd been forced to endure was considered maximum security, it was a posh hotel in comparison to the hell he'd been forced to face. They say prison hardened a man. He was like stone, ice running through his veins. That's why we got along so well.

Turning sharply, I walked toward the SUV, the driver scrambling to open the rear door. As I settled inside, I took one last look at the electrified barbed wire fence surrounding the prison, remaining quiet as Dimitri settled into the seat beside me. Tonight would be just the beginning of a new chapter of the King family.

But first, I would exact my vengeance.

"We'll be back in New Orleans in a couple hours," Dimitri said quietly before handing me a satchel.

I didn't need to bother peering inside, the hefty weight of the duffle indicating a variety of weapons. Dimitri knew exactly what I preferred, including my favorite Beretta.

"I made certain your house was in order. I had the cleaning staff pick up a few things as well. They damn well better have gotten everything you preferred or there will hell to pay," he added.

"I assume you brought the information I requested," I stated as I poured a tumbler of scotch, lifting the crystal glass into the dim light, prepared to savor the rich flavor. Dimitri knew better than to cross me, my ruthless Russian Capo one of the few men I trusted with my life. He also had an innate understanding of my tastes.

He slid a file across the seat, not bothering to glance in my direction.

I'd spent eight months wallowing in a prison cell, treated like a fucking animal. The time had allowed me reflection, especially with regard to the assholes who'd betrayed me.

I took a sip of my drink before even glancing at the file. Only when I'd settled back into my seat did I bother to inspect the contents. The information was exactly as I'd suspected, details highlighting the little prick who'd sold me out to the Feds.

"I assume you know where Ricardo lives, his current place of employment," I said casually as I swirled the glass, studying the snitch's scarred face, my grip tightening around the glass.

"Of course. Shithole down in the French Quarter. Some greasy Italian joint," Dimitri stated, grumbling under his breath. "I should have taken the motherfucker out when I had the chance."

"And deny me of the pleasure?" I chortled.

"Yeah, well, he's been enjoying a damn good life," he railed.

That was about to change. Sighing, I took another sip, filtering through the remaining information. The asshole would soon face my wrath. "And the other item I asked you to look into?"

When he remained silent, I slowly turned my head in his direction.

After a few seconds, Dimitri jerked another file into his hands, his grip firm. "Are you certain you want to do this? I know it's not my place to ask, but you know the Feds are likely expecting retaliation. I mean, this is a federal witness."

As if I gave a shit.

I resisted the rage that had remained pooling deep inside me since the ridiculous hoax of a trial. Even though his tone reeked of insolence, I was also aware of his well-conditioned concern. Someone had used me as a scapegoat and that someone was going to face the barrel of my gun. While the asshole witnessing my handling of business wasn't out of the ordinary, the fact I'd even been arrested meant there was a breakdown in our affairs of state.

The King family owned at least half the police department, and a good number of attorneys and judges. They'd remained loyal through the years and in return, we offered them not only protection when needed but a certain portion of our wealth for their extended… favors. The fact we'd been betrayed meant someone was prepared to enter into our kingdom, attempting to take us down.

My family believed they knew the identity of the assholes behind the ploy. I remained uncertain and refused to start a war based on innuendoes.

The members of the Azzurri crime syndicate, a second mafia family who'd taken residence in our city only twenty years before, were ruthless bastards. However, they'd never attempted something this intricate, their soldiers little more than barbarians who'd eat their young if necessary. This had been something entirely different. I found it difficult to believe they'd dare come after us in such an egregious manner.

However, I would find out.

My arrest and subsequent incarceration had tarnished the King family, hindering not only our business activities but also my family's way of life. I'd been kept apprised of the situation even while behind bars, but there'd been no overtures made by anyone in our family. They'd been too concerned my life would be threatened.

And it had been more than once.

Various enemies had managed to take advantages given our family's tainted reputation. That would never happen again, retaliation necessary. However, to my knowledge, the Azzurris had remained under the radar.

He sighed then slid the file across the seat, appearing more uncomfortable than before. I pulled it into my hands, fingering the edge before turning the flap, a glossy photograph positioned on top. The picture was a surprise, the face peering back at me completely unexpected.

"You are well aware of what's at stake, Dimitri. No one will ever attempt to destroy my family again. No one. This is just the start." As I stared at the photograph Dimitri had captured, I was thrown, a rapid fire of electricity shooting through my veins. Every nerve stood on end, my cock twitching, my balls tightening. Surprised at my body's reaction, I took another gulp of scotch as I traced my finger across the witness's face.

For a few seconds, I was shoved into a vacuum, the face appearing far too angelic and surreal. How the hell was this even possible? The find didn't smell right.

Hunger reared its ugly head, the kind of blatant and sadistic desire that tossed my mind into the vilest places. I took a deep breath as I read over the limited information, finally smiling as various delicious but filthy thoughts filtered into my mind.

Yes, the discovery of the mystery witness changed my course of plans. Perhaps I would enjoy this even more.

While my mother would voice the phrase, 'vengeance is mine, sayeth the Lord,' I would have my revenge in every manner that I desired.

After closing the file, I took a deep breath. "A change in the schedule for tonight, Dimitri." As I thought about what I was about to do, my cock stirred for the first time in months, desire racing into every cell.

The darkness swelling within me refused to be denied.

I was in the mood to go hunting.

Soon the beautiful witness would learn that every action had a consequence, especially when crossing a member of the King family.

I would capture her.

Keep her.

Punish her.

Use her.

Then break her.

And that was just the beginning.

CHAPTER 2

*mily*

"Innocence is the weakest defense. Innocence has a single voice that can only say over and over again, I didn't do it. Guilt has a thousand voices, all of them lies."

Leonard F. Peltier

Exhaustion settled into every muscle, hovering over me like a thick blanket. I could still hear the rumble of thunder as a backdrop of the torrent of rain pummeling against the roof.

I shivered as I stepped into the shower, wishing the blaring television had the ability to drown out the noise. I'd grown to loathe storms, especially when they happened at night.

I closed the shower curtain, leaning against the tile as the stream of hot water cascaded over my aching body. It had been one hell of a week, the sixty-plus hours feeling more like a hundred. Shuddering, I remained chilled to the bone even though the stickiness of the recent heatwave challenged the aging air-conditioning unit. Thank God I had the weekend off, in which I planned doing nothing more than hunkering down on the couch, watching every rom-com in my movie collection.

And maybe indulging in copious amounts of wine.

A ragged chuckle left my mouth as I reached for the soap. My bestie's ugly words regarding getting a life remaining in my mind. While I knew she was right, I wasn't into the bar scene or even catching dinner with friends, at least not like a woman of my age should be. I blamed it on my work schedule but deep down inside, I knew the truth.

Fear.

When I heard the sound of my cellphone ringing, I groaned. If my boss was asking me to work tomorrow, I was determined to tell him no.

Like you've done the dozen times before?

I yanked the scrubby ball from the hook, squeezing a huge amount of soap onto the netting. After a few seconds, the phone stopped ringing. Whoever was on the other end could leave me a message. Maybe I'd turn the phone off for the entire two days. Finally, a smile crossed my face.

I tried to hum, jumping when I heard another boom of thunder. Jesus.

"Goddamn it." The phone was ringing again. What the hell? It had to be Friday night telemarketers.

When the second call turned into a third, I'd had enough, prepared to say a few nasty words to whoever was on the other end of the line. I yanked a towel from the bar, leaving the water running then yanking the phone from the counter.

Julia.

Great.

My bestie was going to nag me about going out. Again. "Stop it. I can't go out tonight. Okay? I'm too tired."

"No. That's not it," Julia huffed, her voice shaking. "Didn't the prosecuting attorney call you?"

"No. Why? What's wrong?" I struggled to secure the towel around my body as I juggled with the phone.

"You gotta… Fuck. Fuck! Do you have your television on?"

"Yeah, but only in the background. Why?" I'd never heard her this way.

"I'm sorry, Em, I really am. Oh, God."

The tone in her voice was enough to fill my stomach with butterflies. "What are you talking about?"

"Go look at your television. Just go. Now."

I hesitated before turning off the water and walking into my darkened bedroom. As I stared at the screen, the horror of what was unfolding sent a wave of terror skating down my spine.

"I need to go," I managed, my body swaying.

"Are you okay? Do you want me to come over?"

"Na… No," I whispered. "I'll call you later." I ended the call and almost dropped the phone before I was able to slide it onto my dresser. My vision was foggy, my heart racing. How could this kind of thing happen?

Danger. Danger. Danger.

"No." It wasn't possible. There had to be a mistake. He was supposed to remain behind bars for at least ten years. Ten.

"This just into the newsroom. Cristiano King, son of the notorious mob boss, Sylvester King, has been released from the Louisiana State Penitentiary where he was serving a ten-year term for second degree murder and extortion. While the information is yet to be confirmed, our sources indicate his early release was due to mistakes made by the prosecution. While there is some question as to whether he will be retried, that will depend on the original judge in the case."

As a photograph of Cristiano flashed across the screen, my heart rose into my throat. Everything about the man terrified me. His angular jaw. His powerful stance. The way he commanded a room when he entered. The gruffness of his seductive voice, the tone leaving me wet and hot all over. Even though I'd been lucky enough to testify behind a screen, his deep baritone had remained with me long after the trial.

But mostly his dark, cold stare, as if the man had no soul, was something I'd never forget. His gaze had penetrated my dreams almost every night.

His eyes were so deep blue that even from the picture, I could swear he was staring right through the screen, a predator hungry to feast on his prey.

The monster had been freed. Free to walk the streets. Free to return to his normal life. Free to put the past behind him.

And I'd live in the nightmare all over again.

Boom!

Another rumble of thunder only added to the jitters, goosebumps trickling over every inch of skin.

Click!

When the television shut off, I yelped, backing away from the screen.

"Hello, Emily." This time his voice was nothing more than a dark growl.

One of hunger.

One of rage.

And one of possession.

Cristiano.

"What… How did you…" Unable to finish the sentence, I swallowed hard, trying to think about an escape route. I dared to look in his direction; the bathroom light created a slight glow over him. He'd reclined in the tattered chair I'd purchased from a thrift shop, the remote in his hand, but I could swear I was able to notice a glint of steel from a weapon. I was able to see the curve of his angular jaw, his voluptuous lips and his long fingers. He was gorgeous, dangerous, and the single man I feared.

"If you're asking how I found out who you are, I assure you that there isn't a form of law enforcement that can keep me from learning what I want to know."

I folded my arms across my chest, shivering, the realization that even if I screamed, no one would be able to hear me creating a rapid wave of terror.

Leaning forward, he placed the remote on the bedside table before rising to his feet, his actions forcing a whimper to escape my mouth.

"You've been a very bad girl, Emily, but you already know that, don't you?" He crossed the room within seconds, gripping both my wrists and dragging me against the heat of his body. He was so strong and much taller than I'd envisioned, his chiseled cheekbones and high forehead only adding to his dangerous appearance.

"No. No! Let go of me."

"Hmmm… Not until I'm finished with you. What you might not have realized, sweet, precious Emily, is that no one crosses either myself or my family without paying a significant price."

The man was going to kill me for testifying against him. I'd been the reason he'd gone to prison. Neither his parade of expensive attorneys nor the threats he'd likely used against other witnesses had saved him from the prosecution's best weapon. Me. The sole witness. The single person who'd given details regarding the vicious crime I'd seen, the wretched violence and blood remaining permanent images in the back of my mind.

Me.

The girl who'd been promised anonymity for the rest of her life.

Me.

The woman who'd fought against the devil and lost.

Now he was going to make me pay.

Inhaling, he tilted his head back and forth, his eyes sparkling in the dim lighting. My God, the scent of him reeked of exotic spices and cedar wood, the fragrance entirely too intoxicating. I was thrown by the haze forming around my eyes as I was forced to stare into his. The same frigid cold, soulless cavern peered back at me but this time, his gaze was filled with something else.

Burning desire.

"Your penance begins now." Ripping my arms over my head, he positioned a single hand around both wrists before jerking the towel away.

I'd never felt so vulnerable, scared to death about what he was going to do. When he backed toward the bed, easing down and yanking me over his lap, my mind began to shut down. I was lost to the fear, my heart hammering to the point the thudding sounds echoed in my ears. Was he going to… no. No! I had to fight him. I refused to become another victim.

The second I began to struggle in his hold, he brought his hand down against my bottom with enough ferocity I was stunned. Pain skittered down the insides of my legs, creating a wave of nausea. This wasn't happening. This couldn't be possible.

Cristiano smashed his hand down again, delivering several brutal smacks in a row. My stomach twisted and I managed to pitch my body forward and backward, realizing in horror that his cock was hard as a rock. He was enjoying this. When I was almost able to roll my hips off his lap, he released my wrists, fisting my hair instead.

"That's not very nice, Emily. I don't think you want to cross me any further."

I hated the way he said my name, the syllables far too seductive. He was spanking me. I was in some kind of shock, my tone turning into pleading. "Please, just let me go."

He laughed, the sound subtle yet even more provocative. "That's not going to happen." He continued the spanking, bringing his hand down in rapid motions, moving from one side of my bottom to the other.

I bit back my whimpers, refusing to allow him the satisfaction of hearing me cry. The anguish was excruciating, and stars floated in front of my eyes, tears of frustration and fear not far behind. *I'm going to die.* The thought rolled through my mind as his actions became rougher, the sound of his palm striking against my ass cheeks floating into the room.

My imagination was getting the better of me, the graphic visions stealing my breath.

When he caressed my skin, rolling the tips of his fingers up and down my heated ass cheeks, I threw my arm behind me in some crazy attempt to stop him.

He wrenched it against my back, his fingers digging into my wrist.

"I can tell you're going to need to be taught a much stricter lesson. All in good time." He slid his fingers across my seared flesh then down the crack of my ass to my wetness.

"No!" I struggled as hard as I could, my actions only allowing me to grind against his legs and the bulge between them. My entire body ached, and I was shocked and humiliated that my nipples had hardened. Fuck. Fuck. I couldn't be aroused.

As he dipped the tips of his fingers past my swollen folds, I let off a series of moans.

"You're very wet, sweet Emily."

"Fuck you."

The spanking began again in earnest, the strikes long and hard. My pulse in my throat, all I could do was close my eyes and pray this would be over soon.

Cristiano pushed his hand between my legs again, this time rolling a single finger around my clit several times before thrusting it into my pussy. "You will learn respect as well as absolute obedience. I won't accept anything less. Do you understand me?"

"You're insane. You're just going to kill me. Just get it over with."

"If I wanted to kill you, you'd be dead already. Death would be too easy for your betrayal."

My betrayal? Was the bastard kidding? I'd done my civic duty, keeping a monster off the streets.

"You're a horrible person." Tears finally flowed, blurring my vision and stinging my cheeks.

"You're right in that account, but from here on out, I'm your master, the man who will determine your fate. But only if you learn to be a very good little girl." He thrust several of his fingers deep inside, flexing them open as he drove them in hard and deep. Every touch was invasive, deliberate. With every plunge of his fingers, he dragged me toward a climax.

My breathing stopped short, my mind refusing to accept what was happening to me.

I was incensed by his words as well as the way my body responded to him. That was the only betrayal. I was sopping wet, aching for him to continue touching me, furious that I couldn't control my reactions.

The bastard released the same damn chuckle, dark and devious yet ripped with the most intensely sultry tone I'd ever heard. I'd been warned about him by the prosecuting attorney, the police, and my best friend. Hell, even my boss had told me the asshole was brutal, capable of killing anyone who got in his way. He certainly wouldn't care about adding someone who'd sent him to prison to the list. I might as well go out fighting.

Bucking hard, I managed to dump myself off his lap, immediately scrambling on my hands and knees in the darkness, trying to reach the safety of the bathroom. I heard his deep sigh seconds before he yanked me by my hair, jerking me against his massive chest. He held me in place for a few seconds before dragging me back to the bed and shoving me onto my hands and knees.

I was out of breath, paralyzed with fear. There was no way I was getting away from him.

"You're a little fighter. I'm going to break you of that, but first things first."

"What the hell does that mean?" I barked, although I knew exactly what his nasty intentions were. I looked over my shoulder, watching as he took his time removing a weapon, placing his gun carefully on the chairside table. As soon as he took two steps away, I lunged forward, almost managing to wrap my hand around the gun.

His hand was around my throat before my fingers were able to touch the cold steel, digging in as he slowly pulled me backward. "That wasn't a good idea, Emily."

Barely able to breathe, I blinked furiously, shivering to my core. He was going to snap my neck. When I was back in position, he removed his hand, patting my bottom then yanking me until my feet were dangling off the bed.

"To answer your question, I'm going to fuck you, sweet Emily, which is exactly what you desire. Isn't it?"

"No. Hell, no!" I clawed at the comforter, using all my strength to kick him, finally able to connect my foot against his stomach.

"That's going to cost you." He brought his hand down several times against my bottom, only adding fuel to my rage.

The pull on my hair was just as painful as the spanking. Within seconds, I was exhausted, panting, aching all over as a wave of electricity shot straight into my core. He stroked his fingers along the seam of my pussy, every move utter perfection, arousing me even more. The man knew exactly what he was doing to me. When he thrust them inside again, I realized I was bucking against his hand involuntarily, driving the long digits as deep inside as possible.

I was sick and embarrassed, horrified and breathless.

"Oh. Oh. Oh." The guttural sounds from my throat were almost unrecognizable. This wasn't me. This had to be a horrible nightmare.

But when I heard the sound of the bastard unzipping his expensive trousers, I sucked in and held my breath, another round of lights pulsing in front of my face.

"I can provide extreme anguish or exquisite ecstasy. The choice is entirely up to you. If you're a good girl and obey me, you'll get exactly what you crave. If you fight me on any level, then the punishment you receive is going to be something you remember for a very long time. Do I make myself clear?"

I couldn't answer him. I had no words, no ability to make any additional sounds. I was lost in a surreal moment, wishing I'd never said a single word to the police, praying I could wake up on that dark and rainy night moments before I'd left the office in search of Italian food.

"Answer me, Emily," he growled.

"Yes. I understand." The perfunctory tone of my voice startled me.

"Good girl," he said in a subdued voice, as if using the softer tone to try to comfort me, to sway me into thinking he wasn't a monster.

But I knew better.

I'd heard all the stories about his family's powerful hold on New Orleans, their wealth and influence just as dangerous as the weapons their soldiers wielded against their enemies. I knew what he was capable of, the horrors he'd inflicted. I also knew of his dark desires, a sadistic man refusing to take no for an answer.

He'd hunted his prey.

Now he was going to cage and use me for his personal pleasure.

And there was nothing I could do about it.

The moment I felt his cock slicing back and forth across my bruised bottom, I stiffened, fisting the covers.

"Relax, precious one. I'm giving you exactly what you need." He purred the words, driving me into a state of desire unlike anything I'd ever known. I'd never been taken so forcefully, disciplined as if I was a bad little girl. The concept took my breath away, leaving me weak and anxious yet a sickening level of excitement continued to build. The scent of my arousal made me sick to my stomach.

Fuck you. Fuck you. Fuck you. The words rolled in my mind over and over again, as if they had the ability to keep me sane.

He kicked my legs apart then pressed the tip of his cock against my slickened folds. "Relax and push back for me. Take my cock like a good little girl."

Obey him. The thought was disgusting but the softness of his voice enveloped me like a blanket, soothing and enticing me into submitting. Maybe if I did, I could finally get away from him. Maybe.

No. No. No! He was never going to let me go.

As he pressed his cockhead past my swollen folds, my body acted entirely on its own, pushing against him. A warm, almost dizzying series of sensations washed over me, shooting straight into my aching pussy. Nothing was going to stop him from taking what he wanted.

He was huge, my muscles struggling to accept the thickness. I was stretched wide open, involuntary moans rushing up from my throat.

"Uh. Uh." My pants were primal, my starved-for-attention body and mind yanking the brazen woman from the dark catacombs of my being.

He thrust the entire length inside, digging his fingers into my skin. His husky growls were cries of satisfaction, his breath just as ragged as mine. "You're tight. So fucking tight."

Every part of me was on fire, my hunger almost as desperate as his. I was crazed from what was happening, unable to process his actions.

Or my body's intense explosion of sensations.

I could tell just how wet I was, my juice trickling down both legs. Horrified, I smacked at the bed, groaning like a crazed animal. When he pulled out, slamming into me again, I couldn't fight the gasps coming from my throat.

"That's it. Take all of me. Every fucking inch." He pummeled into me, the force used rocking the bed. He kept his hand tangled in my hair, holding me in place, as if there was any possibility of escaping. I was his prisoner.

Time seemed to stand still as he fucked me, the monster growling as he ravaged my body. I did everything I could to shut down, but it was no use. Tingling all over, only seconds later, I could feel an orgasm threatening to make the final betrayal, taking me to a place of bliss.

I gasped for air, my moans scattered. And I lost it, the climax rushing up from my toes, slamming into my system with such ferocity I could no longer see.

"Oh. Oh. Oh!"

The same dark chuckle sounded behind me as he fucked me long and hard, filling me completely.

"Such a little tease," he growled, finally releasing his hold on my hair, gripping my hips as he powered into me, yanking me back with every brutal stroke.

I dropped my head, my body nothing but a ragdoll as he thrust harder and faster. I wanted this over with. My muscles continued to clamp and release, another orgasm forcing me to throw my head back, the scream soundless, my body shaking violently.

"Fuck. Yes. Yes," he roared.

As he erupted deep inside, filling me with his seed, another tear slipped from the corner of my eye.

"Why are you doing this?" I whispered.

"Why? You really need to ask me?" He leaned over, curling his body around mine and whispering in my ear. "You fucked with the wrong man, Emily. You see, I take what I want. Now you belong to me."

CHAPTER 3

ristiano

Violence.

I'd always taken everything I'd wanted without hesitation. She'd been no different. The feel of being inside her tight pussy had been a clear reminder of everything I'd missed for far too long. The irony that she was the person responsible for sending me to prison had dragged the primal beast from his lair.

Fucking her had been cathartic, a sweet moment of revenge, but I wanted more.

Required more.

I wanted to feel her pert little mouth wrapped around my cock, sucking as I tangled my fingers in her long strands of hair. I craved sliding my cock into her tight asshole, stripping her of any belief that I was anything other than a monster.

There was some quiet innocence about her, perhaps because she was conservative in her dress, only a hint of makeup covering up her fair complexion. Even in the picture, her silky blonde hair had been worn in a tight bun, as if attempting to hide her beauty. The women I'd been used to had been hardened by status and wealth, well-coiffed, their bodies sculpted by private trainers. While they'd been tasty arm candy, they'd also been devoid of any substance.

This woman was entirely different; a fawn on a spring day, her wide eyes taking in every aspect of her surroundings with awe.

She still had no idea what I was capable of, but she would learn soon enough. I'd fuck her in every hole, break her down to the point that she'd beg me for my touch. After that?

Hell, I wasn't certain.

If I had any decency inside of me, I'd feel guilty for destroying her life, but that simply wasn't the case.

I was a bad man. No sense in trying to deny what came naturally to me.

My initial intentions had been to force the witness to disappear. Of course, there would have been questions, but I'd already worked that portion of the plan out in my mind. My decision was dangerous, perhaps unhinged, but I felt I was due a treat.

I studied her in the darkness, her long blonde hair spilling out over the mangled comforter. She was more diligent in her resolve to escape than I had envisioned, which kept my cock aching and my balls tight. I'd expected her to whimper, cowering like the majority of other assholes who dared to cross me. This girl was entirely different, her will to live creating a spark deep within me.

After taking a deep breath, I fastened my pants, running both hands through my hair before removing my weapon from the table. By my own requirements, I should merely have Dimitri dump her body in a location that would never be found. However, she'd awakened more than the monstrous beast inside of me, hunger remaining just at the surface. Maybe I was crossing a line, but I no longer cared. Spending time in prison had changed my… perspective. Maybe I was even harder than before. Who the fuck knew?

Whatever the case, she now belonged to me, a captured bird I'd keep in a gilded cage.

I laughed softly to myself as I wrapped my hand around her long strands, yanking her to a standing position. She was quivering, her mouth twisting from terrified anticipation of what I was going to do next.

Shifting my gaze, my eyes locked onto her phone. Whoever had called alerting her would be the initial problem to deal with. I dragged her with me as I yanked the phone off the dresser, eyeing the screen. "Now, here's how we're going to do this. You're going to call your friend back. What's her name?"

Grimacing, she was able to shake her head even with my tight hold.

I yanked on her hair, forcing her into a strangling arc. "I suggest you learn that when I ask you a question, you will answer. When I issue an order, you will do so without hesitation. What. Is. Her. Name?"

"Julia. Okay? Don't hurt her."

"I have no intentions of hurting her. That is unless you disobey me. You're going to call Julia and you're going to let her know that you were advised to get out of town for a few days and that you'll call her when you can. Is that something you can do for me, Emily?"

She swallowed hard, her lower lip twitching. "Yes. Yes, I can."

"Good girl. Now, go ahead." I eased my hand away from her hair, prepared for her to fight me. She shifted her gaze toward the phone and reached out tentatively.

I jerked it away and lowered my head. "If you fuck with me or try and signal her, I will be forced to make your friend disappear."

"Such a bastard." She snagged it out of my hand, punching in her security code as she glared at me.

"Speaker phone."

She rolled her eyes but pressed a button.

After I heard the girl's voice from the other end, I pressed one finger over my lips as a reminder.

"Hey, Julia. Um, I think it's best that I get out of town for a few days."

"Whew. Yes, I think you're right. Did you call that asshole of a prosecutor?"

Emily huffed, her reaction quite natural. I was surprised she was as good an actress as she was. "He is an asshole for not telling me such a horrible freak was going to be let out of prison early, and I did. He was the one who suggested I get out of town." She gave me a satisfied look.

"That's good. Where are you going?"

"I don't think it's a good idea to tell you over the phone, but it's a safe place."

Her friend hesitated then laughed nervously. "Yeah, I guess that makes sense. You will call me though, right?"

"Of course. Absolutely," Emily stated with a little more defiance than she should have given her greatest enemy was likely hunting her down.

"Good. You're taking this a lot better than I would have expected."

Laughing softly, she dragged her tongue across her lips provocatively. "I have to."

"O-kay, girl. Just be safe."

"I… will."

I took the phone out of her hand, ending the call, then catching Julia's last name. "You did very well."

"Whatever."

My cock stirred all over again. The woman's chutzpa was damn unusual. It was obvious she either didn't understand or didn't care about the amount of danger she was in.

I slipped her phone into my pocket. It might come in handy at some point.

"You have two minutes to dress. Then we are leaving. If you attempt to fight me or scream, that will be the last thing you do on this earth," I said almost in passing. I knew from her file that she wouldn't be reported missing until Monday at the earliest. By then, there would no way anyone could find her. "Do you understand me, Emily?" Her hesitation pissed me off more than I cared to say. She seemed either oblivious or unconcerned that I had her life in my hands.

"Fine. I hear you. Where are we going?" she asked, her tone just as defiant as before. Another intriguing aspect about the lovely girl. I'd been impressed she'd gone for the gun, as if she had even a slim chance of being able to use it.

"To a secure location."

"Why?" She turned sharply, glaring me in the eye. Her cheeks were wet, a single tear remaining on her cheek.

Unable to resist, I rolled my thumb through the salty bead, collecting it on the tip of my finger. When I pulled it into my mouth, she pursed her lips, an expression of disgust riding her face.

"Because I own you, Emily. I'm going to enjoy breaking you. Two minutes."

She started to take a step away then stopped short. "No man, especially a vile, horrible creature like you will break me. Fuck you."

As she walked quickly toward her closet, I had to smile. I would enjoy every aspect of using her, taking her in every way I desired. And yes, she would be broken.

For I was a sadistic man.

When she cradled the clothing she'd selected and walked into the bathroom, slamming the door, I inched into her closet, turning on the light. The girl certainly lived modestly from her small house to her selection of attire. Perhaps the asshole she worked for wasn't paying her enough.

It certainly hadn't been enough for her level of betrayal.

Smirking, I yanked one of her silk scarves from a hanger, pulling the slick material under my nose. Her scent still covered the thin material; the fragrance was just as evocative as the woman herself, a mixture of exotic spices and just a hint of musk. This would suit my needs for the time being.

When I found the door locked, my cock stirred, pushing against my zipper. I didn't bother knocking, merely took a step away and kicked the door in.

Emily's yelp was my reward, her look of horror a reminder of what she'd done to my life. Her unbridled training was just beginning.

"You should know better than to try and keep me from you."

I yanked her arm, pulling her in front of the mirror and crushing her against the counter, immediately shifting the scarf over her head. When I wrapped it around her neck, twisting the material, her eyes opened wide.

Exhaling, I allowed the hot breath to cascade across her face as I dragged her against me, keeping the silk tight. "I don't think you understand the seriousness of the situation you're in."

She opened her mouth, a few strangled sounds mixing with her scattered breathing, several moans giving her desire away.

"I can smell your arousal," I whispered, the scent intoxicating as hell.

I glared at our combined reflection in the mirror, angry with myself even though the girl deserved every second of punishment that I'd given her.

Her mouth closed, her hands dropping, but not out of acquiescence. She was still rebellious as hell. I wanted to burst into laughter. The audacity of the woman to think that kind of behavior would work on me, perhaps soften me, was ridiculous.

I snorted as I pressed my lips against her heated skin, using my other hand to roll it down her arm. "You are truly a beautiful woman, Emily."

Goddamn, I was aroused by her tenacity and refusal to accept her predicament. I backed off on the strangle hold, still keeping the scarf in place.

She coughed, although she did everything in her power not to react, enough so tears of frustration formed in her eyes.

I hadn't paid a damn bit of attention to what she'd selected to wear, yet the scarlet dress called to me. Another act of defiance. Another way of attempting to break through my defenses. I had to give the woman credit. She wasn't just a fighter. She was a champion bull rider.

After taking a deep breath, I lifted the scarf, placing the soft material over her eyes, tying the blindfold securely. "I'm many things, Emily. That's something you're obviously going to learn the hard way. However sadistic my desires might be, I usually reserve the worst punishments for the lying sack of shit assholes who refuse to accept my leadership or my rules."

She laughed softly, as if this was just a game. "I'm not one of those assholes?"

Satisfied with the knot, I turned her to face me, gripping her jaw with one hand as I stroked her hair with the other. "I believe you're many things, but you're certainly not an asshole. You'll learn to obey me. One day."

When she opened her mouth to retort, I captured her lips, holding her in place as I thrust my tongue inside.

Her reaction was exactly like I'd suspected it would be, her fists pummeling against my chest, her body undulating in order to get out of my hold. But I also sensed something else in her. Lust. I'd felt it before, her pussy so wet and hot that it nearly scalded my cock. There was a strangeness to the connection we shared, the sensations completely unexpected.

The kiss was damning as well as dangerous, my balls tightening to the point of anguish. Toying with her, even considering keeping her as my hostage was bad enough. Actually enjoying the taste of her was ridiculous, perhaps costly. There was a hell of lot to do, including cleaning up several areas of the family's business. I certainly didn't need to be pulled by my more carnal needs.

When she bit down on my tongue, I reared back, lifting my arm to strike her, the reaction instantaneous.

Once again, she didn't cower even though she had to know what my reaction would be.

Closing my eyes, I reined in my anger, slowly lowering my arm then gripping hers. "While I understand your frustration, Emily, you have zero choices. Your entire world now belongs to me. The sooner you learn to accept that, the better off it's going to be for you."

"Fuck you."

"Fucking will definitely be one of those items on our agenda." I pulled the rope I'd snatched from the duffle bag from my jacket, yanking her hands in front of her.

"You disgust me on every level."

"Interesting given your body betrays you. You crave what only I can provide."

"Bullshit."

Leaning over, I took a deep breath, holding her sweet fragrance in my lungs. The scent of her feminine wiles was intoxicating. "Your body betrays you." To prove a point, I rubbed her fully aroused nipple between my thumb and forefinger, my nostrils flaring when she moaned.

"Bastard."

Laughing, I enjoyed another five seconds before dragging her out of the bathroom. "If you make a single noise, it will be your last."

"Why, yes, sir," she muttered with contempt.

I led her out of her house toward the awaiting SUVs, taking a deep whiff of the night air. At least this time I wasn't smelling the rancid stench of chicken bones and grease. Instead, the scent of night-blooming jasmine, the lightly falling rain, and her intoxicating perfume dazzled my senses.

Dimitri attempted to hide his disdain, yet his pinched face was enough to rile me.

She stood like a frail doll in her bare feet, shivering as the rain created droplets on her cheeks. There was something appealing about her innocence.

"We should leave," he stated.

"I'm well aware of the time, Dimitri. As you can see, I was handling a situation."

"What the hell are we supposed to do with her, boss?" he asked as I dragged her closer to the vehicles, scanning the houses surrounding her little abode, prepared for anyone who dared to interfere.

"Have Mario take her to my house. Lock her in one of the rooms." I shoved her against Dimitri, my mouth still watering from the desire to feast on her sweet flesh. I shifted my gaze in Mario's direction, the other Capo usually assigned to my brother.

"Yes, boss," he said without hesitation. "Darren, go with him."

"Will do, Dimitri."

I'd lost four of my best men during the subsequent shootout with cops who'd been given our location by the snitch, Ricardo. Being forced to use Mario, my brother's right-hand Capo as well as a man who'd been on the payroll a short time pissed me off. However, I had no other choices. I walked directly to Mario, gazing up and down the length of him. He and I had sparred on more than one occasion. A true hothead, his lack of control had cost our family dearly and still, my father refused to let him go.

"Make certain she's taken care of, Mario, or you will not appreciate the consequences." I allowed the words to linger as I shifted my gaze back to the lovely woman who'd become my prisoner. While she was shaking, I was impressed with her continued resolve. Now my cock was throbbing like a son of a bitch.

"Absolutely, boss. Glad to have you back. So is Lucian," Mario stated, finally able to look me in the eye.

Lucian. I doubted my brother was happy in the least I'd come back into the fold.

"Are you sure that's wise? The girl, I mean?" Dimitri's Russian accent seemed more intense than usual, his words hushed yet directed. He constantly scanned the street, advised of the rumors that my life was in danger.

I waited until Mario slid into the driver's seat, closing the door behind him before addressing the breach in protocol.

Sighing, I walked closer until we were only inches apart. "Let's get something clear, Dimitri. While I appreciate your continued alliance to the family in my absence, even your work with my brother, if you challenge me again, you will no longer be working for me or anyone else for that matter."

He glared at Emily before shoving her into the SUV. "Understood."

It was obvious that my brother's unusual methods of maintaining control had rubbed off on him. That was about to change.

"Excellent. To answer your question, I'm going to find out everything she knows, including if there was anyone else who's betrayed me."

Dimitri nodded after a few seconds. "That makes sense, of course."

"Find out everything you can about a girl named Julia Maxwell. She's a friend of Ms. Porter," I said quietly.

"I will."

"Time to have a meeting with Ricardo." The little prick had to know a hell of a lot more than the crap Dimitri had heard on the street. Someone had facilitated tipping off the police, especially since I'd left no traceable evidence.

"Just so you know, your family is waiting at your father's house for your return."

I chuckled, shaking my head as Emily lifted her face toward me seconds before the door was closed. "Of course they are. They are going to have to wait for my joyous return." As I moved toward the second vehicle, opening the rear door myself, I took a few seconds to study the girl's small house. While the records indicated she'd purchased the quaint cottage almost a year ago, there was no indication of how she'd afforded the down payment. Certainly her salary wasn't enough to afford that.

I closed the door, immediately moving to refresh my drink. It was time to savor my freedom before all hell broke loose. A part of me reveled in the thought. If the assholes who'd conspired to send me behind bars truly believed they were protected from my wrath, they would find the next few days, even weeks disturbing. I was committed to seeking retaliation, but on my own terms.

When Dimitri climbed in, his usual cool demeanor had returned. I had no intention of splitting the loyalty in my family, but Dimitri would need to learn that he worked for me. Period. While my brother Lucian had been forced to pick up the reins in my absence, I could tell he'd allowed his very different views to interfere with my authority. Never again.

"Have a drink, Dimitri. We might have a long night ahead of us."

He whispered words in his native Russian, ones I didn't care about, then reached for a second glass, selecting vodka as I knew he would. Sadly, the man was predictable; however, his skills precluded his possible elimination. I valued loyalty more than anything in my organization. The former boxer had that in spades.

"He's working tonight," Dimitri added.

He. Ricardo. I'd allowed the man to enter into my realm based on his knowledge of the Azzurri family. I followed the protocol of keeping your friends close and your enemies closer. While there had been peace between our families up to this point, based on my acquaintance with the eldest son, that could always change at a moment's notice.

Ricardo's wealth of information had once thwarted the Azzurris before they attempted to interfere with our business. Then the little prick had changed his loyalty, obviously feeding information to another source while remaining on our payroll. I'd purposely allowed him to remain a free man while I'd been incarcerated, preferring to look the fucker in the eye before he was reminded of the error in his ways.

And it had allowed whoever was responsible to believe they'd gotten one over on the King family.

I swirled my drink, dragging my tongue across the rim of the glass. I'd waited far too long to receive justice. "Then we ensure that his job becomes difficult in the future."

There was a hint of surprise in the Russian's single ragged breath. The truth was, Ricardo could prove to be useful in the future, but only if he reestablished his alliance with the King family.

"Whatever you say," Dimitri grunted.

As the driver rolled into the city limits, I allowed the luminous lights of the city to power my increasing desire.

One of power.

One of anger.

And more important, one of possession.

I rubbed my index finger back and forth across my lips, still able to savor the few minutes with Emily. She had no idea what was in store for her, the dark hungers that would be fulfilled. She would learn soon enough what kind of man had captured her.

Only minutes later, the driver pulled the vehicle to the curb, as usual, keeping the engine idling.

There was no need for instruction. All the soldiers were aware of what was required of them. As I exited the vehicle, I adjusted my jacket, drinking in the sights of the beloved city I'd missed so much. Even the stench of Italian food invigorated my senses, igniting another level of fire. This was a very good day.

Dimitri trailed behind me as I took long strides, moving into the restaurant. As soon as I entered, the terrified looks of the employees' faces gave me a smile. At least I hadn't been forgotten. There was no need to brandish a weapon, no desire to destroy the location. They were merely unwitting citizens who'd worked alongside a worthless pig.

I slapped my hand against the set of double steel doors, moving into the kitchen. Within seconds, the majority of the cooks scuttled away like rats, their faces highlighting the terror in their minds. Only the asshole in question didn't run away. He was smart enough to realize there was nowhere on this planet where he could hide from me.

The steam from various pots still burning on the stove added an interesting atmosphere, the heat in the kitchen oppressive. I scanned the area as Dimitri flanked my side, noticing the fascinating looking knife sharpener attached to one of the steel tables, a large butcher knife remaining in place. I took two additional steps into the room, finally turning my attention toward Ricardo.

He'd eased against another counter, his face completely devoid of any expression, yet drained of all color.

"Mr. King," he said, with a cough afterwards.

"I assume you didn't expect to see me any time soon," I said quietly, moving closer to the knife-sharpening implement.

"I… Well, I heard the news," he said, darting his eyes from Dimitri then back to me, terror riding his face. "It's good you're out of prison, Mr. King."

Dimitri chuckled behind me, shifting closer.

"Ah, you watch the news. Good for you. It's necessary to be informed as to the events occurring in our beautiful city. Don't you think so?" I asked casually as I studied the instrument, smiling before lifting the arm holding the sharpening stone, sliding it across the edge of the blade. When he said nothing, I lifted my head, locking eyes with his.

"Yes… Yes, sir," Ricardo said, his entire body shaking.

I continued sharpening the knife, savoring the sound of the stone as it sliced across the razor edge. Even in the ridiculous lighting swinging from the ceiling, I could tell the blade had already been sharpened to utter precision.

"I knew you would think so," I stated, taking a few additional seconds to perfect my sharpening skills before shifting my full attention in his direction for a few seconds. "I learned a long time ago that a sharp knife produces the best results while a dull knife is much more dangerous." I continued swinging the arm back and forth, the swishing sound echoing in the room. As I concentrated on my actions, my thoughts shifted to the shank I'd sharpened on a craggy edge of the cell I'd spent the majority of my time in. The piece had come into play more than once, likely saving my life.

Swish.

Swish.

Swish.

A single extremely strangled moan pulsed from the asshole's throat.

After a few seconds, I released my hold, standing back to study the reflection of the smooth edge. "That's perfect. A magnificent cutting tool. I'm certain you understand and appreciate the technique." I couldn't help but notice the other cooks had left the room, scuttling out the back door, likely terrified for their lives. "Answer me!"

"Yes!" Ricardo barked. "Absolutely. Sir."

As I rounded the corner of the table, he bristled, his hand clinging to the edge of the counter he was standing against.

"There's no reason to be afraid, Ricardo. I only came here to talk. So, why don't you relax?"

He attempted to give me a smile, his body slumping. "I'm really sorry, Mr. King. I had no other choice."

"No other choice. We all have choices, Ricardo. While some decisions we make can be difficult, even gut-wrenching, it's all about free will. Unfortunately, you made the wrong one." I gave him one of my full smiles before brushing off whatever food debris he'd gotten on his shirt. Then I took a step away, continuing to study the cramped space. So many businesses had suffered, the majority failing after the horrific hurricane years before. It was good to see a local establishment thriving.

I made it a point in my mind to visit the facility at some point in the future.

"But… No, that's not always true, Mr. King."

"Hmmm… How so, Ricardo? Didn't you act alone, determined to bring down the King family? Didn't you alert the authorities that I had certain… business to attend to that night over a year ago?"

Ricardo swallowed hard, his eyes glazing over. "But that wasn't my idea."

"Ah. We're getting somewhere. Then whose idea was it?"

He shook his head vigorously, panting like some unwanted dog. "I can't tell you."

"Can't or you won't?" I eased my hand around his throat, merely holding my fingers in place. "I have faith in you, Ricardo. I think… no, I am certain you want to tell me who set me up on that wretched stormy night. Don't you?"

I could actually hear his teeth chattering as he struggled with providing the needed information. While I wasn't a patient man on any level, I'd realized moments after my arrest that a pig like Ricardo hadn't initiated the bust. He simply wasn't intelligent enough.

Gasping for air, he tried to stand as tall as possible, daring to keep eye contact. "I do, but…"

Squeezing my fingers was such a joy, my heart racing from the prospects of the future. "I feel in a very generous mood tonight, Ricardo. I'm giving you one last chance to confess your sins, but I assure you that there will *not* be another."

"Okay. Yes. I will."

"Good boy," I said and released my hold, patting his face.

"Mr. Vendez. Okay?" Ricardo barely managed to get the words out before shifting into a coughing fit, his chest heaving.

"Vendez?"

"Enrique Vendez. I don't know anything other than a name. I received instructions along with a threat if I didn't do exactly what was on the piece of paper, he'd hurt my wife and kid. He just wanted me to follow you and when you showed up at the restaurant, to call the authorities."

The method was not something the Azzurris would do. What concerned me the most was how the mystery player had learned any of my plans in the first place.

"Enrique Vendez," I repeated, giving Dimitri a look, the Russian shaking his head. It was a name I wasn't familiar with, although I certainly wasn't going to show any weakness to the little pig who'd dared cross me. I'd known all the players over the years, the assholes who tried to slither into our world, taking what my family had worked for generations to achieve. I took a full step back, keeping the smile on my face. "Let me get this straight, Ricardo. You followed orders from a man who only has a name?"

"Yes. Yes, sir. You don't understand. There were pictures of my family. Where my wife works, the daycare. Billy's school. I had no other choice."

“Well, protecting our families is very important. Has he contacted you since?”

“No. I swear to God. Nothing. I will tell you this, he’s not a good person, Mr. King. I heard that on the street.”

Not a good person. It would seem that Ricardo had forgotten exactly what I was made of. “I understand. I really do. There are some people on this earth that allow us to see the worst in mankind. Mr. Vendez is sadly one of those people.” He said nothing as I took two steps away, but I could still hear his ragged breathing as well as his hammering heartbeat. “What else have you heard?”

“Na… Nothing, really, Mr. King.” Ricardo was sweating profusely. “He’s like some freaking ghost.”

No one was able to disappear that easily.

“Okay. I believe you. So, here’s how we’re going to play this, Ricardo.”

I gave Dimitri a look, lifting a single eyebrow. My Capo was well aware of my usual tactics in handling scum like Ricardo. Tonight, I’d take a different stance. There could be certain opportunities afforded to me by keeping the pig alive.

“Yes… Yes, sir?” Ricardo struggled to say.

“You’re going to resume working for me, although things are going to be entirely different.”

“Yes. Yes, sir!” I could hear such relief in the asshole’s voice.

“That means you will do exactly as I order you to do. Any variance and there won’t be enough of you left to find. Are you feeling me, Ricardo?” I shifted toward the knife, running my finger across the blade. Instantly, a trickle of blood appeared on the tip. I held my hand into the light, allowing the stream to flow. "You do understand that. Correct?"

"Yes. Absolutely, sir."

"Excellent. I want you to find out everything you can about this Mr. Vendez. I don't care how small it is. You're going to answer your phone when I call and you will meet with me, providing that information. Am I clear?"

"Yes. Without question, sir."

"Fantastic. Then I think we've concluded our business today." I slipped my finger into my mouth, relishing the coppery taste. I could still hear the worthless fuck trying to control his breathing.

As I moved toward the set of double doors, I exhaled then shifted toward Dimitri. "I think you know what to do from here. Ricardo needs to be taught a very valuable lesson." I pushed open the door, thought about the man's consequences then turned once again toward my Capo, lifting my hand and spreading two fingers.

Dimitri nodded, a gleam in his eyes.

"No. No! Please!" Ricardo exclaimed just as I walked out. There was barely any noise in the crowded restaurant, the customers as well as the wait staff doing their best to keep their distance. I walked toward the front door, stopping long enough to hear an anguished cry.

The asshole was lucky I'd allowed him to live.

CHAPTER 4

ristiano

Dangerous.

Merciless.

Heartless.

The epitome of the King family.

We'd descended from generations of powerful men, our ancestors basic bootleggers during the prohibition. My great-grandfather had been considered a brutal man, raising his two sons to follow in his footsteps. The family's control over the city had erupted in violence more than once, several enemies learning early on that they were no match for my great-grandfather's influence.

He'd learned the art of collecting allies, utilizing both threats as well as promises. Fortunately, my father and his father before him had perfected the art, passing down their lessons learned.

Sometimes the hard way.

With four younger brothers and one incorrigible sister, I knew my parents must have had their hands full. While my father had always been a brutal man, his love rarely shown, our beloved mother had ensured that we'd grown up as normally as possible.

Give or take a few exceptions.

I smirked at the thought as I headed into my father's beautiful estate, the mansion-style house one of the most magnificent in the Garden District of New Orleans. My mother's pride and joy were her gardens, her plants and flowers attended to on a daily basis. Teresa King had perfected the art of ignoring the violence created and often pursued by my father, attending the various neighborhood soirees even though the majority of women were terrified of her.

That was the power of our reign over the city.

As far as my siblings, they were products of wealth and learned class, three of my brothers accepting positions within my father's organization without question. However, Dante was several years younger than the others, pretending that our reputation couldn't rub off on his aspirations. He'd even joined the military in an attempt to rid himself of the stigma attached to belonging to a mafia family.

I'd heard enough even behind the thick walls of my prison cell to know he hadn't been successful. He'd been tormented by his superiors, as if they had no idea what kind of fury could befall them given their blatant stupidity. If my mother's last letter held merit, he would soon reenter the family he had so blatantly left behind.

Then there was my sister, sweet and gullible Angelique. As the baby in the family, she continued to pretend that she was the princess my mother had always referred to her as. While I adored her without question, I knew in my gut it was only a matter of time before one of our enemies attempted to use her in whatever means they believed would help them accomplish their goals.

Destroying our kingdom.

That would never happen.

My thoughts drifted to Emily, the taste of blood still remaining in my mouth. She'd attempted to defy me, refusing to accept her fate. Vile thoughts of exactly what I was going to do to her entered my mind, unfurling like a very special Christmas present.

"Is there anything I should know, Dimitri?" I asked, hesitating before walking in through the front door.

"Nothing you can't handle, boss."

He rarely called me boss, something he'd refused to do from day one of being hired. If any of the other soldiers had dared to confront me in that manner, they would have found themselves on the receiving end of my fist. However, the arrogance in the stocky Russian had been exactly what I was looking for. We'd developed a pseudo friendship after that, although the men I considered true friends I could list on a portion of one hand. He'd earned the right to call me by my first name several years before, his loyalty rewarded with the top-level position as well as the salary to go with it. I was curious as to why he'd picked this moment to use the word.

I chuckled and smoothed down the jacket. I'd be glad to take a hot shower, one where I didn't have to keep a shank by my side.

"And my father?"

When Dimitri hesitated, I cringed.

"Just tell me his condition."

"He's doing as well as can be expected. Some good days, some bad days." Dimitri was holding back.

"The wound?" I asked, the attempt on my father's life something I would never forget. Revenge would be sweet, although given my circumstances, I would need to be careful how I handled that… event.

"He's lucky, at least that's what the doctors told him. No lasting physical effects."

Lucky. Yes, I suppose remaining alive after four of our soldiers had been gunned down, their bullet-riddled bodies displayed on the front of every state newspaper, splashed across both local and national stations could be considered lucky.

I'd grill him further later. Right now wasn't the time and I was certainly in no mood. As far as the information about Mr. Vendez, I would wait to mention it until I had more. There was no sense in getting the entire family riled.

Yet.

Sighing, I thought about the difficult weeks or even months ahead. While I was fully prepared to take complete control over our businesses and our finances, it wouldn't be the same without my father attempting to assert his authority. I would remember that in a bittersweet manner in the years to come.

Dimitri trailed behind me as I walked into the house. Very little if anything had changed, except for the bouquet of fresh flowers my mother insisted be maintained in her favorite crystal vase on the glass table positioned in the center of the foyer. This time, they were white roses, my mother's favorite. I couldn't help but wonder if they were meant as a telling statement, her attempt at begging for peace.

I walked toward the exquisite crystal piece, taking a deep whiff, the sounds of activity floating into the room. Easily able to recognize the voices, it appeared the entire family had been convened in celebration of my release.

Or perhaps condemnation.

My father had expressed his anger during the few minutes we'd been able to spend together after my initial arrest, the man barely breathing from his hospital bed. I'd almost gone off the edge then, ordering full retaliation. Sadly, my arrest had complicated matters. No longer. My calculated plan would eliminate a significant chunk of our true enemy. But my father's heart condition was just another layer of concern. If his health was failing, it was yet another excuse that could be used by the Azzurri family. Complete protection of our family unit was definitely in order.

Family would always come first.

I swaggered into the family room, much like I'd done the last time I was here, taking long strides toward the bar. For at least ten precious seconds, there was no sound in the room, all chatter and bickering ceasing. I even managed to pour a drink before I heard the sound of Vincenzo's booming laughter.

"You know how to make an entrance, brother," Vincenzo said, still chuckling under his breath.

After taking a sip, I turned around, grinning at the group. Only Lucian seemed displeased at my arrival, although Michelangelo appeared distanced. He loathed his given name, using Michael instead, another one of my mother's irritants.

"I'm so glad you're home," my mother said as she approached, wrapping her arms around me. Her somewhat unusual display of emotions threw me off. "How are you, son? Did they treat you badly?"

Badly. I certainly wouldn't tell my sweet mother about the usual horrors that I'd been forced to endure. She didn't deserve to hear any of the gory details.

"I'm fine, Mother. Our father taught us well."

She moved away, giving me an admonishing look as my father snorted from his position in the same overstuffed aging leather chair that he refused to let go of.

I walked closer to the larger than life man, leaning over and pressing my hand against his cool cheek. He appeared exhausted, his skin sallow.

"I'm fine, son. Christ. I don't need to be babied," my father insisted.

"Nonsense. Your father wouldn't last two days behind bars," she said as if everyone knew that. "He's not big and strong like you are. Speaking of which, you're entirely too thin."

Michael spit out a portion of his drink, wiping his mouth as he choked. "Mother," he coughed. "You need to stop babying him."

I moved toward my younger brother first, giving him a bear hug. At least the two of us were closer than the rest. I hadn't been able to comfort him after his significant loss. He'd always been brooding, his beloved bride able to pull him out of a darkness that had threatened to consume him. Thank God he had his two children to take care of.

"How are the twins?" I asked, longing to see my adorable niece and nephew. The amount of suffering he'd gone through since his wife's death was undeniable. Although the horrible incident had been ruled an accident, the entire family was certain they knew who was responsible.

Giancarlo Azzurri, oldest son and a ruthless dictator.

Another issue that would need to be resolved. My gut told me the aggressive Italian, newly appointed Don of his family, would never issue a strike against our family. Besides, there hadn't been a move against our holdings by the Azzurris during my absence, a telling statement.

His eyes twinkled, slight joy returning to his face. "Growing like weeds. They can't wait to see you."

"Soon," I said wistfully. He almost immediately lost the smile, walking toward the bank of windows.

"Our dear older brother doesn't deserve to be treated with kid gloves either," Lucian said under his breath. "My guess is that Cristiano honed his weapons skills while behind bars."

"Lucian!" my mother admonished.

"No harm, Mother." I shot him a look, studying his pensive face. "Is there something you need to tell me, Lucian?"

He polished off his drink without answering. "There's nothing I need to say to you."

"Goddamn it, brother," I started until our father attempted to get out of his chair.

"That's enough, both of you. We work together as a family. Remember?" His gruff voice was even huskier given his refusal to stop smoking his beloved Cuban cigars.

Family.

Perhaps I'd used the term far too loosely in my life. I'd known the second I'd been arrested that Lucian would use the situation to his advantage. While he'd maintained our diamond brokerage business, he'd yet to obtain a road into the New York market, something I'd instructed him to take care of. He'd also come no closer to finding out who'd been responsible for the assassination attempt or why the men and women of law enforcement on our payroll had allowed my arrest and conviction to occur.

It would seem heads needed to roll.

I swaggered toward Lucian, trying to keep my anger in check. He'd aged since my departure, the small lines on his forehead indicating the difficulty he'd faced while attempting to keep the soldiers in line as well as overseeing our other companies. "I think Lucian has been waiting to say something to me for over a year. Haven't you, brother?"

Only two years my junior, he'd been entirely different than me, his studious abilities making him the obvious choice for handling the more refined assholes who ran the diamond market. However, he'd objected to my methods of handling the business since my father had semi-retired years before. Jealousy ran rampant in our family.

Lucian tilted his head, his eyes reflecting a level of amusement. "If I have something to say to you, Cristiano, I have no problems doing that. I'm no longer in your shadow."

"Interesting. I guess that's something you and I will need to discuss." I remained unblinking for a full twenty seconds, the tension between us mounting. My mother's deep sigh was the only thing to break my concentration. I snorted before turning away, determined to let it go for the night.

"However, I do find it fascinating that one of your first stops after being released from prison wasn't about your family, but about exacting revenge." Lucian's voice boomed in the wide open space. He was goading, even sparring for a fight.

"At least I have the balls to handle the affairs of our business as necessary," I retorted. It was obvious there'd been talk about my plans.

"That is fucking enough!" my father snarled. "Tonight isn't about business. This is a celebration. Your brother was released from prison. He endured his time, keeping his mouth shut and his loyalty maintained to the family. I doubt any of you could have handled what he'd been forced to endure."

Lucian snorted, moving toward the bar to refill his drink.

"This is my house," Father continued. "You will honor my wishes. Business will be discussed tomorrow."

The slight chuckle slipping past Vincenzo's lips only further angered him, his harsh glare shifting to the self-appointed playboy of the family.

The awkward silence settled into exactly what I'd remembered occurring the majority of time we were all together. We weren't a happy little family.

"Woo-hoo!" As the front door slammed, the lilting voice of my sister was likely the only thing from keeping my brother and me from spiraling into blows. She stopped short when she was just inside the room, narrowing her eyes as she shifted her gaze from Lucian back to me. "Nothing ever changes in this goddamn family."

"Watch it, young lady," my mother chastised. "I could still wash that filthy mouth of yours out with soap."

I gazed, enjoying the bickering more than I should have. Maybe I'd actually missed the family get-togethers, although they'd become infrequent long before I'd been sent away.

Angelique swished her hips back and forth, blowing a kiss in Dimitri's direction as she passed. "In case you haven't figured it out, Mother, I am twenty-two years old. A worldly woman who lives on her own. You can no longer tell me what to do."

As she locked eyes with mine, a huge smile crossed her face. I wasn't shocked to see her usually gorgeous raven hair dyed an ungodly shade of purple, the free spirit in my sister going strong. She yelped in glee as she ran the rest of the way, jumping into my arms.

"You're home! I counted the days. I was so excited when they told me." Angelique threw her arms around my neck, clinging to me like a lifeline. She and I had a special bond, the kind I'd wished for her and our father. He'd been far too busy when all of us had been growing up to bother with any concept of nurturing.

I could tell out of the corner of my eye that Dimitri's interest in her hadn't diminished over time. While my Capo knew better than to touch her in any inappropriate manner, I knew in my gut that he would protect Angelique with his life if necessary.

When she finally leaned back, sliding to the floor, she gave Lucian a dirty look, forcing me to laugh. "My aggressive little tiger. But purple hair?"

She twirled in a circle, allowing her long locks to flow freely. With every move, she inched closer to Dimitri, finally acting as if she tripped in order to have him catch her.

Dimitri's face reddened if only slightly, the catch planting her firmly against his chest. There was utter silence in the room for a few seconds before my father cleared his throat.

"We are all glad to have you back, Cristiano," my father commented.

"Why do I feel like there is a 'but' attached to my welcome nod?" I asked, taking another swig of my drink.

"Father is worried about the Azzurris," Vincenzo answered.

"What about them?" I glanced around the room, curious about all their pensive faces.

"It would seem that they have every intention of moving in on our particular trades with South America," Lucian continued for him.

The Azzurris were pains in our asses and had always been, but one of the few rules that had been established years before is the clear distinction in our two territories. South America was off the table as far as they were concerned.

"Who the fuck told you that?" I demanded.

"Son. Your language!" my mother huffed.

Sighing, I suddenly remembered why spending time with the entire family had always been exhausting. "Who told you that, oh, brother of mine?"

Lucian cracked a smile for the first time since my arrival, but before he had a chance to answer, Angelique piped in.

"It would seem that Francesco Azzurri has no problem spouting off his family's latest attributes while intoxicated." The smile on my sister's face was both telling as it was infuriating.

Within seconds, I hand my hand wrapped around Lucian's throat, slamming him against the wall. "You allowed our sister to get involved with our business?"

"Stop it. Stop it!" my mother screeched.

"Let him go, Chris," Vincenzo encouraged.

"This is blasphemy!" my father bellowed. "We are a family."

I dug my fingers into Lucian's neck, my rage over the top. "You disobeyed me, brother."

"It's not his fault, Cristiano," Angelique pleaded. "Let him go."

"Then who the fuck's fault is it? Don't say it, Mother. I am allowed to be furious."

Michael walked closer, taking shallow breaths. "Blame me if you need to. I mentioned my concern to Angel over lunch. I had no idea what she'd done until later."

While my anger remained directed toward Lucian, I let him go, ignoring the sounds of his coughing. I'd rarely shown my anger to Angelique. That had never been the kind of emotion that had gotten through to her. She didn't back down, her larger than life persona giving her a defiant look, her expression reminding me of Emily's. For a few seconds, I was thrown by the realization.

I took both her arms into my hands, squeezing with enough pressure that she knew I was troubled. "What did you do?"

"Why does everyone in this family think I did something?" she demanded.

"Tell her, Angel," Michael encouraged. "You know Cristiano. He's not going to leave it unless you do."

She wrinkled her nose, giving me a pouting look but after ten seconds, she realized it wasn't going to work on me. "I might have flirted with him at the art gallery."

"Might have?"

Michael cleared his throat.

Angelique rolled her eyes. "When Michael told me what an informant had said, I remembered that Francesco was on the guest list for one of the art showings."

"Uh-huh," I huffed, giving Michael a hard look. I'd known for a few years that Francesco, the youngest son of the Azzurri family, had been sweet on my sister. There had been some talk about an arranged marriage, something I knew Angelique would never go for.

Let alone the monster inside of me. Even though Giancarlo and I had made a deal of sorts, I couldn't trust that my sister wouldn't be used as a pawn. The Azzurris were the kind of crime syndicate that would eat their own if it meant padding their substantial wealth.

"Okay, so we spent some time together," she offered.

"At your art gallery?" While I knew how much my sister adored running the gallery, a birthday present from our father when she'd turned eighteen, I'd never liked the idea. It was too easy for our enemies to exact revenge on our sister instead of their desired target.

A warm flush swept over her cheeks. "Well, I admit that we went to a club to have a drink. He kept drinking so I started asking questions. And don't you dare be mad at me. I'm part of this family too."

"You did this without protection?" I had more of an edge in my voice.

"I didn't sleep with the asshole, for God's sake," she protested, immediately groaning when our mother walked out of the room in disgust.

"You know exactly what I mean, Angelique, and you know the rules." I shifted my angry gaze in Dimitri's direction. The last thing I'd said to my Capo was to keep an eye on my sister.

"I'm a big girl, in case you haven't noticed. I can take care of myself." Her counter was immediately followed by placing her hand on my cheek, something that had always defused the rage burning deep inside.

I allowed her hand to remain for a few seconds before taking it into both of mine, using enough force she furrowed her eyebrows. "You don't understand the level of danger surrounding us, Angelique. Promise me you won't do something that stupid again."

She opened her mouth to retort but sighed instead. "I promise. Don't you want to know what he said to me?"

A part of me knew damn good and well Francesco could have been tossing something in our direction, although doing so while I was behind bars was surprising. The Azzurris knew better than almost anyone that I had a penchant for retaliation.

I lifted an eyebrow, knowing there was no way to stop her. "Go on."

"Francesco mentioned his family was getting involved in an exciting adventure. I pushed him, but he objected at first. He finally mentioned that his family's decision to move into South America would provide significant business."

"Did he specifically mention certain party favors?" I asked.

She shook her head. "No, but what other business is lucrative in South freaking America?"

I rubbed my jaw, lifting my gaze toward Lucian. "Diamonds."

Lucian seemed impressed I'd have such knowledge, even lifting his glass in salute.

"Whatever the fucking Azzurris are doing, we need to know about it," our father growled. "And soon. I refuse to allow those pigs to take over any of our territory."

"Don't worry, Pops. We'll find out," Vincenzo said. "You need to remember that our big brother has returned. He'll do what's necessary."

"Tonight," my father demanded, obviously changing his mind about only discussing business beginning tomorrow. He was worried, something I wasn't used to.

"It's after nine, Father," Michael said quietly, trying to be the voice of reason.

I could see the instant tension between Vincenzo and Lucian. What in the fuck had been going on since I'd been gone? Tomorrow I'd sort it all out, one way or the other. If I needed to have a discussion with old man Azzurri, then I'd make it tops on my to-do list. However, Giancarlo would be easier to access.

But nothing was going to happen tonight.

"I'll find out the truth. I need the name of the informant, Michelangelo," I stated with no inflection.

"You called him Michelangelo," Angelique teased, her laugh just as I'd remembered and missed so much. "You must be pissed."

"This isn't a laughing matter." I turned to face Dimitri, letting him tell by the harsh expression on my face that I was furious. "And from now on, you're going to have security every time you're working."

Dimitri nodded, standing straighter as if preparing for my wrath.

"Oh, come on," she protested. "Don't you think seeing two hulking masses of grunting men will push away my customers? Sales are already down this year, for Christ's sake."

"As our dear, sweet mother said, watch your mouth. It's time you embraced that this world isn't one big playpen." I knew my words were harsh, but I had the distinct feeling that I was going to walk into a hornet's nest.

"Wow. You've changed," Angelique mused.

"How appropriate. It would seem that prison made our brother even harder than before," Lucian half snarled.

"Cut the crap, Lucian. That's exactly what's needed right now," Michael defended me, as if I couldn't do that for myself.

It would seem my savage methods of doing business had been missed.

"Business is getting more difficult, gentlemen, on both sides of the fence. I suggest we actually take our father's advice and try and work together," Vincenzo almost laughed after issuing the statement.

I shifted back to face them, turning my attention to my father. He'd never wanted to give up the helm, loathing the fact he was getting old. He'd always told me that he and I were just alike—brutal. Perhaps he was right. I wasn't going to take crap from anyone, including from my siblings.

There was far too much at stake, including our legitimate businesses. I finished my drink and moved to place the glass on the coffee table, immediately heading for the door.

"Where the hell do you think you're going?" Lucian's overbearing tone was enough to rile me once again.

"It's been a long day. I'm going home to enjoy a nice glass of cognac." While I had entirely other goals in mind, they certainly weren't going to be privy to hearing what I had in store for the lovely but very disobedient Emily Porter.

My answer brought a laugh from Angelique. At least she and Michael knew that I'd never given a shit about my home before, barely spending any time there.

"Leave him alone," Father barked. "Chris is back in town. He will take care of everything. He will make it right."

As I walked out, I heard Lucian's bitter laughter.

One day our venomous disagreements would come to a head.

And on that day, one of us would be forced to walk away from our family.

CHAPTER 5

mily

Cause and effect.

Behaviors and consequences.

The sentiments played over and over again in my mind like a skipping record, reminding me that every good deed didn't go unpunished. Of course, I'd had no choice in testifying against Cristiano King. The ugliness of the realization had left me unnerved for well over a year, haunting my dreams as intently as Cristiano's chiseled face and carved body.

But I should have known better.

I should have run far away, skipping out of town before the monster had a chance to get his hands on me, but I'd been assured of my safety. I wasn't a fool and certainly didn't believe in fairytales, but I'd bought into the words, lock, stock, and noose around my neck.

As I shifted in the seat, the rumbling engine of whatever vehicle I'd been tossed in almost made me sick. Let alone my bottom hurt like hell from the spanking.

My pussy from the hard fucking.

Don't cry, Emily. Remain strong.

Strong. As if that was an actual possibility. I was suddenly overwhelmed, the full breadth of anxiety gripping every muscle and squeezing, much like the suffocating effect of his brutal touch, claws wrapping around my throat. I would never forget his dark eyes, either in the courtroom or the reflection I'd seen in the cheap mirror hung on my wall.

Soulless and without remorse.

My God. The asshole had taken me like I already belonged to him, almost as if our sinful coupling had been selected in the stars. I bit back an involuntary cry, trying to keep my wits about me. I was exhausted and drained from the experience, the adrenaline rush from before all but nonexistent.

While I'd tried to pay attention to the twists and turns of the road, it was impossible to figure out where they were taking me. Escaping his clutches was the only hope I had. A bitter laugh collected in my throat. As if that was even possible. I sensed a presence in the seat next to me, could hear the assigned thug's heavy breathing, but the bastard hadn't said a single word. There was also a driver, another brutal asshole. I wanted to remember every detail regarding the bastards so I could crucify them. When the engine slowed, another rattling series of panicking fear wrapped around my mind.

I sensed a driveway of some sort, maybe aggregate, but I wasn't entirely certain. The vehicle stopped, still idling, and I held my breath.

Then the sound of a door opening made me cower in my seat, the warm air and light breeze floating across my face uncomfortable.

"Come on," the gruff voice said, yanking me out of the vehicle. There was a hint of a New York accent, crude in tone, almost Italian.

"Let's get this over with," the other soldier barked, cursing under his breath.

I didn't bother asking either one of them any questions. I knew how the mafia worked, the men likely soldiers at best, assigned to all the most ridiculous grunt work possible. I almost laughed at my analyzation of the crime syndicate family, as if I had any idea what the organization was like.

Other than what I'd heard on the news and what little the various attorneys had shared with me.

The men couldn't care less that I was in my bare feet, dragging me along like the ragdoll I'd turned into. Neither bothered telling me to watch my step. The fall on something hard was jarring, the pain in my knees spiking down my legs. "Oh..." I gasped for air, my entire body shaking. I was overwhelmed by racking fear and dread, trying desperately to find a way to fight the asshole even though I knew it was no use.

"Come on. Get up," the Italian snapped, yanking on my arm again. "I got places to be."

I could hear the sound of a door being unlocked and opened. There was a distinct musty smell as I was pulled past a threshold. Then it hit me. This was Cristiano's house. I wasn't certain whether to be grateful or terrified.

After being dragged for several feet, I heard the sound of another door opening.

"We're going downstairs. I don't give a shit if you trip," the second asshole said. There was a clicking sound, as if a light was being turned on. The slender slit of light coming from under the blindfold confirmed it as I lifted my head.

I was no longer shocked by the gruffness of their voices or the hatred in their tone. To the brutal soldier, I was nothing more than the enemy.

Breathe. Think.

"What the hell are you doing?" the Italian snorted.

"There's a special place to put the bitch," the second man huffed.

"That's not what Cristiano wants."

"As if I give a shit. We gotta make certain she doesn't get loose."

The Italian snarled. "Fuck you. I ain't gonna take the rap for your bullshit decisions. You do whatever you want. I want no part of it."

"You're such a fucking pussy. Have some balls for once." He jerked my arm, yanking me with enough force I stumbled.

The stairs were narrow, indicating an older house, which of course made sense in New Orleans. I'd googled Cristiano more than once, but what few pictures of him had landed on the Internet were obviously prepared, except for the ones surrounding his arrest and incarceration. Even then, he'd glared into the cameras, so arrogant and confident that he wasn't going to prison.

As the heavy sound of the man's boots hit a platform of some kind, I shuddered thinking what was going to happen next. The musty stench was even worse, assaulting my senses, the air dense yet chilly. I was in Cristiano's goddamn basement. Another whisper threatened to give away just how terrified I was.

"Stand right here. You move. You die. Got it, sweetheart?" he asked before letting go of my arm.

"Uh-huh."

He laughed, the sound creating ripples of goosebumps dancing down my arms. When I heard a creaking sound, as if an old door had been swung open, I swayed back and forth. "Get on your hands and knees."

"What?"

"You heard me. If I have to ask you again, I just might get nasty." He laughed in a provocative manner, the sound sending a chill down my spine. "If I had more time, I'd enjoy a taste of you."

When he slid his hand to my breast, squeezing roughly, I bit back a whimper then reacted, spitting in the asshole's face.

"You fucking bitch!" The backhand was savage, knocking me to a concrete floor. I was stunned, pain bursting into every muscle. "I should kill you right here." He jerked me up by my hair and I could feel his hot, disgusting breath as it cascaded across my cheek. The stench was horrible. "Do that again and I will. Now, get the fuck in the cage."

While I obeyed his command, slowly dropping to the floor, I finally did something I hadn't done since I was a child. I started to pray.

The jerk fisted my hair, dragging me forward several inches. When I felt a cool metal surface, I was unable to stop the whimper from escaping my mouth. "Please stop. Don't do this."

"I'm not doing anything, sweetheart. Now, if you behave like a nice little bitch, maybe you'll be released on good behavior. Oh, wait. My boss didn't get that opportunity. All because of you."

The clanging sound sent another shot of adrenaline throughout my body. Whatever was planned for me, this was only the beginning.

"Now, you can experience a little time behind bars," he huffed, chuckling darkly.

No. No. No. No!

I yanked my knees against my chest, immediately lifting my arms, able to wrap my fingers around a piece of metal. Bars. Oh, God. Oh… Panic swept through me, my heart thudding to the point I was forced to take gasping breaths. As soon as I heard the brute's boots thudding against the stairs, I ripped away at the blindfold, sucking on my lower lip to keep from moaning. The darkness was horrific, oppressive, and suffocating.

After fighting with the rope that had already chafed the skin on my wrists, I took a series of shallow breaths then reached out, using the tips of my fingers to 'feel' what kind of enclosure I'd been dumped into. Several minutes later, I was forced to accept that I'd been dumped into a basic dog case; metal bars on all sides, the paneled bottom hard and slick.

It was no use screaming. I knew the kind of house Cristiano lived in, well secured and surrounded by as much land as he'd been able to find, likely with a six foot tall perimeter fence keeping everyone, including prying eyes, unable to venture even a single look.

As I settled against one of the panels, I finally allowed more than just a few tears to fall. My life was over, stripped of any concept of a future. I'd followed my conscience and I'd lost. After a few minutes, I closed my eyes, unable to stop shaking, the reality of my new life sinking in.

Never stop fighting. Don't give in. Don't you dare give in.

Myriad thoughts washed into my mind, all the images of the trial as well as the hour spent with Cristiano. Unable to stop shaking, I curled into a tight ball, sliding closer to the bottom of the cage.

Please...

* * *

Humming, I walked into the restaurant, enjoying the scents of Italian sausage and marinara sauce, the odors creating a rumbling in my stomach. The tired and disgruntled face of the worker behind the counter forced me to glance at the old-fashioned clock over his head. It was late, so much so I hadn't even realized the time. A portion of the lights in the dining area had even been turned off in preparation of closing. I'd buried myself in research and financials, perfecting a market analysis study that my boss had requested and hadn't even thought about hunting down dinner until a few minutes earlier. I should have called in my order, but the little Italian place was so close to the office.

The fresh air would hopefully do me some good.

The long hours were supposed to be temporary.

Sighing, I raked my hand through my hair, the strand that had fallen from the bun I'd haphazardly positioned on the top of my head pissing me off all night. The heat inside the small space was sweltering, creating an instant line of perspiration over my lip. I hated the hot summers; the bugs and constant humidity, the constant dampness.

But I adored the city itself, the vibrancy calling to me from the small window in my tiny office.

After ordering, I moved toward one of the booths to wait, rubbing my tired eyes, appreciating the time away from the grind, the darkness a welcome change to the glaring computer screen. The numbers had all started to fade together anyway. Hopefully, Mr. Dublin would call it a day soon. If not, I might quit. I sat back, closing my eyes, barely acknowledging the ringing bell over the entrance or the hard thumping of at least three sets of boots.

Then I heard a voice, the deep baritone forming goosebumps down the length of my arms. Smiling, I opened my eyes, marveling on the sight of what had to be the most handsome man in the city. Tall and muscular, the tailored dark suit he wore was the perfect complement to his stunning physique. His angular jaw and high cheekbones accentuated a chiseled face, his features carved to perfection. Everything about him screamed of wealth, the kind of prosperity that I'd only seen in glossy magazines.

However, the words coming out of his mouth didn't fit his opulent persona.

"Angelo, it would appear you made the mistake of fucking with me," the stranger growled.

"I don't know what the hell you're talking about," the man said in a gruff voice, cursing under his breath.

The fear rolled off the man's tongue and even from where I was sitting, I could tell he was shaking.

A moment of self-preservation kicked into my system and I slid very quietly all the way to the back of the booth, holding my breath.

"Oh, I think you know exactly what I'm talking about. You fucked with the wrong family." As the stranger lifted his arm, I was able to see the glint of metal.

A weapon.

Oh, my God. The man held a gun in his hand.

Pop! Pop!

As he turned his head in my direction, the shimmer in his eyes was something I'd never forget.

Cold.

Soulless.

My mouth watered, which surprised the hell out of me. I hadn't experienced a reaction to any man in months, maybe a solid year. Shivering, I pressed my hand over my mouth

Thump.

Thump.

Thump.

Jerking awake, I blinked several times in an effort to understand what I was hearing, vivid images of the nightmare plastered in my mind. I bit back a cry, still shaking from the ugly visions. Nothing made any sense, including the ache in my arms and legs. The second I shifted, the ugliness of my situation fogged over what was left of my sanity. My mouth was dry, my head aching.

My legs were asleep, yet I managed to push as far away from the cage door as possible, crowding against the back of the container. Then I heard the sound of his rumbling voice, although his reaction was unexpected, sending shivers criss-crossing over every inch of my body.

The roar was unlike anything I'd ever heard, Cristiano's deep baritone reverberating all around me.

Then the clamoring echo of the area surrounded me being destroyed forcing me to hold my head in my bound hands. What the hell was going on?

Seconds later, there was utter silence.

Tick. Tock.

Had a few seconds passed? A full minute? Two? There was no way of being certain.

"Goddamn it," he growled. He was closer. So close. "Fucking Mario."

Mario? Was that the name of the asshole who'd groped me?

Keep it in the back of your mind.

I wanted to say that I was horrified by hearing Cristiano's voice, but I wasn't. The irony was disgusting, pushing me into a wretched mental state. Had the monster actually believed that my body's reaction to him was anything other than attempting to save my life?

Hell, no.

A few seconds later, a splash of light filtered over the cage, the harshness enough I was forced to hide my face and eyes.

After taking several exaggerated deep breaths, he hunkered down, immediately unlocking the cage and swinging the door open. When he reached inside, I cowered as far away as possible, studying him intently.

"I'm not going to hurt you, Emily. You weren't supposed to be dumped into this hellhole." He growled, forcing a series of chills racing down my spine. "Fucking Christ. Did Mario hit you?"

"What does it matter?"

"Fuck. Fuck!"

I wasn't certain whether he was telling the truth as well as feigning concern, or merely playing a game in order to get me to trust him. Then what? I continued to hold my hands in front of my arms, my teeth chattering from the cold as well as the rush of adrenaline. I'd never felt so sick in my life, my stomach churning. When I didn't respond, he rubbed his eyes, slightly shaking his head.

"My Capo didn't follow my instructions," he added, cocking his head as he looked at me.

It would be so easy to get lost in his eyes, to drown in the sexiness of the man as I had no doubt scores of other women had. But I wasn't like other women. I had a backbone. When my reaction was to laugh, his eyes turned cold for several seconds.

After exhaling again, he reached into his pocket, and to my horror, he pulled out a large pocketknife, flipping open the serrated blade.

"No!" I managed, my voice barely audible, a lump forming in my throat.

Cristiano lifted a single eyebrow and leaned forward, struggling to reach me.

"No! No!" I fought him, smashing my fists against his arms.

"Stop fighting me, Emily. I'm going to untie you. That's it. But if you continue to cross me, then I might change my mind."

"How the hell can I trust you?"

"You can't."

"Asshole," I muttered.

Snorting, he gave me an incredulous look. "Do you think I brought you here to dispose of your body?"

"That's exactly what I think."

This time, he yanked at my arms, tugging me forward by several inches, holding my arms in front of him. "You obviously have no clue who I am."

The darkness pooling in his eyes was the color of black granite, hard, cold, and calculating.

"And I don't want to."

He laughed softly then gave me a stern glare. "Don't move, Emily."

"Stop saying my name."

"You have a beautiful name."

"Not when you say it." I turned my head away, unable to watch what he was doing. When my wrists were suddenly freed, I folded my arms against my chest, taking gasping breaths.

The hesitation only fueled the ugliness swimming in my mind. I studied the basement as he grumbled under his breath, almost laughing from seeing gardening tools and several labeled boxes, even cleaning supplies. Just like a normal person would have instead of a monster.

"Crawl to me, Emily."

His command was full of edge, the same huskiness as I'd heard before just as enticing, but I ignored him.

"I said. Come here. I need to get you out of that cage."

"Then what?" I shot back, twisting my head until I was able to look him directly in the eyes.

His voluptuous lips pursed, the coldness in his eyes continuing. Then he moved to a standing position. He was going to leave me in the cage after all. I watched as he moved toward an old wooden table of some kind, leaning against it and crossing his arms.

Was the bastard playing a game of chicken?

I was incensed, furious, another round of rebellion sweeping through every molecule in my mind. I couldn't give into his game. No, I refused to play it his way.

Cristiano studied me intently, his intense eyes burning a hole right through me.

This was little more than a crazy standoff of some kind. I hated that he looked so damn sexy, the ruby red color of his lips reminding me about the kiss. A flush of embarrassment crawled up from my neck when I involuntarily pressed my fingers across my lips.

My God. What was I doing?

The man was a killer, which is exactly what he'd do to me. This wasn't some game of fantasy. This was real life, filled with irrefutable consequences.

Sadly, I couldn't take my eyes off him.

He'd removed his jacket, the crisp white shirt now unbuttoned, the tailored fit only highlighting his muscular physique. The stark color accentuated the olive tint to his skin. I shifted my gaze to his powerful forearms, the cuffs rolled up past his elbows. I'd been able to gather the scent of alcohol on his breath, another sick reason to remember the kiss.

"You and I are going to have a conversation," he said quietly.

"I'm not talking to you."

"Yes, you are and if you lie to me, I'll know. Then I'll use that mouth of yours for something other than talking."

"I hate you." The words were ridiculous, spit out as if they'd matter to a man like Cristiano.

"That we've already established. Now, we can have that conversation in a more comfortable atmosphere or right here. That's entirely your decision, but we are going to talk. You owe me that."

"I don't owe you anything. You were the one who killed that man."

He chuckled and rubbed his jaw, allowing me to notice for the first time the shadow of his two-day stubble. "He needed to be taught a lesson."

"Just like me." The petulance in my tone was increasing. I must have some kind of death wish to push a man like him.

"If there's nothing you learn about me, you should know I have little patience. You have five seconds to determine whether you'd prefer to sit in the comfort of my home for our discussion or wallow in this basement. You do have choices, Emily, but I suggest you choose wisely."

First the bastard was horrified I'd been tossed into a crate then he was threatening me with it.

"Four. Three."

Nothing made any sense, but I had no other choice but to do what he wanted.

"Two."

"Fine. Okay?" I muttered as I struggled to shift onto all fours, my muscles screaming from the cramped quarters. When I crawled out onto the cold, concrete floor, I was almost numb. Every part of me was shaking as I attempted to stand. I was instantly lightheaded and as soon as I took a single step, my body pitched forward.

And straight into Cristiano's arms.

"Shit!" he exclaimed as he caught me, holding me a few inches away. "What the fuck did he do to you?"

"Him? You mean the brute who brought me here? Nothing. You were the only monster who did anything, but that's all you know how to do. Hurt people."

He clenched my jaw, wrenching it, the fire in his eyes exactly what I would expect from him.

"I'd watch your mouth if I were you," he snarled, dragging me onto my tiptoes, hovering over me as if he planned on kissing me again.

A part of me wanted to dare him to. Perhaps that's what I was doing as I arched my back, rising even higher on my toes.

There was the kind of delight in his eyes, raw yet possessive, his hot breath skipping across my face. I was momentarily mesmerized, the exotic, woodsy scent of him filtering into my nostrils, slip-sliding all the way down to my toes. When he allowed his gaze to fall ever so slowly to my chest, I did everything I could to recoil, humiliated that my nipples were rock hard, highlighted by the thin material of the ridiculous dress I'd chosen.

What the hell had I been thinking in selecting the only sexy dress I owned? Was I actually trying to seduce him and if so, for what purpose? Escape?

After cocking his head, he brushed the fingers of his other hand down the side of my neck, swirling the tip of his index finger around my jugular. If he was trying to terrify me, he was doing a damn good job.

"So beautiful," he whispered in a husky tone. "It's going to be a pleasure to take all of you." He wrapped his hand around my neck, holding me in place as he lowered his head until our lips were centimeters apart.

I struggled in his paralyzing grip until his hand tightened, squeezing with enough pressure I knew he could snap my neck. When he pressed his lips against mine, I took several raspy breaths. "Leave me alone. Please."

Cristiano issued a series of low growls, the deep sound vibrating in my chest. "You know I won't do that."

Every part of my body remained stiff, shrinking back as much as his hold would allow.

Exhaling, he pulled away by several inches. Then without warning, he claimed my mouth. I pushed my hands against him, trying to break the connection but it was no use. I refused to open my mouth as he shoved his tongue against my lips but the anguish of his fingers digging into my jaw forced an involuntary action.

His actions forceful, he swirled his tongue against mine, teasing relentlessly. The taste of him was overtly masculine, the flavors of scotch and what had to be cinnamon enticing my taste buds. I did everything I could to thwart his repulsive actions, but he was far too powerful, able to hold me in place with ease. Everything about him was larger than life, the kiss so all-consuming that it sucked all the air out of my lungs. I was lightheaded, stars floating in my periphery of vision.

The same stubble on his jaw I'd found so sexy scraped against my skin, igniting a firestorm of desire burning between my legs. I couldn't believe I was wet, the dampness of my panties adding to the wave of embarrassment. For a few disgusting, irritating seconds, I found myself falling into the kiss, the moment of pure sin unlike anything I'd ever experienced. I was almost drunk on my desire, dizzy from the passion, no longer able to feel my legs. If the brute of a man hadn't been holding me, there was no doubt I'd stumble and fall.

Everything about this was so wrong, bad on every level. I wasn't supposed to be attracted to a monster. I couldn't be. I just…

Some level of rationality settling in, I slammed my palms against him, digging my nails into his shirt and able to break the kiss. The feel of his tight muscles further fueled the sensations, my mouth suddenly bone dry. "What do you want from me?"

"I already told you. Everything. Including the truth."

"My God. I'm really your prisoner. You can do anything you want to me." While I said the words in passing, the sound little more than a whisper, I could tell he was listening intently. When I smashed my fists against him a second time, I was able to break his hold, but the force tossed me to the floor.

When he advanced, there was little I could do. He scooped me into his arms, tossing me over his shoulder and moving toward the stairs.

"You're exactly right, Emily. You *are* my prisoner. Now, it's time to take every inch of what belongs to me."

CHAPTER 6

ristiano

Anger rushed through me like a tidal wave, although my rage had nothing to do with the woman I'd captured. The meeting with my family was the reason. If my brothers had allowed the Azzurris to move in on any of our territories, there would be hell to pay.

However, if Giancarlo had broken our deal, he would die by my hands.

My family knew what was at stake, the viciousness of the Azzurris. My father would like nothing more than to exterminate every one of them. At least they hadn't acted during my incarceration, starting a war that would destroy the city. However, I would need to get to the bottom of the rumors, the attempt on my father's life and even the answer to whether Giancarlo had Michael's wife killed. I laughed at the thought. Could I trust the bastard?

Then there was the issue of Mario's disobedience. He was little more than a thug, although he'd saved my father's life on two occasions, including the attack that had escalated my time spent behind bars. He'd been 'loaned' to me by Lucian in case I'd need additional muscle while leaving the prison, as if the offer held any real meaning. I couldn't stand Mario's arrogance or particularly brutal methods, especially the way he'd handled Emily. While the cage had been placed in the basement for a specific reason months before I'd been arrested, I'd use it as a method of punishment at my choosing, not his.

I'd deal with the bullshit in the morning.

As for now, I was far too hungry.

The shower would wait.

I moved to the stairs, still hating the way the old wooden treads creaked under the heaviness of my shoes. While a significant portion of the house had been renovated before I'd moved in six years before, the refurbishment of the ornate stairway and handrail had been minimal. For some reason, that's all I could think about as I took them two at a time.

She kicked out, struggling to reach for the railing. The sound of her nails scratching the well-oiled surface forced an immediate reaction. I brought my palm against her backside with brutal smacks, one after the other, chuckling as she moaned several times.

"Ouch! Let me down," Emily insisted, pummeling her hands against my back.

"Fight me all you want, little pet. That just turns me on."

"You're a bastard."

Her actions created a primal surge from deep within, the kind of aching need that swept through me like a tidal wave. It was difficult to comprehend why this woman, the very one who'd been able to break the Kings' veil of power, ignited the dark passion within me, but there was no denying my intense yearning.

She was mine.

I stormed into my bedroom, only bothering to flip on the single light on the dresser. As a warm glow filled the room, she did everything she could do to get out of my hold. When she managed to kick me in the stomach with her bare foot, I slid my hand under her dress, wrapping my fingers around her leg.

"I suggest you stop fighting me," I growled.

Whether or not Dimitri had anticipated my actions remained unknown, I'd been pleasantly surprised after entering the house to find the cleaning staff had provided a new set of sheets and a comforter. I'd expected to find Emily in one of the other rooms, secured to the bed and awaiting my return. When that hadn't been the case, I'd almost erupted in rage, uncertain she'd even been brought to the house.

Another thought regarding the cage entered my mind, fueling the anger even more.

I had to get the ugliness out of my mind, at least for tonight. I needed a clear head in order to proceed with certain plans. Rest was in order.

While this wasn't about a romantic moment, I was exhausted, the ebb of adrenaline coming to an end.

That wouldn't stop me from taking what was mine.

I dumped her onto the bed and within seconds, she managed to scramble off the side, grabbing the bedside lamp and swinging it in my direction. I couldn't help but be amused, her jabbing and slashing motions coming dangerously close to connecting.

However, the time for playing games was over.

Ducking, I wrapped my arm around her waist, driving us both into the middle of the bed, the lamp crashing to the floor with a hard thud. I could tell I'd knocked the wind out of her, her mouth twisting, the girl trying desperately to claw as far away from me as possible. Then her lovely doe eyes opened wide, venom still prickling the beautiful flecks of gold surrounding her irises.

Without hesitation, I straddled her hips, jerking first one of her arms then the other over her head, wrapping a single hand around both wrists.

She was going nowhere.

Her chest rose and fell as she glared at me. Still so damn beautiful, so fraught with rebellion.

I was drawn to her like a moth to a flame, although I knew in my gut that my actions could create the kind of combustible fire that could turn into acid, scarring both of us. I was taking a significant chance. Her disappearance would be questioned at some point, although perhaps only by her employer.

I continued to try to figure out why she'd had the nerve to testify against me. The woman was obviously highly intelligent, no doubt well versed in the underground dealings within the city. Our family's name rarely made it a week without being featured by one reporter or another. My instinct told me she was hiding something from me, perhaps the real reason she'd agreed to testify. I would find out soon enough.

No matter how I was forced to obtain the information.

"You're a very naughty girl," I breathed before lowering my head, nipping her earlobe.

She shuddered, her breathing ragged. "Get away from me."

"You know that's not going to happen."

I brushed my lips along her jaw then down and against the column of her neck, allowing my hot breath to cascade across her skin. Very slowly I lowered my hand, swirling my fingers back and forth.

Across her arm.

Across her breast.

Crawling my fingers down to the hem of her dress.

She stiffened, sucking in her breath when I eased the slip of material up to her thigh. I rubbed my knuckles back and forth across her leg, my entire arm tingling from the softness of her skin.

"Oh..." she moaned, turning her head to one side and avoiding eye contact.

I drank in her scent as I swirled my knuckles in lazy circles, moving closer and closer to her heated wetness. The second I pressed my hand between her legs, rubbing my palm up and down her lacy panties, she kicked out, bucking hard on the bed in an effort to free her arms.

"Asshole," she spouted off, her reaction forcing her body to grind against mine.

I was even more aroused than before, my cock fully engorged.

"There's nowhere you can run, no way to get away from me. Now, I suggest you relax, Emily. I can provide extreme pleasure, or I can provide excruciating anguish. As I told you before," I whispered, "the decision is entirely your own. Your destiny. Your life."

"My life," she sputtered. "It's already over."

She squeezed her eyes shut as if she could block me out. I continued rubbing, using enough force I pressed the material between her swollen folds, growling from the slickness covering my fingers, my cock pressing hard against my trousers. There would be no holding back the beast for long, the hunger swelling, my carnal needs refusing to be denied.

"That will depend on just how obedient you become." The harder I rubbed, the more she had difficulty holding back a single sound. She fisted then flexed her hands, shifting her head from one side to the other.

My heart racing, I slipped two fingers underneath the thin elastic of her panties, swirling the tips around her clit.

She did everything she could to buck against me, her head tossing back and forth, her hips rocking.

"So wet. So hot." I adored the feel of her, the extreme heat as well as the surging electricity sparking a wave of energy. "You hunger, the dark and filthy needs you've desired rushing to the surface. Isn't that true?"

"No," she moaned, twisting her lovely mouth, fighting with everything she had to ignore her body's reaction.

"And your body betrays you once again. Tell me."

"No. I just…" Unable to finish her sentence, she darted a glance in my direction, her eyes glassy.

I allowed her to enjoy the pleasure for a full minute, unable to take my eyes off her reaction. Then I released her hands, using both of mine to rip the edges of her dress down her arms, exposing her breasts. The ripping sound gave me a gleeful feeling, the sight of her breasts tightening my balls. She was truly beautiful all over, her porcelain skin glistening in the dim lighting.

Her high-pitched wail continued to ignite the remaining embers, the fire in my belly that of a barbarian.

"Keep your arms over your head, Emily," I directed.

"Bastard." The word was the same, but the tone was new. She was purring, her chest continuing to heave but for an entirely different reason. The fact her blushing rose nipples were fully aroused, hard like perfect diamonds, was just another sign of her growing desire.

Electricity surged through me as I lowered my head, darting my tongue around her hardened bud, growling from the pinched expression crossing her face. I nipped the tender flesh, sucking until I was rewarded with a slight whimper, the sound like sweet music.

Cupping her other breast, I pinched the tip between my thumb and forefinger, twisting and pulling. Her legs flailed, but to her credit, she remained obedient, struggling to keep her arms over her head.

I shifted my attention to her other nipple, sucking and biting down. Her mouth opened into a perfect 'O,' her eyes once against closed tightly.

The very sight of her in the throes of pleasure evoked the sadistic side of me. I'd never been considered a gentleman, my brutal needs something few women could tolerate. There was usually nothing gentle about my touch, no subtle caresses. I took what I wanted.

But this girl, this beautiful and fragile flower required something different. Too bad she'd crossed me. Perhaps in another life, we could have shared exactly what she needed, indulging in days and nights of passion. That wasn't going to be the case. Not now.

Not ever.

Although I planned on thoroughly exploring every inch of her body. I couldn't wait to sink my cock deep inside her wetness, her tight muscles clamping around my shaft like a vise.

When she started to have trouble keeping her arms over her head, I pulled back, moving off the bed, taking the knife from my pocket.

She searched for me almost immediately, her eyes still glazed over, her mouth pursed.

"Undress," I commanded, flicking the switchblade open once, twisting and turning the sharp steel back and forth. Chuckling darkly, I slapped it closed, placing it on the dresser. At some point, there was no doubt in my mind that she'd make an attempt for one or more of my weapons. Perhaps I was baiting her, longing to find out just how strong her resolve was.

That would make breaking her that much sweeter.

Now she stared at me, the hatred from before returning.

I lifted a single eyebrow as I began to unfasten my shirt, taking my time with every button.

Her actions stiff, she climbed off the comforter, lowering her head and allowing her long hair to tumble over her shoulders. "Why are you doing this?"

She actually had the nerve to ask me why for a second time? Why not just kill her instead? That's exactly what she was asking, although she was terrified of my answer. I snorted, tugging on my shirt until I'd managed to release it from my trousers. When I didn't answer her immediately, she tipped her head in my direction, studying me intently.

"Because I enjoy beautiful things." The answer was the most truthful I could provide. Any other reason and I would be lying.

Especially since I wasn't entirely certain myself.

Nodding, she seemed to accept the answer. I was surprised there was no pushback. She simply stood, tugging on the bottom of her dress, shimmying her rounded hips back and forth until the material fell to the floor. Her shoulders heaved, but her hesitation was only minimal before she slipped her fingers into her thong, shoving the lace down her long legs, kicking out of them with vigor.

I was surprised when she covered her breasts with one arm, her other placed in front of her smooth mound. She certainly wasn't the kind of woman I'd played with from time to time. Her humility and shyness, the warm blush creeping up from her neck was beguiling.

It was too bad I was such a monster, incapable of caring about anything or anyone so precious.

I turned toward the dresser, removing my watch, the one my father had given me the last Christmas I'd been a free man. He wasn't into holidays, at least not usually, our mother arranging for whatever presents seemed appropriate. My father had been responsible for giving me the gift, the stunning piece holding more value because of what it represented.

The watch had been in the family for decades, my father having received the gift from his father, a grandfather I couldn't remember. That Christmas, my father had turned over the reins in their entirety, the watch the clear indication.

To the entire family.

Perhaps that's why Lucian hated me so much. He'd been the one to stroke our father's ego, doing everything he could to follow in the man's footsteps. Lucian believed his academic background as well as his reputation amongst our business associates was the right fit for taking over as Don.

I'd seen the crushed look on my brother's face, finally storming out of the room only minutes later. There had been bad blood between us ever since. Today had been no exception. I placed the piece of jewelry on the dresser before unfastening my belt. I stared at my reflection in the mirror, able to tell she was watching me intently, trying to figure out who or what the hell I was.

I slowly slipped the leather strap through my belt loops, able to hear her subtle yet strangled sighs behind me. I coiled the belt, placing it on the dresser next to my weapon.

Every action I made terrified her. Good. She needed to be afraid of me.

As I unfastened my pants, I shifted my eyes away from her briefly. That was all the time she needed in order to race toward the door, able to make it into the hallway before I reacted.

Damn, the feisty woman was a handful, a brat who needed to be tamed.

Unfortunately, she wouldn't like my methods.

Hissing, my patience had just been tossed, my frustration with her reaching a place of no return. She needed to learn her lesson one way or another. I took long strides, catching her just as she'd made it to the top of the stairway, my fingers digging into her arm and giving a solid yank.

She shrieked, the sound high pitched, jerking around to face me and throwing a hard right hook. The shock of her actions stunned me momentarily, enough so she yanked out of my hold, almost tumbling down the stairs.

"Get back here!" I snapped, shaking my head as I lumbered down the stairs, catching her again within seconds. I dragged her against me, taking her forearms when she attempted to punch me a second time.

"Let me go. I hate you. I hate you! Murderer."

If she expected the words to sting, she truly had no idea what kind of man she was up against. "As usual, sweet Emily, you are correct in your assumptions, something you're keen to continue forgetting. You're going to be punished severely."

"Of course. Why not? That's all you understand. Violence."

Growling, I pulled her with me and into the room, once again dumping her onto the bed. "Get the fuck on your hands and knees."

"Why bother?"

"Because I instructed you to do so. Do it or I assure you that your punishment will be worse." No one had challenged me like the woman glaring at me with such a hateful expression. No one. No matter the enemy, or the harsh decisions I'd made, no one had attempted to thwart me more than once.

And lived.

While I was riled, my desire took precedence over the anger that threatened to turn me into the hard, cold bastard I'd enjoyed portraying the majority of my life. The fact she'd managed to get under my skin was something that I found difficult to deny.

Or refuse to continue enjoying.

Emily dropped her head, her breaths scattered before moving into the position I'd demanded. However, I heard the exclamations said under her breath, her wishes for my demise. My death was a distinct possibility.

I yanked the belt from the dresser, trying to control my breathing, curtailing the last of my rage. While she required discipline for her abrupt and wretched actions, she didn't deserve the wrath that encompassed the majority of my being.

She shifted back and forth, undulating her hips in the usual provocative manner. Even though my cock ached to be inside of her, the fact she'd attempted to get away from me couldn't be ignored. I inched closer, closing my eyes briefly as I rolled the tips of my fingers across the expensive leather.

To think I hadn't been able to wear a belt in prison, fear that I'd commit suicide or worse the reason. I almost laughed at the thought. Inhaling, the same scent of our combined desire almost pushed me into a drunken state. I'd craved the taste of a beautiful woman behind bars more than once.

When I pressed my fingers against the small of her back, she shivered, clenching the comforter. "You're going to finally learn what it means to fight against me, Emily."

"You will never break me."

I laughed softly, more to myself as I ran the tip of my finger down the crack of her ass. "We will see."

As I folded the belt, she shuddered once again, the sound of her breath doing little more than fueling the brutal man inside. I pushed her legs apart, running my fingers along the slick wetness of her pussy before issuing a single crack, the thick leather slicing against her bottom with ease.

Emily's body jerked, her reaction meshed with a single moan.

I smacked her backside two more times, languishing in the slight but beautiful blush erupting like a bloom of fresh flowers across her skin.

She bucked a few times, tossing her head back and forth.

Every move she made further ignited the darkness within me.

After taking multiple deep breaths, I brought the leather strap down several times, my aim utter perfection.

Her cry of fury, indignation, and pain couldn't stop the cravings I had.

To subdue her.

To make her submit.

To drive her to acceptance.

I heard her continued words of hatred as I pressed on with the round of discipline, bringing the belt down several additional times. The beast inside of me was mesmerized by the crimson color spreading across her buttocks. I sucked in my breath and caressed her bruised bottom, enjoying the heat radiating through my fingers. She had no idea what she was doing to me, the yearning that remained at the surface.

"You're doing very well," I said almost too casually.

Every sound she made was one of anxiety as well as her own level of anger. I knew she hated me, her body refusing to accept my domination. It would take time and diligence.

That would be utter joy that I was prepared to feed on with my needs.

"I want nothing more than to feel the heat on your bottom against my body as I fuck you."

My words brought another litany of anguished sounds, creating a smile on my face.

I brought the strap down four additional times, the adrenaline rushing through my body and consuming every cell and muscle. My needs would require fulfillment soon. I'd almost lost count of the number I'd given, every tendon constricting as my cravings increased.

"Oh," she moaned as she struggled, taking several shallow breaths. "I hate you."

Let her hate me.

"If you try and escape again, your punishment will be much worse." The warning was one I knew she'd attempt to defy. That was her nature.

After issuing the final few strikes, I tossed the belt across the room, almost gasping for air, the hunger furrowing in my system unlike anything I'd ever experienced.

But I had to admit, the thought of tasting her before fucking her was just as overwhelming.

As she collapsed on the bed, I stepped back, finally relieving myself of the tight confines of my pants. My cock was at full attention, my balls aching like a son of a bitch. I put my hand between my legs, stroking my shaft, running my fingers up and down the length, my actions rough enough a strangled sigh pulsed from my lips.

I couldn't wait to fill her with my seed for a second time.

A low-slung growl erupted from deep within as I approached, flipping her over on the bed. Her look of surprise, both in her eyes as well as her pursed lips was exactly what I would have expected.

When I crowded between her legs, only then did she let off an intense moan, her entire body quivering. I shoved her thighs wide open, pushing her knees against her chest as I lowered my head, continuing to make savage and very guttural sounds.

Emily pounded her fists against the comforter, tossing her head back and forth.

"What... what are you... doing?" she managed to ask.

"Feasting, my sweet Emily. Feasting."

I rubbed my lips and face against her inner thigh, studying the stunned look crossing her face as I dug my fingers into her skin. Every muscle in her body was tense, her legs stiff to my touch. When I darted my tongue across her clit a single time, she jerked up from the bedding, acting as if she was still prepared to fight my actions once again.

A hard smack against her pussy lips was enough to force her to settle down, her body thumping against the bed. She covered her face with her hands, releasing ragged moans.

And I could hear every word she muttered, the statement of hatred doing little more than giving me a smile. I swirled my tongue around her tiny nub again, enjoying the sweet taste as I concentrated on my efforts. She was so wet, her pussy juice trickling against her inner thighs. All I wanted to do was to drag my tongue through the tasty droplets, savoring the flavor. But my hunger was too great.

I buried my head into her delicious folds, taking my time to lap up her cream.

"Oh… God…" she breathed, her murmurs filtering into the room.

Lifting my head, I breathed across her pussy before sliding my tongue past her slickened folds. When I added a single finger, rubbing it up and down before thrusting it as deep as I was able, her legs began to shake involuntarily. I added a second and third finger, flexing them open as I plunged inside, curling the tips in an effort to rake them across her G-spot. I refused to take my eyes off her as I satisfied my thirst, driving my tongue beside my fingers.

"Uh. Uh. Uh…" She half laughed, her hand still covering her face, goosebumps erupting across every inch of her naked skin. She was sexy as fuck, including the glisten blooming on her cheeks. She was unable to mask her beauty, even with her hand covering her face.

I consumed every inch of her, dragging my tongue up and down slowly. There was nothing like the taste of a woman incapable of acknowledging her beauty.

With every swipe of my tongue, I brought her closer to climaxing.

Sadly, the ruthless bastard in me wanted to ensure she knew exactly who was in charge of every aspect of her pleasure. Easing away, I licked my lips then brought three fingers down in rapid succession, smacking her pussy lips hard and fast.

Whimpering, she jerked up, her doe eyes opening wide. This time, her mouth was twisted in confusion as well as horror.

I pressed my lips against one inner thigh then the other as I snaked my hand over her stomach. "Never forget that every inch of you belongs to me."

While she didn't utter a word, the contempt in her eyes was the same as before.

She clenched her eyes shut, trying not to react as I resumed licking, driving four fingers inside her wet heat while I used my thumb to tease her clit, the tender tissue now swollen.

With every swipe of my tongue, Emily did her best to ignore the raging sensations dancing through her. Every part of her was shaking, her chest rising and falling rapidly. Almost a minute later, she had no ability to hold back, her body bucking as an orgasm began to sweep through her.

"Oh. Oh. Oh."

I drilled my fingers inside brutally as I sucked on her clit, growling, savoring every drop of her sweet cream. As a single climax turned into a second, I buried my head against her wetness, licking fervently. Her cream filled my mouth, sliding down the back of my throat. I couldn't seem to get enough, sucking on her tender tissue as I plunged my open fingers in even more savagely than before.

Emily's moans were scattered, her entire body heaving, her fingers white-knuckled as she fisted the comforter. Very slowly, I eased my legs between hers, the heat of our combined bodies combustible. There wasn't a cell in my body that hadn't erupted into a raging fire, the beast within me roaring his pleasure.

As well as his impatience.

Even before her body stopped shaking, I crowded over her, pressing the tip of my cock against her wetness. If she sensed what I was about to do, she didn't react, although her whimpers continued.

After positioning my cockhead at her entrance, I planted both hands on either side of her, leaning over until our lips were only a few inches apart. "Now, I fuck you."

My words finally caused a reaction, the voluptuous woman losing her ability to open, pressing both her palms against my chest in a frail attempt to push me away. She stared into my eyes, her fingers caressing my aching muscles.

The dark hunger that had lured me to her in the first place took over. I thrust the entire length of my cock into her pussy, my breath rattled as her muscles immediately clamped over my aching shaft. The heat was explosive, the warmth attempting to chisel away at the brutal man inside.

She gasped from the force used, the shimmer in her eyes a mixture of excitement as well as uncertainty. The woman was fighting our attraction, the natural instinct that I'd felt the first time I'd taken her. But when she arched her back, her fingernails scratching down the length of my chest, there was no doubt she was sliding into the throes of ecstasy.

"Agony or ecstasy. Something for you to remember, Emily," I whispered.

I pulled almost all the way out, leaning further over until our lips were finally touching. As I held the stance, I gathered additional confusion playing out in her mind. She had no understanding of what I was doing or why I'd kept her alive for this long. Obviously, she had no comprehension of the fact she'd become my possession, my private little pet to play with.

As I rubbed my lips back and forth over hers, she mewed, her mouth opening up like a rose petal, waiting for me to explore the soft velvet. Unable to resist, I swirled my tongue around her mouth before easing it inside. Once again, I drove my cock deep inside, the harshness of my actions slamming the headboard against the wall.

I crushed her mouth, enjoying her constant hesitation yet her willingness to surrender, at least for moments at a time.

Soon she would be begging for more, her hunger becoming insatiable.

Soon she would surrender in every way, body and soul.

Soon she would fully comprehend the wrath of a dangerous man.

And after that? She'd accept her ultimate punishment.

CHAPTER 7

Emily

Dangerous.

Damning.

Delicious.

The array of emotions rushing through me was disgusting, creating a self-loathing that left a bitter taste in my mouth.

Or at least it would have had the taste if the brutal, unforgiving man not been so incredible. I remained furious that my body responded, the chill coursing down my spine all about the extreme pleasure I'd already experienced. Even the game of cat and mouse had induced excitement, yanking on the kind of darkness that had consumed Cristiano long before he'd ever met me.

There was no light in his eyes, only a pitch-black glance into his soul. He enjoyed toying with me, doing everything he could in his power to break my resolve. That wasn't going to happen.

Everything about the man confused the hell out of me, including the furniture in his bedroom. The oversized canopy bed was massive, the mattress positioned several more inches off the floor than normal. The posts were carved in an ornate design, the wood inlaid with gold. While there was no mirror over the bed, the thick truss-like wooden slats reminded me of a cross.

Every other piece of furniture was just as oppressive, likely costing most than the majority of cars. Nothing in the room fit him, not the brutal man who'd taken me by force.

I bucked my hips as he continued thrusting his cock inside, my pussy walls aching from the size of his shaft. There wasn't a muscle in my body that wasn't tingling from his rough touch, the way he'd manhandled me. He was so powerful, much stronger than I had the ability to fight, yet I refused to accept some crazy willingness to succumb to his desires.

Or his requirements.

But still my heart was racing, my cells erupting from the fire-power of heat, his skin searing mine. As the kiss became just another brutal taking of my body, some level of common sense finally shifted into my mind. I pummeled my fists against him, but his body refused to budge, his cock filling me completely.

When he finally broke the kiss, he sucked then nipped my lower lip, several growls pushing up from his throat. Every-thing about him was so masculine, forceful. Perhaps I'd always craved a dominating man, although I'd never admitted or dared to explore the option.

What the hell was I thinking?

This *man* was a monster, a murderer.

I couldn't begin to tolerate or like a man who'd already sold his soul to the devil.

But as the savage fucking continued, I found it more difficult to block the beautiful bliss crowding into my space, taking over my rational mind.

The fact he'd already made me orgasm was horrible, the scent filtering into my nostrils just as disgusting. I struggled against him, although with every involuntary jutting of my hips, I only pushed his cock in even deeper. He was all consuming, pounding into me relentlessly, growling like the wild beast I already knew him to be.

I was almost crushed underneath the weight of him, but somehow our bodies molded together. Shock and embarrassment rode me hard, the realization that I was deriving absolute pleasure from his savagery pushing me to the brink of losing faith in myself.

And losing my mind.

When he slowed his rhythm, pulling almost all the way out then sliding in as if I was a delicate flower, he brushed his jaw across my cheek to my ear. Even the way the stubble of his slight beard scratched against my skin left me breathless, my nipples aching. As he whispered into my ear, the seductive tone smooth and velvety, stars floated in front of my eyes, twinkling brightly.

"Do you want to come, little flower?" he asked.

"Na... No," I lied, uncertain I would even be able to stop my body's reaction.

He chuckled in his dark and demonic manner as he swirled his tongue inside my ear. "I told you never to lie to me. Do you want to come?"

I gritted my teeth, terrified of answering either way.

But I did.

The single word slipped past my lips before I could stop it.

"Yes."

"Good girl." He picked up his rhythm, moving in and out, the sound of my wetness pulsing in my ears.

I tried to fight the insane arousal, doing everything I could to push the orgasm out of my mind, but it was to no avail. My entire body was quivering as the climax began to slide along the insides of my legs.

"Then come for me, sweet Emily. Come."

I gasped for air, digging my nails into his arms, rocking against him like a bucking horse.

"Come," he commanded, his tone more forceful.

I couldn't resist him or what was happening deep within, as if I was awakening from a delicious dream, taken to the heights of exquisite ecstasy. As I clung to him, I clenched my eyes shut, pretending this was the beautiful start to a magical time shared.

Instead of just the beginning of my nightmare.

As the orgasm swept through me, building to the point of an amazing frenzy, I opened my mouth and screamed. A single climax erupted into a second, then a dazzling third. Nothing was real any longer.

Not the moment.

Not the fear.

Not the anticipation of what was to come, the horrors I'd be forced to endure.

Only this incredible, breathtaking moment. Gasping for air, I opened my eyes, blinking several times in some crazy effort to focus.

His chuckle remained as he powered into me, his hips rocking against me in such a provocative manner. He'd risen onto his elbows, his cold eyes staring straight through me, lust swirling around his corneas. I was shocked how mesmerizing they'd become, as if he was drawing me into his world.

Or keeping me locked down in his lair.

Panting, I licked my lips, every cell in my body on fire. How could I feel this way? How? What the hell was wrong with me?

There was no warning. Cristiano merely pulled out, crawling backwards then flipping me over and yanking me onto all fours. He smacked my already bruised bottom several times before pushing on the small of my back, forcing me to press my face against the bedding.

"Now, I fuck you in the ass."

The words were just as chilling, the harsh sound of his tone of voice another reminder that he was nothing but an animal.

A rush of adrenaline and apprehension shot through me, the pain from the harsh smacks coursing through every tendon and muscle. I'd never been taken in the ass before, not once.

The thought was revolting, hardcore in ways I could barely comprehend.

Then why was excitement drifting into every vein, keeping my muscles taut and the butterflies increasing?

He caressed my bottom with both hands as he spread my legs further apart. Just the feel of his fingers was enough to create a series of moans. I was shaking all over, tears forming in my eyes. When he shifted a single finger down the crack of my ass, I tensed, trying to keep from squealing.

"I bet you're tight as hell," he said, his tone dominating. So deep. So dark.

So enticing.

I tried to concentrate on the sound of his voice to abate my fears, but I couldn't process what he was going to do.

Just take what he wanted.

Refusing to accept no for an answer.

And while the excitement remained, the fear of the unknown sent a powerful message straight to whatever rational side of my brain was left. Before I knew what I was doing, I scampered toward the head of the bed, preparing to jump off.

The husky growl booming into the room echoed in my ears. He snagged my hair, entangling his fingers in my long strands, yanking me backwards and closer to the edge of the bed. Several painful slaps against my backside were his way of reminding me to behave.

I could hear his heavy breathing as he tugged again, lifting me to the point I had to steady myself on the tips of my fingers.

"You shouldn't have done that, little flower."

"I can't do this."

"Can't? Oh, I assure you that you can and you will. Like I told you, every hole belongs to me." He delivered four additional cracks in rapid succession. The pain was excruciating, the excessive heat telling me in no uncertain terms that I would be sore in the morning.

Or maybe for days.

Was that his intent, to remind me that for every misbehavior I could expect a hard spanking?

I gritted my teeth as he rolled a single finger down the crack of my ass again before sliding it into my pussy. The same ecstasy I'd felt before shot through me, but it was short-lived. He pushed the same finger between my ass cheeks, sliding just the tip inside. The feeling was uncomfortable as hell, the invasion filthy.

He refused to let go of his hold as he pushed harder, shoving against the tight ring of muscle.

"Oh… I…"

"Yes, just as tight as I knew you'd be," he growled, inserting a second finger, thrusting both all the way inside.

The anguish was instantaneous, a ragged moan spouted off toward the heavens above. I couldn't believe anyone actually enjoyed this. I was mortified, so damn embarrassed. There could be nothing more humiliating.

I almost laughed at the thought. Yes, I was certain there could be, especially if the bastard had his way. I held my breath to keep from screaming as the searing pain sent a crisscrossing of electric jolts tearing down the back of my legs. Several tears slipped past my lashes, ones of anger and frustration.

When he forced me to arch my back even more, I gritted my teeth, refusing to give into his tyranny. This monster would not tear through a single layer. Not one.

"Relax, little flower."

"I can't relax. I've never…" I couldn't even finish my statement. Why the hell would he even care that I'd never done this before? He had no conscience. He had no care, certainly not about me. I was just an object to him.

He stopped pumping, taking a deep breath then exhaling slowly. "A virgin. How interesting."

A bitter laugh escaped my lips.

The bastard inserted a third finger, still driving them into me but more gently.

Slowly.

"Just breathe for me, sweet Emily. Breathe."

There was no other choice but to breathe, although I couldn't control my pulse or the rapid rate I was sucking in and releasing air. The pain was biting, my muscles stretched to the limit, my body bucking as I clawed the comforter, trembling all over.

Yet I realized in horror that I was wet, my pussy throbbing. This was actually turning me on? My God. I clenched my eyes shut.

This isn't real. This isn't real!

But it was.

Cristiano removed his fingers, taking his time to caress my aching bottom.

What the hell was the man waiting for?

He ground his rock-hard cock against me, rubbing back and forth. Then he thrust his shaft into my pussy, pumping several times before sliding the tip to my darkened hole.

I bristled, unable to stop the series of moans, my mind reeling from what he was about to do.

He said nothing as he pushed his bulbous head inside, teasing my muscles.

"Oh, God. Oh. Oh…"

"That's it, little flower. Open up for me."

When he continued pushing, the anguish returned, but only for a few seconds, my muscles finally accepting. He was so large, the pressure intense, yet a level of warmth I had never experienced replaced the pain.

"That's it," he murmured. "Take all of me."

The moment he was fully seated inside, he threw his head back and roared, the sound strangely melodic.

Blinking away the tears, I took several deep breaths as my muscles spasmed, drawing his thick cock in even deeper.

He gripped my hips, thrusting harder. There wasn't a cell or muscle, tendon or synapse that wasn't on fire, tiny sparks fluttering all throughout my body. I could no longer breathe, my heart hammering to the point I fell into a dark abyss.

But the pleasure was incredible, sensations that had never been alive awakened as if from a deep slumber.

"Oh… Uh. Uh. Uh." The guttural sounds coming from my throat sounded foreign, my tone husky. While I continued to claw the bedding, I was confused that a smile had crossed my face. Enjoying what he was doing to me was crazy.

Sickening.

Amazing.

I could tell he was close to coming, his breath skipping even more than before. The second I clenched my muscles, his entire body tensed, a low rumbling sound floating into the entire room.

Then I heard the word, one he'd said before but this time, I feared it even more.

"Mine."

Cristiano didn't move for several seconds yet his body continued to shake. When he finally backed away, I slumped against the bed, trying to catch my breath. I heard his footsteps as he padded away. A cold chill shifted down my legs, more from the loss of the extreme heat of his body being pressed against mine. Every muscle ached. I was exhausted, drained from the ordeal and unsure of what to expect next. I tugged at the covers, creating a pillow before shifting in order to see what he was doing.

Just seeing his naked body took my breath away. I'd never seen a man so carved in all the right places. Every muscle was in perfect proportion, chiseled as if his entire body was made of the finest stone. And his buttocks? I bit my lower lip as he walked toward what appeared to be a bar in the corner of the room. I was able to envision him in a tight pair of blue jeans.

My God. Why the hell was I thinking like some wayward waif? I purposely turned away, cringing as I heard the clink of glasses. Was this supposed to be the romantic post-sex discussion? I certainly doubted we were going to cuddle or share any niceties. I chewed on my cheek, continuing to dig at the covers in an effort to slide underneath for warmth.

Or maybe in an effort to hide.

I managed to find the beginning of the sheet and crawled under them, pulling the edge over my breasts. I couldn't take my eyes off him as he poured two drinks from an elegant crystal decanter. There was something so strange about what he was doing.

As if this was… normal.

When he turned around, the expression on his face was stern. "Who told you that you could cover up?"

"I…" Another blush swept up both cheeks.

"Drop the covers." His demand was even more authoritative than before.

I had to bite back a retort, but I did as he commanded, allowing the sheets to fall around my waist. While his gaze was heated, filled with lust, the same cold and dangerous look appeared in his eyes as he approached.

He stood almost stoically, staring down at me for a full five seconds before handing me one of the drinks.

Which I refused to take.

His sigh was exaggerated. "Take the drink, Emily. I'm uncertain why you still believe you can ignore my requirements."

"Because you don't own me."

It was obvious he was amused by the smirk forming on his mouth. "Take the drink. Now."

I finally reached out, wrapping my hand around the glass, loathing not only the fact our fingers touched but that electricity skittered down every inch of me. I wasn't much of a drinker, but tonight whatever was in the glass was appealing. I hid behind the crystal, licking the rim and looking away as he crawled onto the bed, plumping the damn pillows before placing two of the four behind his back and shoulders.

As if he was king of the hill.

Cristiano crossed his legs at his ankles and sat back.

I shifted my gaze anywhere but at the man, trying to nurse the bitter liquor. Maybe if I got drunk, I would be able to handle the rest of the night.

"Look at me, Emily."

His voice was even gruffer than before. I gulped hard, taking not one but three sips of the drink, barely able to swallow. I did as I was told, finally turning my head, hating that my lower lip was now quivering.

He studied me as he swirled his drink, finally sucking down half of it. When he placed the tumbler on his leg, folding his arm behind his head, only then did he say anything else. "You were in the restaurant."

His words were in the form of a statement, not a question. "Yes. Picking up a to-go order."

"Interesting since you don't live anywhere near the area, a place full of fleabag motels and seedy clubs."

I shook my head. "I work around the corner. I had few options for employment, and I needed a job."

"What were you doing there at night?"

How the hell was I supposed to answer that? "I was working late, which is something I've done several times. And I was hungry."

"Which is why you walked by yourself to a shithole of a restaurant in what is one of the highest crime areas in the city."

"The office is on the outskirts in a new complex and I really love… or loved…" I realized I was whispering.

He took another sip of his drink, his stare even more intent; however, I could tell he was trying to place the location. Damn, the man made me nervous. "I know the building. I guess I should have paid more attention to the businesses located in the surrounding area.

"The name?"

My first thought was surprise that his battery of attorneys hadn't told him part of the information. Then I realized it was in some crazy effort to keep me safe.

You failed. You failed. You failed.

My inner voice nagged at me, laughing as if I was nothing but a fool. "Bayou Market Analysis."

I could see such surprise on his face as well as another round of amusement. "What the hell does that make you, an office administrator?"

To be incensed that he thought I was only smart enough to be an administrator was ridiculous. What the fuck did I care what the asshole thought? I snorted before I realized it. "I was the lead market analyst for the firm." The firm. There were eight employees, two of which couldn't find their way out of a paper bag. While I'd been the fool to volunteer for additional work, the kind that kept me locked down in the office until all hours of the night, only my boss had any kind of real title.

As if I had to tell the jerkoff anything.

"Well, one formidable lady on all regards," he said quietly, laughing softly to himself.

"I'm sure that by now one of your goons already figured out almost every aspect of my life. I graduated with honors from the University of Pennsylvania with a degree in finance, earning my bachelor's in three years. Subsequently, I went on to earn my master's degree in one year. You are absolutely correct that I am one formidable woman." The defiance in my voice was likely to piss him off. What the hell? Why not shoot the moon.

"Very impressive indeed."

The quiet that settled between us was just as horrifying as the man barking orders. I tried to concentrate on the glass, realizing the damn thing was Waterford crystal. Jesus.

"This bed, the entire bedroom doesn't suit you."

"You mean a killer."

While I knew we weren't going to have normal discussions, getting to know each other like a couple, I was curious. "A self-appointed ruthless man."

He chuckled. "The truth is that the bedroom suite came with the house. I thought about trashing every piece, but I've grown used to it. Does that mean you like it?"

"Every piece is beautiful, majestic, but I'm not certain it fits the house." I realized I had a smile on my face as my hand moved to the nightstand, fingering one of the carved sections. I felt the heat of his stare and cringed.

"Why did you agree to testify?" he asked, his voice almost inaudible.

So much for the small talk.

"Because it's my civic duty."

It was his turn to snort. When he jerked off the bed, I cringed, prepared for whatever new form of punishment he was going to issue.

He took his time pouring another drink before returning to the bed. "While I do understand that there are people who feel it's their requirement to testify even for violent crimes, I've known few people in my life that actually volunteer to testify against certain factions of criminals."

"You mean mafia members."

Chuckling, his eyes lit up. "Exactly."

"That's because people like you threaten anyone who dares to cross you."

"We do what's necessary to keep our business going, Emily, but I have never threatened a witness."

"Until now."

He thought about my two little words, finally nodding. "There's a first time for everything, especially when it's necessary."

"Why did you kill him?" I knew he wouldn't be honest with me and what did it matter anyway?

His face pinched, he appeared to be thinking about my question. "My family is most important to me. They are the fire that fills my soul, the only love I've ever known and the very reason I've considered myself so lucky all these years." He shook his head, his upper lip curling. "Lucky. Well, maybe that's not the correct word. Family means everything. When one member is challenged, there is nothing that will stop me from protecting my own. Nothing."

"So you're saying a member of your family was hurt?" I could see some crazy kind of sincerity in his eyes.

"It was a necessary and vital decision. That is all I'm going to tell you. What I find interesting is why you would volunteer for this civic duty. You obviously knew the reputation that the King family has acquired."

I shuddered from his question because the sad truth was that I couldn't tell him the reason why. I had no understanding of why the prosecuting attorney had coerced me into something I'd initially refused to do. Of course I'd figured out exactly who Cristiano King and his family were. The entire ugly scene had been splashed across the news, speculation that the murder had been a hit on every nightly report for almost a week. I'd made the mistake of going to the police prior to having any knowledge of who the person responsible was, something I'd regretted almost instantly.

While I was the kind of woman who believed in doing the right thing, I also wasn't some kind of ridiculous fool. I enjoyed living, for God's sake, and I wanted to continue doing so. I closed my eyes briefly, still able to see the vicious face of the attorney as he'd accused me at being an accomplice to a member of another equally horrific group of criminals.

"I know this isn't something you could understand, Cristiano. It would appear that you've always gotten everything you wanted in your life easily. However, I am a woman of integrity and honor. I believe in the good of mankind and when I was forced to see you kill that man in cold blood, I couldn't… I would never be able to look myself in the mirror if I hadn't gone to the police and testified to what I'd seen."

The quiet in the room was palpable.

"Are you telling me the truth, Emily, because if you aren't, your punishment will be severe."

Severe. He made the statement as if what he'd already done to me had been nothing. "I'm not lying. Maybe you don't know anyone who follows the rules, but I do." As soon as I issued the words, I sucked in my breath. I'd fallen into a trap of my own making.

Cristiano chuckled again and I knew he was getting off the bed. Maybe to retrieve his gun. I held my arm, my other hand shaking. I wasn't certain I cared what he did to me. I wasn't going to be threatened on a daily basis.

"I'm very glad to hear that you're the kind of woman who follows rules, which means that you will follow mine. It's time for bed."

I took one last gulp of the drink, jumping when I heard a sound then daring to open my eyes. He'd placed his glass on the bar and walked toward his dresser. I was right. He was going to kill me. I pressed my hand over my mouth to keep from whimpering.

"We will discuss this further in the morning."

When he turned around, my eyes fell to the pair of handcuffs in his hand. I scuttled back on the bed, struggling to place the glass on the nightstand, blinking furiously in some crazy effort to hide my tears.

He followed my gaze, smirking in his usual sexy way. "This is just for the night until I can make better arrangements. I know you will attempt to get away and I simply can't have that."

I jerked backward, hitting the nightstand.

"Unless you'd prefer to spend the night in the cage."

"Can I at least go to the bathroom?"

He cocked his head, nodding after a few seconds. "Fine. Don't take too long. Do not lock the door. I will not hesitate to kick it in."

I rushed toward the bathroom door, my entire body shaking, fumbling to find the light. When I closed the door, I slumped against the counter, struggling to catch my breath. Crying wasn't going to do any good. Nothing would help the situation or to get me out of this. No one was coming to help me.

Very slowly I turned around, looking over my shoulder at the redness covering my bottom. I ran my fingers across my skin, cringing from the buildup of heat. I would be sore in the morning. A laugh threatened to bubble to the surface. As if my aching buttocks were anything to worry about.

I turned on the water, leaning over the sink. An ugly memory flashed into the forefront of my mind, the horrible words the attorney had said to me.

"If you don't want to go to prison for a long time, you are going to help us."

"I didn't do anything!" I exclaimed, uncertain of what the hell he was getting at.

He laughed, rearing back as he glared down at me. "And you and I know better. Does this look familiar?"

As he dropped several pieces of paper in front of me, scattering them across the table, I tried to catch on to what he was getting at. The letterhead was from the company I worked for, but I didn't recognize anything else. "What are these?"

"Incriminating evidence that your firm is nothing more than a front for one very dangerous man. So here's how we're going to play this. You're going to provide a very secure deposition and you're going to continue working for Bayou Market Analysis, only you're going to provide us with information."

I should have known the entire situation would get me killed.

The hard knock on the door jerked me back to reality.

"It's time," Cristiano said with no emotion.

Time.

Time had no meaning any longer.

When I opened the door, he took the time to shift his dead eyes to my toes and back to my face before stepping away from me. As I made my way back to the bed, all I could do was shiver. After getting under the covers, I stared at the ceiling, doing everything I could to block out the horror I was facing.

"Arm over your head, Emily."

There was no point in arguing. I simply did as I was told. Within seconds, he'd attached the cold steel around my wrist, the other section placed around a hook attached to the bed. My God. He'd done this before with another woman.

"Is that too tight?" he asked, brushing his fingers down my extended arm.

"No." *Asshole. Jerk. Bastard.* I didn't have the courage to mutter the nasty words any longer. I was far too tired, running out of steam.

"Good."

Leaning over, I could swear the man was going to kiss me goodnight. Then he simply turned, moving swiftly to the dresser and retrieving the gun and his knife before turning out the light.

I continued to cringe, trying to adjust the covers over my shaking body. There was no way I would be able to sleep.

While I knew he'd gotten in the bed, he made no sound, none at all.

The darkness was overwhelming, creating monsters in my mind. As I tugged the covers even higher, I realized that the creatures I'd seen in nightmares as a child were nothing in comparison to the beast lying next to me.

When I closed my eyes, I made a vow to myself.

Somehow, some way, I would manage to kill him.

In. Cold. Blood.

CHAPTER 8

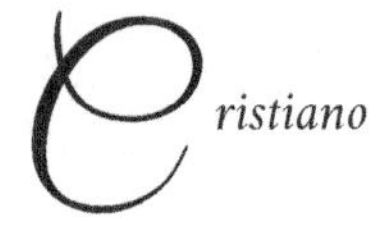

ristiano

Nightmares.

I'd had them my entire life, often awakening me in a cold sweat. While I almost never remembered any details, I knew in my gut they were bloody as fuck. If I had to guess, I'd say some psychiatrist would have a field day, telling me that my guilt was the reason.

Bullshit.

I knew better.

But as I stared at the ceiling in the darkness of my own home, I was beginning to wonder what the fuck I was doing with my life. I had significant wealth including from cash, stocks, and real estate. Hell, I even owned three of the most expensive sports cars that had ever been manufactured. I could have any woman I wanted on my arm.

But there was no joy in my life.

Except when I handled the business of the King family.

Sighing, I could sense her presence in the darkness, the scent of her covering every inch of my body. My cock ached just thinking about being inside of her, taking her without hesitation. I hadn't really thought about the fact I'd only spent a few nights next to a woman in my bed, hell, any bed for that matter. I'd never wanted to be that close, exposing any concept of a weakness.

The single woman I'd allowed into my life had been… difficult, our coupling a product of families attempting to make peace instead of war. I'd wanted no part of the glitzy attempt at putting us together, a possible arranged marriage. I'd made no bones about that fact with my father.

Only to be met with his rage.

This was something entirely different, a catch that had seemed simple at first. And now? There were far too many complications, as well as reasons I'd snatched her from her home. Keeping her a secret could prove to be an additional path of undermining the family.

Fuck.

I thought about Emily's reaction to the bed and smiled. I'd seen the light in her eyes as she stroked the wood. I had no idea why the fact she appreciated pieces of furniture made me happy.

But it did.

I shifted onto my side, able to catch a slight glimpse of her from the slender strip of moonlight coming in through the blinds.

She'd also turned onto her side and away from me, although I had my doubts that she was asleep. Her fear of me remained, her anxiety over what to tell me, if anything, obvious. I also was well aware she was lying to me about why she'd testified. There was something significant she was hiding.

Terror of what I would do or something worse?

My instinct told me the latter.

Whatever it was, she still had no understanding that she'd awakened the beast. I reached out, almost touching her shoulder then yanking my hand away. This wasn't about some romantic getaway. There would be no caring shared between us, no trust built. How could there be?

I purposely rolled over, refusing to grasp that I actually liked the girl. She had nerve, defiance that refused to take into account the power I wielded. That took the kind of courage few men had ever shown. Frustrated, my cock still aching, I slid my hand under the sheets, rolling my fingers around my cockhead. I'd enjoyed every second of taking her. As I closed my eyes, I tried to think about my next steps.

Finding out what the hell Lucian had actually accomplished in my absence.

Finding out the reason I'd been set up in the first place.

Determining if I needed to retaliate against the Azzurris.

Then… I'd determine the fate of sweet, beautiful Emily.

A luscious flower.

A precious gift.

A noose around my neck.

* * *

Shifting, I slowly opened my eyes, reeling immediately from the fact daylight was streaming in through the blinds. My instincts kicking in, I snapped my hand around the gun even before I planted my feet on the floor, tossing the fucking covers that had weighed me down. I scanned the room, certain that I'd heard a noise, an intruder in the house. When I realized there was nothing but quiet, utter silence, I was forced to take several deep breaths.

While I lowered the weapon, I refused to allow it to leave my hand.

Huffing, I took long strides toward the open doorway, peering into the hall. The same blissful quiet continued. No longer did I have to hear the clangs of prison doors as the morning wakeup call slammed the heavy metal against the concrete walls. No longer would I have to endure the bullshit growls and groans of the fucking assholes who were imprisoned in the system. And no longer would I have to conceal the shank every single time I attempted to take a shower.

The fact I hadn't been given solitary confinement was a testament to the legal system. Somehow, our influence had bypassed the various men on our payroll. The attorney and the judge had been determined to make an example out of me.

Fuck them.

They would have their day in court.

After chuckling at the images in my head, I remembered that I wasn't in the bed alone.

Or was that the case?

Exhaling, I shifted my attention back into the room, slowly padding toward the other side of the bed. The sight of sleeping beauty eased the tension.

Even though her presence was damning.

As I peered down, I could tell she'd attempted to tug her wrist from the manacle, the red marks and scratches indicating she'd almost succeeded. While her fingers were beautiful and long, her bone structure was slight, a fragile bird.

A delicate flower.

A woman with a warrior's heart.

At least she was sleeping peacefully.

I took a glance at the clock. After seven. There was far too much to do. When I returned my gaze to my captive, her stark, cold eyes were waiting for mine, her entire face pinched from fury and frustration.

"Good morning, Emily."

"So very formal," she hissed.

"You shouldn't have struggled, although I knew you would, which is why I can't trust you." I moved toward the dresser, finding the key to the handcuffs, placing my gun on the edge.

"Trust. You spout off words like trust to me?" she laughed, the spunk from the night before even more intensified.

I was surprised that spending a night beside the man she called a murderer hadn't quieted her fight. Then again, I did enjoy a good sparring event. "I have a very busy day today." As I attempted to unlock her from her overnight shackle, she did everything she could to fight me.

Without hesitation, I wrapped my hand around her throat, pinned her against the bed. "You need to listen to me very carefully, Emily. I will not take a single minute of your misbehavior today and I will have no problem tossing you back into that cage. Do you understand what I'm telling you or should I give you a firm reminder of what you might be facing for hours at a time?"

She blinked several times, her eyes glassing over. "I'll… be good."

"Uh-huh. And you're going to learn respect. For me. For my house. For my soldiers. You have one other alternative." Squeezing, the power I had in my hand was unlike the sensations I'd experienced while controlling or condemning assholes who chose unwisely to turn against me. This time, my conscience sparked, something I loathed. However, I didn't need to warn her any further.

Her eyes held compliance instead of rebellion.

When I released my hold, she didn't move, although her body continued to tremble. I unsnapped the cuff, immediately rubbing her wrist. "You're going to bruise."

"So what?" She recoiled after issuing the words, hugging the covers over her body.

Exhaling, I left the shackles attached to the bed. They would likely come in handy at a later time.

"I need to take a shower."

"And what about me?" she asked in a whispered voice.

"You're coming with me." I yanked her out of bed, pulling her behind me, snagging my weapon before entering the bathroom. "Get in the shower."

I heard a single whimper before she complied, slipping inside the oversized bathing area. Showers had always given me a respite, much like indulging in a glass of cognac or a good cigar. Today was entirely different. Just seeing her voluptuous body as she crowded toward the back was more arousing than I'd felt the night before.

With the gun placed on the counter, I turned on the water, immediately stepping inside. As I lowered my head, allowing the hot water to cascade over me, I could still hear her ragged breathing. After running my fingers through my hair, I turned to face her, inching closer as I allowed my mind to wander to all the lurid, sadistic things I craved doing to her. At some point, I'd introduce her to my playroom, a location that I'd insisted on having, yet one I'd never used.

I almost laughed at the thought. My sexual appetites were considered far too extreme for the majority of women, even those who frequented some of the most intense BDSM clubs. However, I'd never had the opportunity to indulge in every aspect of training an innocent, someone who had never been introduced to the dark art. With this woman, I would enjoy taking the time.

Shackling her.

Disciplining her.

Marking her lovely body.

Breaking her.

And fucking her as often as I desired.

I was a sick man, one capable of doing heinous things.

When I planted my hands on either side of her, she lifted her chin. Still so blatantly defiant. Still so utterly exquisite. And still refusing to accept my authority.

I lowered my head, drinking in her delicious scent, filling my lungs with her fragrance.

Her breathing remained scattered and she planted her hands against the cool marble, studying me just as intently as before.

"If you're trying to look into my soul—"

"You have no soul," she interrupted. "None. And your heart is pitch black."

"Interesting for a woman who's only known me a few hours."

"I know your type. You enjoy displaying your power, using violence as your only tool of interrogation as well as intimidation."

I gave her words consideration. "Perhaps you are right. However, utilizing intellectual conversation with basic thugs hasn't been well received."

"Then maybe you need to enter into another business."

Chuckling, I leaned further over until our lips were only centimeters apart. "That's a very good point, Emily."

"Stop saying my name."

"What would you prefer I call you?" I asked as I rubbed my face against hers, the softness of her skin creating another wave of hunger burning deep within me. "Kitten? Pumpkin? Pet?"

"Nothing."

I brushed my lips against hers, expecting her to recoil, but there was so much electricity sparking between us that her body shifted involuntarily, her back arching. Her slight actions pushed our lips together, leaving me tingling all over, my cock now at full attention. As my cockhead pushed against her stomach, I captured her mouth, holding still for several seconds and enjoying the taste of her.

She shivered but parted her lips, allowing me to dart my tongue inside. The connection was undeniable, the vibrations shared between us more powerful than the night before. I took my time exploring the dark recesses of her mouth, swirling my tongue back and forth.

While she remained still at first, trying not to engage in our moment of passion, her resolve crumbled with each passing second, her tongue shifting against mine.

I became more forceful, crushing my mouth against hers, pinning her against the wall as the act of intimacy intensified. As I dominated her tongue, she moaned into the kiss, her slender hands pressing against my chest.

Only she wasn't pushing, attempting to force me away. Her fingers were digging into my skin, kneading my muscles. Just the way she touched me drew me further into a delicious haze of longing, thirsty to taste every inch of her, hungry to fill her mouth, pussy, and tight asshole with my cock.

I fisted her hair, wrapping my fingers around her long strands as I allowed the kiss to continue. I couldn't seem to get enough of her, my tongue dancing against hers in a wild ride of passion.

This was tenderness, a closeness that I hadn't expected to enjoy. When I finally broke the kiss, I tugged on her hair, exposing the long length of her neck. Everything about her was stunning, her skin glistening from the few droplets of water. Growling, I licked across the seam of her mouth before nipping her lower lip, moving ever so slowly to her jaw. Even the taste of her skin was delicious, adding fuel to the already raging fire in my loins.

"Oh..." she whimpered, closing her eyes, her mouth pursing.

I continued my exploration, sliding my lips down the length of her neck, allowing my teeth to graze across her porcelain skin. As I lowered my head, rubbing my lips over her shoulder, she slid her hand further down. Was she longing to touch me? The monster she hated? When she crawled her fingers even further, I lifted my head, realizing there was a slight smile on her face.

"Are you attempting to tease me, my pet?"

Huffing, her eyelids flitted open, her eyes glassy.

From desire.

From an unsated need.

From a rush of adrenaline.

We were more alike than she realized, our needs dark, even dangerous. Yet I knew I couldn't stop my actions, the yearning that would remain with me for hours, even days.

When she wrapped her hand around the tip of my cock, I filled my lungs with air, holding it for a few seconds as the sensations increased. I was lightheaded, my heart racing. Never had I felt this way with any woman before.

Another series of growls pushed up from the depths of my being. I resumed licking her delicate skin, moving closer to her rounded breasts, blowing across her already taut nipple. "You're hungry this morning."

While she remained quiet, she rolled her fingers around my cockhead, creating extreme friction. Stars danced in front of my eyes, the beast dwelling within attempting to maintain control. I was shocked at my body's reaction, the needs that continued to swell. As she pumped up and down, twisting her hand, I engulfed her nipple, pulling the tender flesh between my teeth.

"Oh… I…"

Her whimpers only added gasoline to the fire, every cell electrified. I moved from one nipple to the other, swirling my tongue around her hardened bud before biting down. When I shifted one hand down her side, sliding it between her legs, her moans filtered into the space. Every sound she made, every ragged breath, created a wave of energy.

I fingered her clit, rolling my finger back and forth, realizing that her tiny bud remained swollen from the night before. My excitement heightened as I eased my fingers down, slipping them into her tight channel. The way her muscles clamped around the invasion forced another series of growls. I was nothing but a barbarian, preparing to consume every inch of her.

She parted her legs even further, allowing me additional access. I shoved several fingers inside of her, pumping in a brutal manner, flexing my fingers open as her muscles yielded. She was so hot, her juice slickening my fingers.

I knew I wouldn't be able to wait for long before shoving my cock inside.

When I lifted my head, gazing into her eyes, she dragged her tongue across her lips. "What do you hunger for, my little flower?"

Her bold demeanor seemed to crumble before my eyes, her expression one of longing.

The same carnal needs.

The same savage desires.

The same hunger to let go.

"Everything," she managed, half laughing after issuing the single breathless word.

I intended on providing exactly what she craved.

As I thrust my fingers inside, pumping vigorously, she slid her hand away from my cock, her body undulating as she rolled the ten tips of her fingers up my chest, caressing every muscle along the way.

After fingering her for several seconds, I yanked her against the side wall, the water from the second spigot peppering over us, creating another series of tingling vibrations. She panted, her eyes opening and closing as she gripped my forearms. When I removed my fingers, pushing them into my mouth, she watched every move I made. I licked and sucked then slipped them past her pursed lips.

"Suck my fingers, little flower. Lick every drop of juice."

She obeyed my command, wrapping one hand around my wrist as I drove my fingers inside. When she stopped my actions, taking control and delicately licking up and down each finger, I was mesmerized by her gentleness, entranced by her beauty.

The sounds she made were more like purrs, so catlike, ripped with thirst. She was no longer able to deny our connection, even her pretense stripped away, revealing the woman who'd been locked inside.

Inhaling, I finally removed my fingers, pressing both hands on her shoulders, forcing her to her knees. "Suck me. Take every single inch."

Her head tilting, she darted her eyes back and forth, her mind processing my command. Even as her body continued to tremble, she rubbed her hands over my legs, tickling my darkest needs as she brushed them up, cupping one around my balls, nestling my cock in the other.

I resisted touching her, at least at first, fisting my hands against the marble in an effort to remain still. I spread my legs apart, allowing her all the access she needed, jutting my hips forward. Every move she made was tentative, as if she'd never been allowed to indulge in the joy of sucking a man's cock.

She would soon learn what it was like to please her master. I closed my eyes briefly as she toyed with me, running my testicles through her fingers. They were so damn swollen, aching with the need to fill her with my seed.

There was something almost sweet about her actions as she pressed the tip of my shaft back and forth across her mouth, finally darting a single lick across my sensitive slit. The volts of current jetting through me were explosive, my heart thudding savagely against my chest. With every slice of her wet tongue, every squeeze of my balls, she was dragging the true barbarian from his lair.

I tipped my head back, enjoying the way the heated water splashed over our ignited bodies, savoring every minute of this private session. The ugly business of the day would keep me from engaging any further than this morning.

But tonight would be a different story.

A smile crossed my face as she lifted my cock, licking down the underside, crowding even closer. When she took one ball into her mouth, using her strong jaw muscles to suck, I was unable to stop a ragged growl from erupting. Every muscle was tense, my pulse skipping. Her delicate ways were driving me to the point of madness.

As she continued taunting me, shifting her attention to my other testicle, licking and sucking as if she was enjoying a lollypop, my entire body shook from the rush of adrenaline. I intertwined my fingers in her hair, holding her in place as she tormented the fuck out of me. She knew exactly the buttons to push, keeping me on a sharp precipice of desire while taking her time to savor her duty.

Every sound I made was guttural, the breath coming from my lungs scattered. I could no longer feel my legs as she mewed, dragging her tongue back and forth across my cock before pressing her open mouth against it. She took her damn sweet time easing to my cockhead, licking around the tip in lazy circles.

"Suck me, little flower. If you continue teasing me, there will be hell to pay." My words were barely audible, a fog drifting over my eyes as I attempted to gaze down.

She either didn't hear me or didn't give a shit, continuing her methodical actions for a full thirty seconds. When she finally took the tip of my cock into her hot, wet mouth, I let out a ragged roar.

"Fuck!"

Emily seemed fueled by my harsh word, continuing to squeeze my balls with enough pressure the ache increased. As she opened her mouth wide, taking the tip inside, her tongue shifting back and forth, I slammed one hand against the wall, my frustration growing.

With every inch she took, I became more rattled, my needs growing.

My heart racing.

My balls tightening.

For a man who'd always taken everything he wanted, refusing to accept anything less, providing her with sheer indulgence was almost too much. My patience was being tested, my control placed on the spot. Perhaps she was pushing me on purpose, trying to determine my limits. Unable to hold back any longer, I gripped both sides of her head, rising onto the balls of my feet and driving the entire length of my cock into her mouth. When the tip hit the back of her throat, the gagging sound she made was the perfect music, innocence personified.

I'd never felt this alive, every cell and muscle so electrified. She had a way about her that embroiled my senses, pushing me to my limits. While her body continued to quiver, she acted as if she was in control, snapping her fingers around my legs, shifting the angle of our bodies so she could move up and down on my cock.

Refusing to allow her to take over, I slammed my shaft into her mouth, driving in rapid and steady motions. She finally clung to my legs, her doe eyes staring at me as I pumped into her. I was relentless, brutal, enjoying the sounds erupting past the thick invasion.

I had no idea how long I ravaged her mouth, but as beads of perspiration trickled down both sides of my face, I could no longer hold back from taking her. There would be plenty of time for her to suck me dry.

Over and over again.

I pulled away, immediately jerking Emily to her feet, yanking her arms over her head.

"Oh..."

Her yelp only made me smile.

"What are you doing?" she dared to ask.

"Fucking you." I held her in place, my fingers entangled with hers as I shifted my hips, the tip of my cock slicing up and down her pussy. "That's what you crave."

"No," she whispered, once again denying what we shared.

I continued grinding my hips against her as I crushed her against the marble. She fit perfectly against me, her body molding with mine. "What did I tell you about lies?"

"I'm not lying." She tossed her head from one side to the other, even though she refused to take her eyes off me.

"Yes, you are. Tell me the truth."

With the heat of our bodies increasing, she was forced to take several gasping breaths, her body jerking against mine.

"Tell me."

After a few additional seconds, she let out a strangled moan. "Yes."

The single word would be the only admittance I'd receive, but it was merely icing on the cake. I yanked one leg around my hip before sliding the tip of my cock past her swollen folds. With one hard thrust, I drove every inch inside, shuddering from the way the touch of her seared my nerve endings.

I fucked her relentlessly, pumping in rapid motions, filling her completely. I was on fire, unable to stop the beast from taking over, the brutal force slamming her body against the wall. She moved with me, mirroring my actions. We were nothing more than carnal beasts, our needs turning to the most basic in man and woman.

With every sound we made, the hard slapping of our bodies moving as one, the sadistic side of me came closer to the surface. I pounded into her long and hard, my hunger knowing no bounds. Even the way her muscles strained to accept what I was doing to her yanked me closer to nirvana.

When she wrapped her other leg around my upper thigh, her fingers digging into my shoulders, every action became even more brutal. The feel of her pussy muscles clamping then releasing was telling. She was close to a climax yet still fighting what she considered to be an ugly betrayal. But she was glowing in the dim lighting, her face glistening from both my harsh actions as well as the steam floating between us.

"Oh, God… This is… No, I…" Unable to finish her sentence, she stiffened, her eyes opening wide. The moment the climax rushed into her, I pressed my lips against hers, her scream erupting into my mouth.

And I refused to stop my crazed actions, drilling into her pussy, slamming her against the wall. When a single orgasm turned into a beautiful wave, I couldn't stop shaking.

Seconds later, she sagged against me, pushing until she was able to break the kiss. Her heavy breathing was a delicious reward.

However, I wasn't finished with her yet.

Easing her down, I yanked her to face the wall, once again shoving her arms over her head. There was no need to issue any command. She arched her back, keeping her legs wide open as I ground my hips back and forth across her bruised ass.

"You belong to me," I reminded her before driving my cock into her pussy, gripping her hips and pulling her away from the wall. I knew I couldn't hold back for long, my needs far too great. She gasped for air as I powered into her, pulling out then slamming into her again and again. In the frenzy of taking her, I could barely breathe, no longer able to think clearly.

I simply needed to fuck her, to consume the woman who'd dared to defy me, the one that I would possess.

Her ragged purrs spurred me on, and I lost myself in the moment, fucking her like a wild animal until I could take no more. As my balls filled with seed, I drove her onto her tiptoes and the moment I erupted deep inside, I heard her cry of anguish.

As if I'd broken through another barrier.

As if she longed to submit.

And as if she hated the woman she'd become.

CHAPTER 9

mily

Numb.

I was completely numb, barely able to function. Even the coffee cup in my hand threatened to fall, dropping to the perfectly polished wooden kitchen floor. Everything seemed surreal, nothing really mattering any longer.

I stood at the kitchen window, staring out at one of the most gorgeous landscaped areas that I'd seen in New Orleans. There was an abundance of greenery, everything very tropical. Even the vibrancy of the flowers reminded me of something I'd seen in a magazine, not the coiffed grounds of a murderer. There was even a glorious lagoon-style pool and I could swear I heard the water as it tumbled from the fake rocks positioned in one corner. Everything I'd seen was luxurious, a product of his wealth.

His family's influence and power.

Yet he seemed disenchanted by his surroundings, as if he couldn't care less where he lived. I'd grown up in a family with little money, yet he probably spent more on the expensive bottles of wine I noticed than I could manage on my house payment even now.

Gluttonous pig.

One that had managed to rip away almost every layer of protection. Even the way his scent continued to cover my body was a disgusting reminder of his power.

I pressed my hand down on the dress, the rip in several seams making the frock seem tawdry. He'd forbidden me to wear panties, just another thing to hate him for. I had nothing of my own. No clothing. No makeup. Nothing. And my cellphone was nowhere in sight.

I heard him talking on the phone. Him. I could barely say his name or even think it. Every part of me ached, but not just from the spanking he'd given me or the rough sex during our shower together. The way I felt was a direct correlation to the fact I'd let my guard down.

I'd actually enjoyed the asshole fucking me.

I'd relished the touch of his fingers, the way every brush of his thumb scalded my skin, the surge in my desire that had kept me wet.

Even during the middle of the night.

The moment he'd rolled over in the middle of the night, placing his arm around me, I hadn't been able to hold back the whimper. It seemed so damn... normal. But there was nothing that was normal about this. He'd abducted me from my own home under threat of hurting me. He'd forced me into a cage, awaiting his return. While his remorse at finding me locked behind bars seemed genuine, I could tell by his eyes that seeing me in such an incapacitated manner had fueled the hunger that never seemed to go away.

He was enjoying every minute of this and nothing could tell me otherwise.

I tried to take a sip of coffee, my hand shaking to the point the liquid sloshed. What was going to happen now? Would he lock me away, keeping me like the pet he seemed to enjoy? I closed my eyes, leaning my head against the window. While I didn't notice he'd ended the call and hadn't heard any footsteps entering the room, I felt his presence.

He was larger than life, a true predator.

When I opened my eyes, I caught his reflection in the sunlight streaming in through the window. His face appeared pensive, his body looming over mine. And sadly, he looked amazing in his crisp white shirt and black suit, the selection of a dazzling cerulean blue tie highlighting his stone-cold eyes.

I had the distinct feeling he was preparing a war.

Cristiano flanked my side, peering out the same window, only once glancing at my cup. Five seconds passed.

Ten.

An awkward twenty.

Was I supposed to say something to him?

"You didn't enjoy your coffee. If there is something else that you'd prefer, let me know and I'll have someone pick it up for you," he said in such a casual manner. We hadn't just enjoyed a crazy but wonderful one-night stand. He wasn't forced to be accommodating, even sweet in his stiff and impersonal conversation. He could simply offer me bread and water, enough nourishment to keep me alive for his sexual appetite.

"Why bother?"

I hadn't realized the words had slipped from my mouth until I heard him chuckle.

"Because that's the civilized thing to do, Emily."

I hate you. I hate you.

He was going to continue to use my name, spouting it off as if we gave a shit about each other. Fuck him. Fuck this.

"I'm not thirsty," I said after a few seconds.

Stiffening, I could tell he had no idea what to make of my yin and yang of defiance. I wasn't trained in being a good prisoner. I had no understanding of what mafia men required. A laugh bubbled to the surface as I envisioned a *Book of the Week*, the concepts needed to survive being abducted by a murderous pig.

That would be a best seller.

"This doesn't have to be difficult, Emily."

"What is this, Cristiano? Or am I allowed to call you that? You've abducted me from my life, acting as if you were going to kill me, disciplining me like a bad little girl then handcuffing me to your bed. Now, you offer me coffee of any type, flavor, or choice that I'd prefer. What is next, breakfast? Maybe breakfast in bed."

There was no sign of amusement or anything else sweeping across his gorgeous features. He was simply blank, remaining unblinking as he stared out at his own lawn. But I could swear it was like he was seeing it for the first time.

"I've lived my entire life in New Orleans, but I've never really appreciated the architecture or my surroundings. I was always too busy. School. Work."

Perfecting a kingdom forged in blood.

I dared not say the words.

"My family means everything as I told you, but business is what keeps me awake at night. Enjoying the wealth our family created over the decades has never been on the forefront of my mind. You see, my father taught his children to work hard. That's what matters in my life. The simple pleasures I now realize I took for granted. Coffee. Fine wine. A juicy steak."

Where the hell was he going with this?

When he finally turned his head in my direction, I noticed something I hadn't before. Anguish.

"That's what you miss the most when you're stuck in a six-by-six-foot cell, the concrete walls thick, the bars rigid steel. You think about the little things, including being able to sleep without hearing a man's agonizing cry because he's losing his mind. You being able to take a hot shower without worrying about some freaking asshole attempting to make you his bitch. And you long for nothing more than food that isn't greasy and bread that isn't stale."

I was taken aback by the vehemence of his words, the coldness in which he said them.

"So, when I ask you about a choice in coffee, accept that as a privilege, Emily, one that could be taken away as easily as you took my choices away from me."

"Are you asking me for an apology?" I asked indignantly.

"I'm asking you for some kind of realization that while you may see this house as something that was gifted to me, you would be wrong. As I told you, I am a bad man, dangerous on several levels, but I'm a human. We all have several sides, even a monster like me. You have been given choices. I suggest you think about that today. For your loyalty, you will be rewarded. For your continued betrayal, you will be punished. There is no in between."

My loyalty? What the hell was he getting at? I wanted to be shocked at his stern words, but I wasn't. This was... no, I was just a matter of business he was attending to, a way to get back at his enemies. And all I had to do was play along then maybe I could remain alive. I had no way of reacting, no ability to fight with a madman. I was just a simple girl.

That's not the truth.

The inner voice nagged at me again. I'd been used as a pawn in a vicious game. Only I'd be the one to lose.

"Can you do that for me, Emily?" he asked after several seconds.

"Yes."

He closed the distance between us, the sound of some kind of chime igniting the look in his eyes. We had a visitor. Leaning down, he kissed me on the forehead, gripping my shoulder as he did so. The act was even more intimate than anything we'd shared.

Gentle.

Tender.

Loving.

I was confused as hell but when he stepped away, I was able to catch a glimpse of his gun nestled in a holster under his jacket. He was prepared for battle.

"My Capo is going to stay with you while I'm handling business today. When I return, we are going to continue our discussion over a nice dinner. Do you understand me?"

"Yes. Yes, sir." Why I offered the word of respect was beyond me. Maybe my instinct in order to stay alive. Maybe I was falling for his lines of bullshit. I wasn't entirely certain. I returned my attention to the area outside his fortress once again, trying to keep from shaking.

I heard the sound of footsteps, a brief but pointed discussion although the words were muffled. Then there was the sound of loud voices, anger in Cristiano's tone of voice. I strained to hear what was being said then walked closer to the door. My choice of eavesdropping might not be the best idea, but I was determined to find out exactly what was going to happen.

And what the bastard was made of.

"Why are you here, Lucian?" Cristiano asked.

"I thought you wanted to have a discussion."

"Yes, but now isn't the time."

I heard another laugh, the man called Lucian even snorting. Then I heard footsteps coming in my direction. I backed away, shifting toward the kitchen counter, gripping the edge with my other hand.

"I don't appreciate you barging in. I have business to attend to," Cristiano barked.

"As do I, brother."

Lucian.

Now I remembered the glorious photograph I'd seen both on the internet and used by almost every television station. The family was beautiful indeed; five brothers and a sister, both the mother and the father still alive. They were all extremely good looking, the smiles on their faces as if they were the happiest of families, but I knew they held secrets.

Conditions on employment within their hallowed grounds.

Threats made on government officials and law enforcement.

When the brother walked inside, he was more than just shocked to see me. His eyes glassed over as he studied me, slowly easing further into the room. "Well, you do work fast, Cristiano. Barely a few hours out of prison and you've found a companion."

Cristiano followed him inside, attempting to block his view. "She is of no concern to you. We can discuss business later; however, you will answer me this. How is the entrance into the New York market?"

Lucian kept his gaze pinned on me for a few seconds. Before he turned to face his brother, his brow furrowed. "Are you certain you wouldn't like to discuss this in private?"

Laughing, Cristiano didn't bother looking in my direction. "The question is a simple one. We can get into the specifics later. Have you gained membership into the elite area within New York?"

I could tell there was unbridled tension between the two, the kind of bad blood that often led to family feuds. I also gathered that Lucian's appearance was unexpected, further angering Cristiano.

"I've had several discussions with our contact, but he seems disinclined to garner entrance into the exclusive club."

Lucian's answer only further infuriated his brother. I'd read enough to know the Kings owned several legitimate businesses, or at least according to tax records. I'd also heard rumors that their foray into the world of expensive and exclusive diamonds was merely a front, giving them an entirely different market in which to launder money from their sale of illegal drugs.

"And the reason?" Cristiano hissed between clenched teeth.

"Let's just say our notoriety didn't suit their conservative tastes."

Cristiano remained quiet, taking his time before answering. "That is unfortunate."

It was Lucian's turn to laugh. "There are certain issues you aren't aware of, brother, ones that should take precedence."

"We will discuss this further. Now, I have business to handle. I suggest you gather all the reports and financials. We will meet at the office later." There was such utter contempt in Cristiano's voice, a growing anger than was only partially due to whatever animosity they shared with each other.

"Very well, brother. Aren't you going to at least introduce me to your friend?"

"As I said. She is no concern of yours. Period. You can see yourself out."

"Friend, or did you take matters regarding your incarceration into your own hands?" Lucian asked.

Fuming, Cristiano closed the distance between them, his face pinched. "Leave it alone, Lucian. From what I've learned, you've ignored enough of your duties that you should be concentrating on ensuring that I'll be able to pick up the broken pieces. If not, you'll be the one to face my wrath."

"Be careful threatening me, brother. I was one of the few who really had your back. That's something for you to keep in mind."

They remained in their tense positions for a full twenty seconds before Cristiano finally chuckled. "You should leave."

"Yeah, I guess we have nothing to talk about. Enjoy your... business."

Lucian glared at him for several seconds before storming toward the door.

Cristiano cleared his throat. "There is just one more thing. Mario. He is never to be placed on my detail again."

His brother barely darted a look over his shoulder, but once again, his eyes settled on my face, leaving me even more uncomfortable than I was. "Be careful, brother. You're already alienating everyone who attempted to pick up the pieces after your... actions." He left without saying another word. The sound of the front door slamming was jarring, only further fueling Cristiano's rage.

When he turned to face me, the look in his eyes left me trembling. I backed away as he took long strides closer and in a split second, raked his hands over the counter, knocking coffee cups and a crystal bowl of fresh fruit onto the floor. The sound of smashing glass was followed by his angry bellow.

He took several exaggerated breaths before walking toward the same window where I'd stood, smacking the glass with enough force the panes rattled.

The seconds that passed were agonizing.

"While I'm sorry that you had to see that exchange, it would be wise of you to remember that you are a guest in my home. What you might hear is not to be repeated. Not to anyone, including me. There are some aspects of my business that are off limits."

I shrank back against the counter then looked away. The emotional rollercoaster he was on was as terrifying as the man. "Yes, *sir*." The contempt in my voice was likely to push him over the edge.

Instead, he laughed. "Every family has issues."

Before I could even think of something to say, another chime dragged his attention to toward the front door. Hissing, he glanced at his watch before walking away.

Only then was I able to take a deep breath, trying to calm my nerves. He was volatile, hiding behind thinly veiled at resuming the command. I had the distinct feeling that the battle he was about to wage would be deadly.

Another male voice.

Another set of footsteps.

Thump. Thump. Thump.

They were getting closer.

"Emily, this is Dimitri."

I resigned myself to turn around, staring at the scarred blond from the night before. "We've met."

The man smiled curtly, his eyes locking with mine briefly before glancing down at the wreckage on the floor. There was no look of admonishment or desire. He was simply a soldier. Jesus. They lived as if every day was going to become a battle zone. I couldn't imagine a life where burly men dressed as mercenaries, carrying a wide array of weapons became everyday life. That wasn't living.

"Lucian?" Dimitri asked.

"Unfortunately."

"You will do everything that he tells you and you will not fight him. Is that understood?" Cristiano asked softly.

"Yes. I understand."

"I will purchase some clothes before I return. You'll be allowed to wear them as long as you remain obedient."

I wanted to bite his head off, but I merely nodded. I knew now wasn't the time to challenge him on anything.

"If she gets out of line, you have my permission to discipline her. However, she is to be left unharmed," Cristiano continued.

"Yes, sir. I'll take care of her," Dimitri answered.

"I know you will." Cristiano gave me another stern look before moving quickly toward the door, slapping his hand on the threshold. “Leave the mess. I’ll have one of the staff come in.”

He didn’t bother saying another word before walking out, only this time, the slamming door didn’t bother me.

Dimitri stood exactly where he was, tense, even awkward. When I heard him muttering something in Russian, I turned my attention to the broken glass, bending down.

“You don’t have to do that,” Dimitri remarked, although his tone had little sincerity.

“I might as well be useful while I’m here. Is there a broom and a dustpan, or is there no cleaning equipment in this house of glass? I doubt Cristiano had ever had to lift a finger his entire life.”

I heard his deep chuckle behind me. “You have no understanding of the King family. None. You Americans are all alike.” This time, the words he muttered I knew were exclamations, curse words said in frustration of being saddled with me. He walked past and into another room, returning with exactly what I asked him for.

“And what does that make Russians?”

He cocked his head, looking away after a few seconds. “We are a proud people who understand the concept of hard work.”

“Then it must make you angry that Cristiano and his family live a life of luxury. How can you stand to work for him? How? I don’t get it. My guess is he treats you like some servant. I’m surprised he didn’t command you to clean up the mess he’s made. Isn’t that what you do? I can only wonder where you live.” I bit back any additional retort, knowing I was pressing my luck.

I could tell I'd angered him. I concentrated on cleaning up the mess, my own rollercoaster of emotions finally breaching the surface.

He backed away after a few seconds, still remaining in close proximity. Too close. I wanted him gone, away. I needed some peace and time alone to process all the shit that had happened in such a short period of time. That wasn't going to happen. There were no landlines that I'd seen while being escorted down the hall. There was a massive security system that I had no doubt couldn't be breached.

Then there was the cage in the basement if I was a bad girl.

A single tear slipped past my lashes, one too many. Crying wasn't going to do me a damn bit of good.

And why the hell was the asshole hovering around me?

"To answer your question, my life in Russia was a shit show. My family had no money, my parents taking any job they could to try and make ends meet. My father died because of his work in a factory. There were no precautions taken so he was forced to breathe in toxins for years. He died when I was only seven years old. After that, I did what I could to protect and care for my mother, ending up working for a man who you would consider the devil reincarnated. I won't tell you about my experience in a Russian prison because if I did, you would have nightmares for the rest of your life. Coming here was a godsend. Working for the King family is amazing."

The statements made by two dangerous men were gut-wrenching but didn't give either one of them an excuse to take lives when they saw fit. Yet as I gazed into his ice blue eyes, I could see compassion and such respect that I was surprised. "I'm sorry, Dimitri."

He snorted. "Cristiano has been very good to me. I have a little house and a yard. I have clothes and a vehicle. And I have money to feed myself, enough to send to my sister who refused to leave Russia. I'm the one living a life of luxury."

I nodded, unable to find any words.

Moving quickly, he took the broom from my hand, resuming the task of cleaning up. "I do anything that Cristiano asks of me. Anything. That is called loyalty. And as far as Cristiano. He knows the meaning of hard work and sacrifice as well. His father is very tough, refusing to give to his sons. They must earn their place, which Cristiano did after years of struggling to please his father. Not an easy task. I suggest you keep that in mind before you condemn him."

I backed away, studying the scar on his face, taking a deep breath as I thought about what he was saying.

"He kidnapped me, and I have no doubt that when he gets tired of me, he's going to kill me. That's all I can think about."

Dimitri swept the rest of the glass shards from the floor before rising to a standing position. "If he wanted you dead, Emily Porter, I would have already disposed of your body."

I realized my lower lip was quivering. "Then what does he want?"

He thought about my question, exhaling before answering. "Love."

CHAPTER 10

ristiano

Death.

I'd never feared death while growing up. I'd been invincible, the kid who refused to take no for an answer. I took a deep breath, gathering the hint of several types of flowers. They often gave me comfort but not today.

Misery continued to wrap around my heart, the ache more powerful than usual. If only things could be different.

The beautiful day did little to ease the pain I always felt when I came to such a bleak, cold place. I studied the bouquet, fingering the few roses before kneeling down, gently laying them across the beautiful patch of green grass. Everything was just as manicured as I'd remembered, the grass always cut to a perfect design.

Yet nothing felt right.

Sadness wrapped around my heart as I brushed my hand against the granite tombstone, tracing the letters of her name.

"Sweet Bella."

There wasn't a day I hadn't thought of her since she died, not a single day. Her smile. Her laughter. The way she flipped her hair when she was angry.

The memories were precious. The ugliness irrevocable.

Death now held an entirely different meaning.

The monster responsible would be found.

One day.

And on that day, the angels would sing, the asshole writhing in anguish.

"I've missed you." My words seemed so hollow. I couldn't help but wonder if she was looking down on me, frowning about my actions, especially with regard to Emily. I'd accepted the fact I had no conscience a long time ago. Something had snapped inside of me, erasing all the joy and happiness.

That day was one I would never forget.

I closed my eyes, allowing an image of Bella's face to form in my mind. It wasn't as difficult as it used to be, but today I found it debilitating, my anger surging.

I'd never been particularly religious, but in honor to my mother, I made the sign of the cross, pressing the tips of my fingers to my lips then pushing them against the gravestone. "I'll be back when I can, Bella. I promise I won't be gone for that long again and you know I always keep my promises."

As the wind whistled through the trees, I tipped my head toward the bright sky, my heart aching. This had been more difficult than I remembered.

After standing, I walked back toward the car, my hand remaining on the handle for a full ten seconds before I was able to open the door.

I had to face the fact I'd taken Emily for two entirely different reasons.

One, to make her suffer like I had, kept away from everyone I loved.

And two, because the glimmer in her eye had reminded me of Bella's.

What in the fuck was wrong with me?

Without any further hesitation, I jumped into the Ferrari, roaring the engine to life, forced to wipe the tears from my eyes before backing out. When I zoomed out of the area, I glanced into the rearview mirror. I could swear I saw a vision of Bella, her long hair blowing in the breeze.

"Fuck."

The word tumbled from my mouth as I pressed down on the accelerator, doing everything I could to push aside the sadness. But there was only one other emotion I was capable of.

Rage.

I was furious not only with my brother but also with myself. His accusations had pushed me, something I tried never to allow. While I knew Lucian was doing it on purpose, I'd fallen for his goading. He almost never came to my house, preferring to meet at the corporate offices or at family gatherings.

He'd come with a purpose in mind and if I had to guess, I'd say that Mario had talked, telling my brother about Emily. I hissed as I realized I hadn't thought the plan through well enough. While it was my life to live, every action I made during the next thirty days would be scrutinized.

Confrontations.

I'd been required to deal with them my entire life. I'd been the big brother, the kid who made certain there was no one who laid a hand on my siblings. I'd gotten into dozens of fights over the years leading to expulsion from several prominent private schools. When I'd been tossed out of the last one my parents considered worthy of our family, they'd finally reached their limit of my bad behavior.

While military school in another state had been their only choice, the time served in such a stern environment had hardened me. I'd come away from the four years with a better understanding of my father's regime as well as the school of hard knocks. The kids hadn't taken kindly to a gangly brooding asshole, especially given my family's reputation.

I'd been on the receiving end of their bullying.

Until I hadn't been able to take it any longer.

To this day, I remained surprised that I hadn't landed in a detention facility. I'd only found out after graduating from college that my father had bought off the prominent senator, the cash exchanged just one of the 'gifts' he'd offered in exchange for the man's silence. When the senator became the previous vice president of the United States, I'd truly embraced the power of my father's influence.

From that day on, I'd done everything I could to return to my father's good graces. As I eased the Ferrari into the parking lot of the Italian restaurant, I laughed softly. I wasn't entirely certain why I'd thought about my earlier life, the years ones I'd just as soon forget about. Maybe the recent incarceration had made me soft. Or maybe I was fighting with the demons that had plagued me ever since.

My reminiscing wasn't going to do me any good. I had to get control of my anger, especially with regard to Lucian. I'd been able to read between the lines of Lucian's troubled statements. The Azzurris might have interfered with our representation within the exclusive Diamond Dealer's Club in New York. There were too many questions, almost all of them leading to the forced meeting I was about to engage in. While my father had dabbled in diamonds early in his career, he'd become determined to utilize the lucrative market to boost our family's reputation as well as our wealth.

In my mind, the move had provided just another complication. While Lucian ran a small diamond brokerage store, the real money was in the Diamond District in New York City, a single day of trading usually bringing in four hundred million dollars. Were the authorities correct in that we could use the operation to hide other monies obtained through our less scrupulous operations? Yes.

But not until we were established in New York, something the Azzurri family was also interested in. And I knew they would stop at nothing to try to achieve what they wanted. It was time to ensure that the brother who'd replaced his father as Don understood that they would never venture into our territory.

I found a parking space in the back. After checking the amount of ammunition, I got out of the car, scanning the surrounding area. I'd chosen to track down Giancarlo without using backup. This was a place of business after all and we were civilized men. I adjusted the button on my jacket, tugging on my sleeves before closing the door. I'd used the word more than once today.

Civilized.

Perhaps there was nothing refined about our methods of handling business, but both families were smart enough to know that starting a war would take careful consideration. Now wasn't the time.

Unless…

Giancarlo was only two months younger. We knew each other well, his attendance at the same military school more of a coincidence than anything else. Only he'd landed in prison not long after turning eighteen.

To call us friends would be an overstatement, but we'd come to an understanding in the past few years, at least I thought we had. While our fathers were determined to remain bitter enemies, savoring the thought of annihilating every member of the respective families, both Giancarlo and I had determined to shut down the old ways, the brutal methods that had plagued both families for centuries.

Our deal had been made on a handshake alone, a statement of honor. However, that had taken me several years to accept. Was it possible the man had no honor at all? There was no way to shove the thought back in the ugly black box at least for now.

Not until I'd confronted him.

Deal or no deal.

The Azzurris could have a portion of New Orleans, stretching their claws into parts of Texas and further west. Our territory also included Texas, the runs from Brazil much easier to handle, but our operations extended to Florida. However, this would be a different kind of breach altogether. I had to know if they'd decided to move onto our turf during my absence.

As I walked into the restaurant, almost immediately four of Giancarlo's soldiers moved from positions lurking in the shadows, prepared to handle the situation if necessary.

Or if ordered.

I waved my hand, glaring from one to the other. "Tell your boss I need to see him."

All four looked at each other, one finally nodding before heading into one of the darkened dining rooms. They didn't need to ask my name.

Only a few seconds later, the soldier returned. "Lift your arms."

"You're not going to frisk me," I said as quietly as possible as I opened my jacket, allowing them to see the Beretta. "And this will remain with me."

The soldier looked uncomfortable, shifting his hate-filled gaze toward one of the other before motioning me to follow. The moment I entered the dining area, every person in the room stopped what they were doing, the looks on their faces the same as always.

Fear.

A few glanced toward Giancarlo's table nervously, prepared to race out of the restaurant if necessary. I smirked as I passed by, noticing Giancarlo was eating by himself, an unusual occurrence. When I moved closer, he rose to his feet, wiping his mouth on the cloth napkin and tossing it onto the table.

The Italian turned toward me, gazing down then lifting an eyebrow. He hadn't changed, his olive skin and dark eyes giving him a sensual quality. He'd even tackled a stint at modeling after being released from prison, living in New York against his father's wishes. After that, he'd become a ruthless businessman.

"He's packing, boss," the scarred soldier told him.

Giancarlo took his time before answering. "Leave us alone, Tony."

"Yes, boss."

He glanced over his shoulder, watching as Tony left. "If you're here carrying a weapon, the conversation must be serious."

"It's important. I need answers. If they're not the ones I hope for, my father will make certain decisions that will affect both families. I believe you know what I mean."

He rose to his full height, locking eyes with mine. There wasn't a sound in the room. After a few seconds, he grinned, yanking me into a bear hug. "Of course I do. Good to see you a free man, Chris."

He was the only person, other than my brother, who I dared allow to call me Chris. I'd hated my given name while in school, doing everything I could to disassociate myself from the family's murderous legacy.

"Good to be seen and not in blazing orange."

His boisterous laugh was one thing I always remembered about him.

As well as his uncanny marksmanship abilities.

"Sit. Sit. Would you like to join me for lunch?" he asked as he waved one of the waiters over, easing down onto the chair.

"I'm sorry I can't today. As you might imagine, I have much to do since my release."

"At least have a glass of wine with me, old friend. Yes?"

While this wasn't a social visit, I gave a respectful nod. He was trying too hard, a telling fact.

"Excellent. More vino."

I almost laughed given his accent was much stronger than normal. He'd spent almost no time in Italy, educated at Harvard. He was egging it on, likely for a reason.

Only after the waiter poured another glass of wine from a very expensive bottle of Masseto Massetino did he speak. "I anticipated your arrival."

"Is that why you're celebrating?" I held up the glass, swirling the dark liquid.

He laughed heartedly. "I could never get anything past you, my friend." He lifted his glass. "Salute to your freedom. And it's good to have a chance to talk man to man."

"Agreed." My thoughts drifted to the soliloquy I'd given Emily only two hours earlier. Freedom. The kind of life our families had chosen to live precluded any concept of real freedom. "Why were you expecting my arrival?"

Giancarlo took another bite of his food before pushing the plate away. He sighed before leaning over. "I am aware of the word on the street. You're here to confront me about our involvement with having you arrested."

I weighed my words carefully. "I'm here to ask you about the assassination attempt on my father's life, and a subsequent plan on moving in on our territory, including precious gems. I'm also curious if you have any information on the murder of Michael's wife."

He opened his eyes wide, anger sweeping across his face, bristling as I'd expected. The man's fuse was as short as mine, his penchant for reacting without asking questions well known. He took a deep breath, holding it for a few seconds before expelling.

"We've known each other a long time, Cristiano. While our fathers have no love for each other, you and I came to an understanding a long time ago. For you to accuse me of doing several egregious acts isn't what I'd expect."

"Yes, we agreed to leave family out of our respective businesses. However, sometimes there are required casualties that are regrettable but necessary. I want the truth, Giancarlo. I can't hold back my father unless I get it."

Giancarlo narrowed his eyes. "If this is some kind of riddle…"

"You know I refuse to play games. I need to hear it from you that you had nothing to do with the attempt made on my father's life."

While I could tell he was still incensed, the tension eased visibly. "You come to my restaurant carrying a piece. Then you accuse me of several crimes. I'm insulted, Cristiano. But

I have to give you credit. You have balls the size of melons. Your father should be proud."

I said nothing, turning my head and noticing the way two of the soldiers were itching to enter into a fight. "I'm not like my father, Giancarlo. Neither are you like yours."

"And I'm glad for both. All right. I give you my word on my mother's life that I had nothing to do with the attempt on your father's life and from what I heard, the death of Cassandra King was an accident, which is still tragic. If she was murdered, I've heard nothing on the streets. What you're accusing me of is not how we conduct business, at least not with the King family. As far as moving in on your turf, you know me well enough that I take what I want. Our deal is still viable."

"And the diamonds?"

He grinned, shrugging his shoulders. "I've made inquiries and nothing more."

I studied his eyes, finally nodding again. "I'm glad to hear that. I would hate if my first act after my release was to begin a war."

"I would hate that as well, especially since you'd lose." He grinned after issuing the words, but there was a strange glint in his eyes.

"I must ask. There is also a nasty rumor that you are preparing to move into South America."

He seemed uncomfortable. "Where did you hear that?"

"It would seem Francesco is sweet on my sister."

His frown remained, a spark of anger in his eyes. Then he laughed heartedly. "You know my younger brother. His dick speaks for him the majority of the time. We have made explorations, nothing else. There is much business to go around. Don't you agree?"

I could tell he was incensed that Francesco had said anything. I realized that attempting to corner the South American market could be a mistake. At least Azzurri would owe me. "Agreed."

He exhaled, tapping his fingers on the table. "I was thinking. Perhaps a more permanent connection between our families would strengthen our hold on gulf states."

I burst out laughing. "If by that you mean an arranged marriage between Angelique and Francesco, that will never happen. My sister is far too… disobedient."

He laughed with me, nodding several times. "That she is, and my brother needs to learn when to keep his mouth shut."

A quiet settled between us.

"Then I can easily report to my father that you have no desire to attempt to maneuver into our territory." I wasn't asking. I was stating.

He shook his head, leaning against his chair. "Of course you can. I can see that you've gotten right to work, likely talking to your informants. Warring over turf isn't what has created the unrest in our beloved community."

"What aren't you telling me?"

He finished off his wine, reaching for the bottle himself. "It would seem there's another player in town, although I haven't been able to make sense of what I've been hearing."

"I heard rumblings while in prison. What is the latest?"

"That offers are being made to certain... officials that have been accepted."

Interesting. "Which means the new deals supersede various deals previously made."

He nodded several times. "Unfortunately, I haven't been able to find any evidence to corroborate what I've been told."

"Told by whom?"

"I have my informants. You have yours."

"What have you heard?"

A twinkle formed in his eyes. "That the witness in your case has certain connections."

Instantly, my body bristled, my heart racing. "What kind of connections?"

"To the very individual who may be responsible for the rumors we've both heard."

I sat back, shoving the wine further away. He watched me intently, narrowing his eyes. "As in this witness never saw anything in the first place?"

"Possibly. That I don't know for certain, but I do think that whoever he or she is working for has designs on both our operations. Think about it. An assault on your family would lead you to assume we were responsible. This entity wasn't able to remove your father; therefore, when you gave them an opportunity to remove you out of the picture in an entirely different way, they devised a plan that would make it foolproof. Now, I doubt this person was prepared for you to be released from prison so soon, so I would be very careful if I were you. There's a good chance that you were always the target."

"Meaning?"

"Meaning given you run the family operations, they'd want you as far out of the picture as possible. There are also few people who don't know about your love of family. You would turn over any boulder in order to find out the person responsible for doing any harm, no matter who or how powerful that individual is. True to form—"

"I made certain that happened," I finished the sentence for him.

"Exactly. I might be off base, but that could be the case."

His warning was well noted, the fury rumbling in my chest. It should have been clear to me that Emily had been lying to me all along. Even the information on her could have been leaked as a ploy. I sucked in my breath, trying to calm my pulse. That wasn't going to happen any time soon. "I appreciate your candor."

"You are welcome, my friend. All that I ask in return is that you desist from making accusations. I am a patient man, but I refuse to tolerate certain... let's just say damning words. I do have a business to run."

"Understood, Giancarlo. I believe what you've told me. Thank you for the wine."

"If you like, I'll be happy to send you a case."

I laughed as I stood, patting him on the shoulder. "You were always a man who enjoyed life to the fullest."

"We should both know that life can be cut short in an instant, without warning." There were a few seconds of sadness in the man's voice, much like the haunting feeling that remained pitted in my system. The loss of his first wife had been just as tragic as Bella's untimely death.

"Agreed."

"Let me give you a piece of advice, Cristiano. Find someone you care about. The only time we are allowed to show weakness is with regard to a woman. That is also about the only thing that keeps us sane."

"That may be true."

"Just one more thing. The Kings weren't the only ones recently affected. I found out that two of my men had been betraying me, supplying information. I had to handle the situation."

"Did you learn who they were working for?"

"They refused to talk, even after my best men interrogated them."

"Interesting." His soldiers had been more afraid of whoever they'd sold out to than the torture and ultimately death they'd receive at the hands of Azzurri's men.

Giancarlo huffed. "Enjoy some freedom, my friend. That much you deserve. Business can wait. Beautiful woman on the other hand." His laugh was just as gregarious as before.

As I walked away, passing through his sea of soldiers, I realized that there would never be a woman I could trust. Not with my life. Not with information.

And certainly not with my heart.

As I walked outside, the scent of sauce and Italian sausage didn't have the usual effect of making my mouth water. This time, the stench churned in my stomach.

She'd lied to me.

Now she would pay the price.

* * *

I went over every word of the conversation I'd had with Emily, trying to make sense of any of it. One thing was certain. She wasn't the innocent flower that I'd believed her to be. I'd bought the entire story, even feeling guilt for having captured her.

No longer.

The plan had been brilliant, one I'd even fallen into. Emily would talk. She'd tell me everything I needed to know.

As I sped through the city, the sound of my phone only fueled the increasing anger. However, this was one call I needed to take. I pressed the button on the steering wheel, shifting down as I hit traffic. As Consigliere and the family attorney, Joseph Carello had been the man responsible for getting me released from prison. While I'd never liked the man, he was completely loyal to my father.

Hell, the man should be after the amount of money my father had placed in his bank account.

"Joseph. I haven't had the opportunity to thank you."

"Don't thank me just yet, Cristiano. There's already talk of a new trial date."

"I thought this was dead."

"Yeah, so did I. I think we need to have a discussion," Joseph said, his tone more urgent than I was used to.

I switched lanes, moving around a string of slow cars. I had my own sense of urgency to get back to the house. I was also planning on having some of my men do a sweep of her entire place. While the chances of finding anything leading me to whoever she was working for were slim, mistakes were often made. Emily Porter was certainly no professional at the game. "It's going to have to wait at least until tomorrow."

"I don't think it can."

"Why is that?"

"Because not only do I know about Emily Porter, I am well aware you abducted her from her home."

I hissed, correct in my earlier assumption regarding Mario spilling the beans. He'd gone straight to Lucian, who in turn had called our attorney. "Fine. Where are you?"

"At my office."

"I'll be there in ten minutes." After ending the call, I took several deep breaths. From here on out, I had to think clearly, developing an entirely different kind of plan. I jammed on the accelerator, blowing through several lights, the sound of horns and screeching tires forcing me to sneer.

My father had once told me that my disregard for life could get me killed one day. Perhaps that was the case. In the meantime, I planned on taking Giancarlo's advice. I was going to enjoy my life.

One way or the other.

"Mr. King. So happy to see you."

I grinned seeing Mary. She'd worked for Joseph for years, had treated me like a son the majority of the time. "You look fabulous, Mary. Just gorgeous today."

She blushed, rolling her eyes. "Always the flirt. What a shame you aren't a few years older."

"What? You don't like younger men?"

"Incorrigible. He's waiting for you."

I winked before walking down the hallway. She certainly didn't deserve my pissed-off mood or a second of my ire. I didn't bother knocking, walking in without hesitation.

Joseph looked up from his computer, shaking his head and pushing back from his desk. "You don't waste any time. Do you?" He moved toward the corner bar in his office, pouring two drinks without asking.

That meant the conversation was serious.

I shifted toward the massive floor-to-ceiling window in his office, the location with the most incredible view of Bourbon Street. Even in the daylight, the people walking the streets were colorful, enjoying their time, pushing their comfort zones. I accepted the drink, waiting as he flanked my side.

"I've heard it's going to be an intense Mardi Gras this year," he said quietly.

The event was months away. The man was obviously nervous about the case as well as the recent events. "Why don't we just cut the crap, Joseph? Go right ahead and chastise me, but from what I've heard, my decision to interrupt Ms. Porter's life was well founded."

"And just what have you heard?"

"That she was not merely encouraged to testify in court, her entire story was actually a fabrication and that Ms. Porter is possibly working for someone who has every intention of stripping away a certain business faction of our family. As you can understand, I couldn't allow that to happen."

He turned his head very slowly. "Do I need to know where you heard this... information?"

"I have my sources. I assume that Lucian told you I retrieved her."

"Retrieved?" he snorted, walking back to his desk. "She's not a dog or a file that was lost. She's a human being and when the authorities find out she's missing, who the fuck do you think they're going to come to?"

"And I'll have an alibi prepared."

"Jesus Christ, Cristiano. This isn't some kind of game. You can't bully or threaten your way through this one. You're still facing a minimum of five years in prison, four if they allot the time you've already spent behind bars. However, my guess is the retrial will be on a charge of murder one this time. I had a chat with Griffin Williams just a little while ago. He told me that he has a press conference scheduled which will simply be the beginning of his effort to crucify you as well as the entire King family."

"Nothing new."

"Yeah? Well, this time it would appear he has you dead to rights. From what he told me, there's additional information, possibly another witness, although the cagey fuck certainly wasn't going to play his hand."

"I thought you ended this bullshit."

He shook his head. "I'm damn good at what I do, Cristiano. I've protected your family for decades; however, I can't do my job when you go off on the deep end, which you did. Our influence has taken a major dip as well as our reputation. You knew the mistrial might not be the end of the case, yet you felt compelled to abduct the witness. I just don't understand you at all. Do you have a death wish?"

I refused to take my eyes off the street, marveling in the neon lights and colorful buildings. I had taken everything for granted for far too long. That was going to stop.

"I wanted to talk with her." My words were ridiculous.

"That's bullshit. There's more to this and I know it. So what is it?"

Sighing, I couldn't admit that I simply adored Emily's picture, that my entire body had been set on fire from one glance at a photograph. Yeah, that would go over well.

"Wait a minute. You like the girl. That's it. Isn't it?" Joseph demanded.

"As I said, I felt it was prudent to talk to her."

"My God. I should have known. You're exactly like your fucking father. Impetuous. Never thinking about anyone else."

I shifted to face him, walking closer, reining in my fury. "I'm nothing like my father."

His smirk was grating enough I wanted to wipe it off his face. Instead, I turned away briefly, rubbing my eyes as I took several deep breaths.

"Exactly why haven't you been able to shut down this retrial? From what I know, we still own enough people you should have been able to convince them to drop this case. What the hell do we pay you for?" I'd never challenged Joseph to this degree. "Reputation or not, we hold secrets on half the freaking police department, including the police chief. If I need to drag that out in the open, I'm happy to do so."

"How dare you, Cristiano. I was lucky that you didn't get life for killing that man in cold blood. You lost your temper, just like you have dozens of fucking times before. How many goddamn times did I have to bail your ass out of jail when you were younger?"

Far too many.

He huffed when I didn't answer him, taking a gulp of his drink then walking to the second window in his office, peering down at the street below. The silence was awkward as hell. "I did my best, but there's something going on, Cristiano. I've tried to tell your father that his regime is being challenged by outsiders, but he seems to have blinders on. I think his health has really taken a toll on him. Plus, your absence was something he couldn't get over. He counted on you."

Counted on me. The way he said the words was a clear indication that I'd let my father down.

Again.

"What about Lucian? He was given the reins when I left. What the fuck has he been able to accomplish in my absence?"

He shifted a single glance over his shoulder. "Lucian has done his best. He really has and he gives a damn about you, whether you want to believe that or not. He's managed to keep everything afloat, increasing profits and ensuring that none of our clients make a move against us, even with ugly rumors surfacing that the King family had lost control. However, he's not you. His concentration is on the great diamond market, not on running the business at hand. And you and I both know that neither Vincenzo nor Michael can handle the operation. Vincenzo has never taken the King dynasty seriously and Michael has the children as well as the Throne Room. Hell, the man has turned the club into a New Orleans destination." His laugh was anguished. Bitter. He also looked rattled, something I'd rarely seen in him before.

The Throne Room, a glorified club for the rich and powerful. My father has insisted on keeping the venture, a former speakeasy from the past. It at least offered an opportunity to obtain a handle on those with enough influence to alter our course of business.

"And Dante?" I asked.

"The last time I heard, he's on his third deployment in Afghanistan and will be for at least six more months."

"That news will certainly disappoint Mother." Dante would do anything to stay away from the family, including extending his tour of duty in the military. I rubbed my eyes, sheer exhaustion settling in. "How has our business been affected in my absence?"

"Nothing outright or egregious from what I've been able to tell. However, one of the suppliers from South America threatened to pull out when Lucian wasn't able to provide what they believed to be adequate protection. From what I was able to decipher, it was a ploy to alter the split. Lucian managed to handle it, but I'm not entirely certain what concessions he made in doing so. The legitimate businesses are all doing well, quite profitable in fact."

From the look on his face, I could tell Joseph had additional information. "What haven't you told me?"

Sighing, Joseph appeared even more uncomfortable, his body language and pinched expression giving him away. "I've worked for your family for years, but your father remains my friend."

I wanted to tell him to get the hell on with it, but I yanked in my patience, allowing him to finish.

"I don't have to tell you that the old way of doing business was ruthless, actions made considered cruel today, but I stood by your father, advising him of whatever options became available." He shifted his gaze in my direction, his expression one I couldn't recognize. "Well, let me cut to the chase. I fear that one of your father's old enemies has returned, although I have no proof that's the case."

"Then why are you telling me?"

"Rumors. While you have your informants, I also have mine."

"Get on with it, Joseph. Are you trying to tell me that the person responsible for the attempted assassination of my father is familiar?"

"I don't know for certain. Just my instinct; however, the information I've received continues to speak to someone else entirely, a relatively new player in town." Joseph continued to appear uncomfortable as hell.

"Just give me a name."

"Enrique Vendez."

I wasn't taken aback. "Vendez. I'm hearing the name for a second time in twenty-four hours."

"Meaning what?"

"Meaning I had a chat with the informant who squealed. Evidently, Vendez is behind my father's shooting and tarnishing our reputation. The question is what do you know about him?"

"Unfortunately, not much. The man is as elusive as he is secretive. He was supposedly a two-bit player down in South America."

"That's not much to go on."

Huffing, Joseph lifted his glass. "I'm well aware. That's the case anyway until about five years ago. From what I've been able to find out, he slowly made his way up the food chain. Then he disappeared, likely developing his business plan. While there are a few rumors on the street that he's connected to Carlos Morales, there's nothing concrete that I could find. Hell, the information I obtained was because I called in a couple favors."

Carlos Morales was the head of a notorious cartel out of South America. The man was nothing more than a brutal dictator, eradicating anyone he thought was getting in his way. He was certainly not a friend of my father, even accusing him once of overstepping his bounds. Something wasn't adding up.

"Where did you find this Vendez?"

"Well, there's a thing called public records, which no legitimate business can hide from, even though it's obvious he tried. He's the owner of record of a corporation out of Baton Rouge, EV Holdings. Underneath the corporate umbrella is a string of profitable businesses strung out through the south. The corporation is mostly a shell, but he does have dozens of employees."

"Including businesses in New Orleans," I said, resisting laughing at the thought.

"Yes. While some are legitimate, others are questionable, but there's little information to find. The man is very careful in what's on the internet. Given he earned his stripes in South America..." Joseph allowed the sentence to trail off.

"He's taking over the run from South America and spreading his wings."

"Exactly, but I don't think he's stopping with party favors and that's not the most damning part." He pulled a single piece of paper from a file on his desk, keeping it in his hand as he walked closer. "Do you recognize any of the names?"

I glanced at the papers, running down the list. When I stiffened, he pulled it away from me.

"Bayou Market Analysis." Another jolt of electricity surged through me.

"Yes. Emily Porter works for them," he said quietly, allowing me time to reflect on the news. "They handle the market analysis on various stocks and trades, including in the diamond market."

Jesus Christ. The asshole was attempting to move in on two fronts.

"And as you know, South America has a healthy diamond mining industry," Joseph continued.

What Giancarlo had told me was accurate. I closed my eyes, the grip on the glass becoming crushing. "She fucking lied to me." Just saying the words out loud left a bad taste in my mouth.

"Well, I'm not certain what or if she's told you anything, but she might be a pawn and nothing more. From what I've been able to find, she was at the restaurant that night in question. That could be a coincidence or that could be some odd twist of fate. Either way, you have a significant problem on your hands."

"You're still not telling me everything," I stated.

He half smiled. "You're so like your father. Intuitive. Refusing to succumb to fear. Even brazen." There was another hesitation before he continued. "If my sources are correct, there is a price on your head. Also, I have reason to believe that Ms. Porter is now considered expendable."

There was certainly no chance that her disappearance had been discovered, unless she'd been watched. "Interesting." Thoughts about the past entered my mind. My life had certainly been threatened before and would likely be again. I wasn't surprised, except for the timing. My release from prison had obviously disturbed some course of action.

"What I've told you is not to be taken lightly, Cristiano."

"Why Emily Porter?"

Joseph exhaled. "I'm not certain, unless she is innocent in what occurred, simply used as I suspect is the case."

"But you don't know that for certain."

"At this point, nothing is certain. Keep in mind that just as the King family's methods of doing business has required a shift in practices over the years, there are dozens of other entities determined to gain a foot in the market. Your death would send a clear message that New Orleans is ripe for another change."

His point was well taken.

"Do you have a picture of Vendez?"

Joseph chuckled. "That's part of the problem. There are no photographs of him, other than a couple of grainy shots from the side at a distance. He could be anyone. Hell, he could be using a pseudonym for all I know or actually be a compilation of different people. I've checked with all my sources. While it would appear than Vendez's name is on several ten most wanted lists, several countries attempting to apprehend him, to date, he's never been arrested."

"Fuck. Fuck!"

"Don't lose your temper, Cristiano."

"Too late for that. As far as my father's enemies, I need a list from you as to who they are. I will find the bastard responsible. No one threatens my family."

He nodded. "This could work very well in our favor, but only if we play the cards right."

"Meaning what? That I need to kill her? I'm not going to do that. I can't."

The smile on his face pissed me off as much as my outburst. "I was right. As soon as I saw the picture, I knew you'd find her attractive."

"That no longer matters. This family and our business must be protected. Getting the asshole out of our territory is vital." I paced the floor, furious with myself. What the fuck had I been thinking? The truth was I'd been thinking with my cock instead of my head.

"While I don't disagree, you do have options, the ability to send a message of your own that the King family will not be taken down easily."

"Options. What in the hell options do I have, Joseph?"

He walked closer, gripping my shoulder. "Marry her."

CHAPTER 11

ristiano

The thought was ridiculous, blasphemous. I had no intention of marrying the woman. While Joseph had taken the time to explain the reasons I should, including she could no longer testify against me and that I could acquire additional information at some point, I wasn't interested. I'd instructed him to find another way before walking out of his office, disgusted with the entire situation.

Instead of returning to my car, I walked Bourbon Street, drinking in the sights and sounds. Music blared from several locations. Various scents of food floated out the doors. And everywhere there was joy and happiness.

While the calculated idea of forcing our nuptials was practical, some families continuing what I considered to be an ancient practice, even my father hadn't stooped to anything so low in his thinking. We were Americans, free to choose what we wanted to do and who we desired to be with. Love was difficult at best, the majority of women unable to handle the business let alone the lifestyle, but this was entirely different.

How the hell would I be able to trust her? She'd run away or worse, attempt to kill me. Emily had enough strength and resolve to do so.

Unfortunately, I knew I had to give it serious consideration. If there was indeed no other choice, then Emily would make a beautiful bride.

Chuckling, I entered one of the upscale women's clothing stores in the city.

"Can I help you?" a clerk asked as she approached. I could tell she recognized me immediately. "Mr. King. I'll be happy to find anything you'd like."

As I gazed around the store, I was pleasantly surprised at their selection. "I need an entire wardrobe for a friend of mine."

"What do you have in mind?"

"Dresses and lingerie. Shoes if you have them. Oh, and I'll need several."

Her eyes lit up with dollar signs. "I think I can find everything you need. What's her size?"

I laughed, shaking my head. "I have no idea, but she's about your height and build."

"Well, excellent. Then follow me. My name is Sheila, by the way. Please make yourself at home while I select a few items. Marty, bring Mr. King a glass of champagne. We have a lounge over to the right. It won't take very long at all."

"Thank you." I laughed softly to myself as I pictured Emily. "She's very beautiful, Sheila. The kind of woman who holds an aura around her like sunshine. A lovely flower. Please make sure that the selections you make are feminine with a touch of magic."

She smiled, a thoughtful look crossing her face. "You care about her very much, this friend."

I thought about her question. For whatever reason, I did care about her, likely too much. "Yes, I do."

"Then I'll select only the most beautiful dresses that we carry."

"One more thing, Sheila. Do you happen to know a bridal shop in this area?"

Her smile grew, her eyes twinkling. "Of course. I can help you with that as well."

* * *

I hadn't been to the office in over a year. Benson Tower was an architectural beauty, our offices located on the twenty-sixth floor, taking up a significant portion. My father had always insisted that we generate our business in a corporate environment instead of some sleazy back room in a bar or old warehouse. He'd also insisted on suits and ties, demanding that we look presentable at all times.

I'd missed the atmosphere, the mainly glass building and various water effects. Perhaps our business had become more profitable, our clients appreciative of our diligence to what we provided. I chuckled as I moved into the elevator, pressing the button for the top floor. Then again, I'd been very selective about the clients I'd allowed to walk into our office suite.

As I walked into the office, I was surprised that there were very few employees. It was obvious Lucian had let them go for the day.

He appeared in the hallway, taking a deep breath before turning and heading into his office. While I followed, I took my time, closing the door once I was inside.

"I think you need to tell me exactly what's going on. In business and with regard to rumors in the streets." I had no inflection in my voice, but I certainly had contempt for him in my mind.

"I'm certain Joseph told you enough," Lucian said, a hint of resentment in his tone. "Business is stable, but I don't know for how long."

"Joseph mentioned that a man named Enrique Vendez is attempting to move in on our turf, likely the very reason that you haven't been able to get into the Dealer's Club."

"That's what I suspected as well."

I walked closer, doing everything I could to curtail my temper. "And you didn't choose to tell me this before?"

He turned sharply, glaring me in the eyes. "What the hell were you going to do behind bars, Cristiano? What? You couldn't do a damn thing. If Joseph told you what he expressed only two weeks ago, the man is a total mystery. I've pulled every resource I can in hopes of finding this individual, but either he's paid people to keep their mouths shut or worse. There is a stench of fear on the streets, as if there is an impending course of actions that will derail several of our businesses. If I had anything concrete, I assure you that I would tell you."

"I would hope that you would, Lucian. Did you know about the witness?"

He shook his head vehemently. "Not until Dimitri was able to locate her identity just a couple of days ago. The justice department did a damn good job of keeping her a secret. Our people inside the department had been shut out, perhaps because they're low level employees."

"But you have your doubts."

"I always have doubts, Cristiano. I did learn something about our father's way of doing business. By the time Dimitri found Ms. Porter, we'd just been made aware of your release. At that point, I knew it was something you'd want to handle personally, although I certainly didn't think you'd have the balls to kidnap her."

Sighing, I had no doubt he was telling me the truth. "You were right in your assumptions and how I handle the woman is entirely my decision. What about the shipment from South America a couple of months ago? I heard there were incidents."

He laughed. "The bastard Julio wanted sixty percent instead of thirty. He was told in no uncertain terms he would be cut off from any future business opportunities."

"Did he accept?"

"Only after I had one of his boats torched. I'm certain our good friend Carlos Morales was angry about the loss of party favors, but he was intelligent enough not to make a threat."

The Morales Cartel wouldn't take the loss of product lightly. There would be an attempt at retaliation at some point.

However, I hadn't expected the answer and couldn't help but smile. My brother had never had an affinity for violence. I gathered he was finally understanding the necessity in some circumstances. Perhaps he had learned a few things from our father. "A good decision."

"Wow. My brother actually can give a compliment. Maybe Emily is good for you."

Tensing, I resisted lashing out. We needed to work together at this point.

The tension was even higher than usual.

"Look. I'm sorry that you were forced into carrying the load. From what I've heard, you've done a good job."

He gave me a hard look. "Vincenzo actually stepped up to the plate when necessary. Even Michael was on board with providing aid. We are a family after all."

I was glad to hear the others had been useful. "You need to get a handle on New York."

"What about this Vendez?"

"Once found, he will need to be eliminated, but not until I figure out exactly what he's attempting to do. However, I have a bad feeling that whatever his plan, it's going to happen quickly."

"I agree with you. And Emily?"

A rush of heat boosted the level of adrenaline. "I haven't decided."

"Well, that is something you need to do and quickly."

"Joseph told you that I've kept her. Of course he did."

"You're right in that whatever you do is your decision, but I suggest you try and keep in mind that she could be nothing more than a plant."

"So I've been told."

He snorted before walking around his desk, pressing down on his keyboard then turning his laptop around to face me.

I walked closer, eyeing the face of a man who'd been a thorn in the family's side for years. Griffin Williams was the lead prosecutor in the state department, an asshole who'd been determined to bring us down. He'd held a press conference, just like Joseph had mentioned.

"Let me turn the sound up for you," Lucian said.

"What are your intentions with regards to Cristiano King?" A reporter swung the microphone in his direction, her face beaming at being close to the man. Griffin stood on the steps of the courthouse, the large crowd gathered around him mostly reporters. He'd always adored the attention, exploiting his impeccable win record as if he should be honored.

However, for the half dozen times he'd attempted to bring down the King family, he hadn't succeeded. He hadn't even been the one to handle the prosecution in my case and was likely fuming from the fact.

"I've been assigned to the case and I plan on ensuring that the people of New Orleans and the entire state of Louisiana are protected from every thug, including Cristiano King. He is a criminal who should spend the rest of his life behind bars. Trust me. I intend on making that happen. New evidence has come to light that will enhance my case." Gloating, as Griffin stared into the camera, he smiled, likely speaking directly to me.

New evidence. What the fuck was the asshole getting at?

Lucian switched off the link, shaking his head. "I don't like this, Cristiano. Griffin is a pig, but he's been itching to take us down for years. You need to listen to Joseph. This thing is about to get ugly."

Ugly wasn't the word I would use. This was going to get bloody.

Whatever decision I would make regarding Emily would need to be done tonight.

By the time I finished the business of the day, it was already dark, the slight moon only creating ominous shadows as I drove down the streets. Anger and sadness remained furrowing in my mind, my gut churning from the volley of information I'd received. If Vendez was attempting to eradicate the family, he had to be found quickly.

The rest was… unsavory.

I sat in the driveway for a full two minutes before easing from the car, yanking the bags into my hands. My anger had abated to a manageable degree, but she would need to be punished for lying to me. She was a smart girl. I refused to buy that she had no idea about what was going on. As I walked inside, I heard music coming from another portion of the house. Music. What the fuck did Dimitri think this was? Some kind of freaking day off?

Dumping the bags, I took long strides down the hallway, finding no one in the family room. Fuck. What the hell was going on?

My anger swelled as well as fear, real fear. There was also a chance that her life could be placed in danger. All the prosecutors needed was her previous testimony. If she'd been used as a pawn, then she was expendable. I couldn't rule out any of the possibilities. When I didn't find either one in the kitchen, I stormed outside, bristling the second I noticed Emily with her feet in the water, Dimitri standing in the shadows.

"What the fuck is going on?" I bellowed as I approached.

Immediately, Dimitri moved into the dim light, a pensive look on his face. "She wanted to see the pool. I didn't think you'd mind."

There was no hesitation. I took long strides in his direction, backhanding him across the jaw.

He stumbled, his weapon almost slipping from his hand.

"Cristiano!" Emily yelped as she scrambled to her feet. "What the hell are you doing?"

"My soldier knows better than to allow you outside. There are far too many dangers."

Dimitri rubbed his jaw, collecting himself yet not looking me in the eye. He knew he'd failed me. "I'm sorry, Mr. King. I honestly didn't think there'd be a problem. The ground is secure. I made certain of it."

"Yeah? Well, you weren't thinking, Dimitri. That's the fucking problem. You know as well as I do what's at stake." I could barely control my anger, the rage all but consuming me. I ran my hands through my hair before scanning the perimeter. While the property was as secure as possible, there were still plenty of weak areas where a sharpshooter could easily get off several shots.

"Yes, Mr. King. I understand. I'm sorry." Dimitri took two steps away, his chest heaving. There was a hint of defiance in his voice, as I'd come to expect from him, although I knew he'd go no further for fear of facing my wrath.

"You're such a fucking monster. There aren't boogeymen hiding behind every shrub, Cristiano. You're paranoid." Emily huffed and tried to storm past me.

I grabbed her arm, yanking her against my chest and lowering my head. When I lifted her chin with a single finger, her glare was icy cold, reeking of venom. "That's where you're wrong, little flower. This isn't about paranoia. This is about experience as well as knowledge of the kind of people I've dealt with my entire life. You don't understand what I'm up against every day. Danger is real, something you need to keep in mind."

She twisted her mouth, her eyes darting back and forth. "How very sad, Cristiano. What a wonderful life you lead, never being able to enjoy your surroundings." She managed to yank her arm away, cursing under her breath as she hurried toward the house.

I let her go, fisting one hand and pressing the other against the handle of my weapon. Then I turned my full wrath on Dimitri. "You made a serious mistake. I have reason to believe that there will be an attempt made on my life and perhaps Emily's as well."

He shifted his gaze in my direction but there was no surprise in his eyes.

"Yes, sir. I'm aware. It won't happen again."

"You're right. It won't. As far as I'm concerned, you're nothing more than a foot soldier." I knew my words were cruel, heartless, and unforgiving. At that moment, I didn't give a shit. I was angry with the world, prepared to take on anyone who got in my way.

He opened his mouth as if to try to provide an excuse then thought better of it. "Let me know who you'd like by your side and I'll see that it happens. Again, I am sorry. I promised you that I would never let anything happen to her, and I intended on keeping that promise, even if it meant losing my life." He turned, slowly walking toward the door.

I rubbed my forehead, hissing under my breath. "Dimitri. Just… You're relieved for the day. Be back here at eight in the morning. Bring Nick with you."

"Nick?" Dimitri asked. "Why?"

I wasn't in the mood to be second guessed. I was well aware that Nick was still new to our operation, holding the lowest ranking. However, I had hopes he'd become an enforcer. "It's time for him to get his feet wet. I'll need you with me tomorrow to handle some business. You do believe he's trustworthy."

"Very much so. He's also eager."

"That's what I'm looking for. Also find out everything you can about Enrique Vendez. His possible involvement was confirmed."

The silence was deafening. He narrowed his eyes, finally nodding. "Yes, Mr. King."

His perfunctory words were biting, but perhaps deserved.

"I did check on Emily's friend. I can find no connection to any of our businesses. She seems clean."

Sighing, I waved him off.

When he entered the house, the slight click of the door still gave me a snarl. If I wasn't careful, I would lose it, and that couldn't happen. The next few days were crucial, the plan of operation now required to change. I stared at the pool, the LED lights just giving me another reminder of all the things I'd ignored in my life. A snicker formed, my head aching.

At some point things had to change.

Before walking into the house, I thought about what I was going to say to her. Nothing would matter at this point. She would remain nothing more than a hostage, but one of vital importance. Maybe my instinct to capture her had been right after all.

I entered the house, taking several deep breaths. As expected, she was nowhere to be found. The music was still playing, the melodic sounds doing nothing but fueling my anger. I found her in the kitchen, a wineglass in her hand as she stood in front of the window. She sensed my presence immediately, twisting even more to avoid eye contact.

"You lied to me," I stated, my tone stern.

"What the hell did I lie about? I already told you I don't want to be here. I stated with clear emphasis that I witnessed your horrific act. What else do you want from me?"

"The truth."

She shook her head with an exaggerated exhale. "I have told you the truth."

"Then how were you able to purchase your lovely home? You have zero money. No stocks, no savings."

Hissing, she jerked around to face me, venom the only expression I could read. "How dare you. Purchasing that house took every penny I had. Why do you think I know every Goodwill store in town?" She shook her head. "Wait. You think I was paid off for my testimony. My God."

"I have to entertain every avenue."

"You should hear yourself, Cristiano."

I could see the hurt in her eyes, but she was telling the truth. "I believe you."

"As if I give a shit. What the hell was that about with Dimitri? Were you just trying to be the big man, some ruthless asshole? What dangers are in your freaking backyard?" When I didn't answer right away, she laughed, taking a swig of her wine. "Of course you have no comment. What else would I expect?"

I inched closer, gripping the edge of the counter, noticing that she'd positioned a second glass by the open bottle of wine, a gesture that I couldn't comprehend. With my voice as low and emotionless as possible, I answered. "There has been danger surrounding my family my entire life. There are people, enemies, that would stop at nothing to destroy my family."

"Well deserved."

"You know nothing about me."

"And I don't want to know anything else," she spouted, recoiling slightly. "Other than why you killed that man. He was nothing but the owner of a restaurant, for God's sake.

What kind of danger could he pose to you, especially since you're a merciless killer?"

"That man is responsible for my father almost being killed."

She seemed taken aback, blinking several times. "How? Why?"

"Why? Because he betrayed my family."

"I don't understand."

"Of course you don't understand." I closed my eyes briefly. "I have four brothers and a beautiful baby sister. My mother is more like an angel, her devout faith something that allows her happiness. My father? Well, he's a great man, although he was rough on every one of us growing up, but just recently he's enjoyed family gatherings and holidays. I know he regrets missing so many as we were growing up. My siblings are loving and vivacious, trying to enjoy their life."

"Wow. You sound like a Hallmark card," she said defiantly.

I took another step closer, surprised that she didn't budge an inch. "There have been four attempts made on my father's life, including the one I mentioned. There have also been two on other members of the family. My father almost died almost two years ago because that asshole from the restaurant sold his soul to someone else."

"Who? Who would dare defy the great King family?" she challenged.

The truth allowed the guilt to continue. "I don't know."

"You don't know yet you murdered him?"

"I did what I had to do to send a message to others. I would do anything to protect my family and the men and women who work for me, all of whom have a target on their backs and will even if they discontinue their employment. That is the pledge I've made to them. That is a requirement."

The slight smirk on her face was nothing but a continuation of her rebellious nature and her lack of understanding my life. She would learn the hard way that disobedience allowed weakness, which in turn created an avenue for my enemies to break through our defenses.

"As I said before. Your life is very sad. I'm not certain why the bars in prison bothered you. You've been living behind them your entire life."

The words were poignant and so damn accurate.

"Maybe so, Emily, but even if I had steel bars on every window, that wouldn't mean I was safe. I assure you that while I have the finest security system, men who would die to keep me alive, there will always be an enemy waiting to assassinate one or more of my family. And I assure you that you've already become a target. Do you understand what I'm saying to you? Your life is in danger."

She swallowed hard, blinking several times. "Why would your enemies kill me? If what you're telling me is the truth, they should be reveling in what I managed to do for them."

"Because I own you. Because you are important to me."

Whether or not she accepted what I said I wasn't certain, but she seemed to soften as I closed the distance.

"I'm important to you? I'm just a possession to you and nothing more." Her wistful words were said with regret, almost as if she wished what we shared was more.

"You belong to me, Emily. It's time you accept the fact. Now, we are going to talk because your lies will not continue."

"I've told you ten times. I'm not lying to you."

"Who required you to testify against me?"

"No one required me to." She moved around me, sliding the wineglass on the counter and moving further away.

Someone had coerced her and she was hiding the reason.

As I'd done before, I grabbed and yanked her arm, pushing her over the edge of the island. "Let's try that again."

"What are you insinuating?" she snapped, struggling in my hold.

"That you know more than you've told me. You are going to be punished for lying to me. You knew the rules. You broke them."

She narrowed her eyes. "Rules? What rules, Cristiano? To stay the good little pet while you're gone? To stay behind locked doors, unable to catch a glimpse of the sunlight? I don't know anything. I did what was required of me."

I yanked on her dress, dragging it up to her waist. "Until you decide to tell me the truth, you're going to be punished."

She did everything she could to get out of my grasp, bucking against me. "What is wrong with you?"

"What is wrong with me?" I asked as I yanked open one of the drawers, finding exactly what I was looking for. The wooden spatula would suit my needs at least for now. I brought the implement down several times, moving from one side to the other in rapid succession, the thudding noise ringing in my ears.

"Stop. Just stop!"

"You deserve to be punished." The words were harsh, the sentiment exactly what she needed to hear. The time for her lies was over. I smacked her six times, enjoying the almost instant crimson blooming across her bottom.

Emily gasped, still trying to push away from the island, her legs kicking out.

I pushed her down, running my fingers over her bruised buttocks, kneading her tender skin before starting again. I was methodical in the spanking, covering every inch of her ass, the tops of her thighs. After thirty seconds, she stopped squirming, her moans mixing with the solid snapping sound of the wooden implement connecting with her skin.

While she deserved the harsh discipline, there was no immediate joy in what I was doing. However, she needed to recognize her place. After four more smacks, I caressed her ass cheeks, taking deep breaths in my resolve to calm the remaining anger. She wasn't to blame for what had occurred. I was almost certain she'd been used, her position within the company Joseph mentioned the reason.

I smacked her a few additional times, taking my time as I shifted from side to side.

Her breathing ragged, she had stopped fighting me altogether. She clung to the edge of the island, her knuckles white from the pressure. A moment of contempt for the situation rushed deep inside. I tossed the damn spoon and pulled her against me, taking deep breaths.

"You're working for Bayou Market Analysis."

"You already know that," she whispered.

I pulled her head against my chest, thinking about my words. "You were coerced into testifying. Weren't you?"

A single moan slipped past her lips, her body quivering. "Why does it matter? You're a free man."

"That may not be the case. The lead prosecutor had every intention of retrying. And I assure you that if that happens, he will stop at nothing to uphold the original sentence if not lengthen it. That isn't going to happen."

"Why is this attorney pushing so hard?" she managed.

"Because Griffin Williams has attempted to prosecute my family for years. This is his one way of succeeding. All because there is a witness. You."

After a few seconds, I released my hold.

She took purposeful steps away, shuddering. "Fine. You really want to know the truth? Yes, Cristiano. I was pushed into testifying by the prosecuting attorney. Me. Mr. Reynolds threatened me that if I didn't do so, there would be severe consequences."

"Why?" Reynolds wasn't a name I recognized from the prosecutor's office.

"I honestly don't know. He said he had evidence against me and that I'd go to prison because of it if I didn't provide a formal statement."

She grabbed her wine, her hand shaking as she brought the glass to her lips.

"You need to tell me everything," I said, jerking the bottle of wine into my hand and pouring a second glass. My patience was gone.

"I don't know what to tell you, Cristiano. The asshole acted as if I was the criminal. He was insistent that I was covering up for criminal activities within the company, which is bullshit. I do market research. I spend hours on the computer."

I waited, allowing her to gather her thoughts. "Go on."

"Mr. Reynolds mentioned that the work I was doing was illegal. He had papers showing that reports I'd created were actually for a bogus company. What little I could gather from his inflammatory accusations was that money laundering had occurred on several occasions through this particular company."

"What company are we talking about?"

"Look, I know that Bayou is just a subsidiary of a larger firm, a corporation. I've seen certain documents with EV Holdings, including my checks. But I was hired to do a job and that's what I've done for the last two years."

"What kind of research?"

"Mineral rights and markets."

"Diamonds," I said, half laughing. At least the information Joseph had discovered was accurate.

"How did you know?" Emily narrowed her eyes.

I shook my head. "That doesn't matter, Emily. Why the hell did this attorney threaten you, unless you know more than you're telling me? Were you working on additional projects?"

Her lower lip quivered. "No. I provide reports, which I assume allows the board of directors to determine what industries they are going to invest in. That's way above my pay grade. I don't have any information about the corporation or whoever owns it. I work for Franklin Dublin and trust me, he's not a mastermind criminal."

"Do you know the owner of EV Holdings? Has he ever come into the office?"

"Mr. Vendez? As far as I know, he's merely the man who signs my checks. I've never met him and Mr. Dublin hasn't mentioned him to me. Who is he?"

I studied her expression as I thought about the tone of her voice. Perhaps she was telling me the truth. "That's not necessary for you to know."

"What aren't you telling me?" She inched closer, her brow furrowed. "You think I had something to do with your father's assassination attempt. Don't you? My God, you do."

"I've remained alive by not sharing information, Emily."

"I'm not your enemy, Cristiano, at least not the way you're implying. I am very sorry about your father, but I had nothing to do with it. I'm glad he survived. And I assure you that the job isn't what I want to spend the rest of my life doing. It pays the bills and nothing more. It's obvious that you've already checked my bank account, but if you haven't, let me save you the time. I have less than a thousand dollars in savings and barely more than that in my checking account. My car is twelve years old and I worry every day that the damn thing will need an expensive repair. I haven't purchased any new clothing in over a year and the furniture that you've already seen is secondhand. In other words, I live paycheck to paycheck. No one paid me off to turn on you. I did what I thought was right."

"The conviction in your voice is admirable; however, if I find you are lying to me, I will have no choice but to handle the infraction in a method that you won't enjoy."

She huffed, nodding several times. "So you've made certain to tell me more than once."

Sighing, I took a gulp of the wine. Scotch was more to my liking at this point. "I purchased some clothes for you and other items. You should find everything you need."

"Thank you," she said curtly. "What happens now?"

"Now?" I repeated. "I need to make a few phone calls. Then we will enjoy dinner together."

"And after that?"

I knew the answer, although I wasn't ready to say anything to her at this point. The less she knew the better. "I don't need to remind you that if you attempt to escape, I will find you. There is nowhere you can run. Not in this city. Not in this state."

I studied the way the lighting over the island highlighted her features, my cock stirring.

She was mine.

Soon that would mean forever.

CHAPTER 12

Asshole.

The word refused to leave my mind. I glared at him as he walked away, his threats leaving a bitter taste in my mouth. I took another sip of wine, hoping the rich cabernet would hide the nastiness. Sadly, the wine did nothing, including calming my nerves. I'd actually found myself enjoying a portion of the day. While the gruff Russian had refused to allow me to wander the house by myself, I'd seen enough rooms to know Cristiano lived a solitary life, one devoid of the usual clutter than the majority of people had in at least one room of their house.

There were no pictures of family or friends, no way to know what kind of taste he had in books, music, or movies. Everything was organized, perhaps done by the cleaning staff, but I had a feeling that Cristiano was very particular about everything he owned.

Including me.

I'd tried to ask Dimitri questions only to be stonewalled. He'd said very few words, only making a single phone call and his conversation had been in his native language. Only when I'd asked to go outside had he actually talked to me other than the pointed conversation over the broken glass.

But I would never forget what he'd said.

"Mr. King has taken to you."

"Doesn't he have a wife or a stable of girlfriends?" I'd retorted more than asking a question. Cristiano's love life didn't matter to me.

Dimitri had walked closer, staring down at the shimmering pool water before answering me. "He's never been married and has cared for a single woman."

"I'm not his girlfriend."

"No. You are more."

Then he'd retreated to the shadows, watching every move I made. I'd wanted to ask Dimitri what he'd meant but Cristiano had burst in, acting as if I'd performed a mortal sin.

He was even angrier than before he'd left. Whatever news or information he'd gathered had been disturbing.

Danger.

And what was he trying to get at with questions about my employer? Nothing made any sense.

Just before Cristiano walked out, he stopped in the doorway, turning his head slowly. His gaze was just as heated as before, the look in his eyes one of absolute possession. He lifted his head then walked away, his gait steady.

A cold shiver trickled down my spine.

I'd kept something from him on purpose and I wasn't certain why, yet the lie was one that I found difficult to continue keeping. I had a bad feeling that I'd been used.

I was unable to shake the feeling that the nightmare was far from being over. Exhaling, I placed the wine on the island before venturing into the hall, noticing the dozen or more colorful bags. As I walked closer, I wasn't expecting the giddy feeling from seeing the number of packages. While I had no doubt that he'd gotten one of his soldiers to purchase the items, I knew the name written in cursive lettering splashed across the bright pink bags. The store sold high-end women's fashion, the price tags on almost every item far exceeding my budget.

After making two trips, I managed to bring all of them into the kitchen, placing them on the table. Even the beautiful tissue paper carefully wrapping the contents was luxurious. Sadly, it was just another reminder of how the rich and famous lived while the rest of the world survived from paycheck to paycheck.

When I pulled the first two pieces from one of the larger bags, butterflies formed in my stomach. The dresses were exquisite, made from the softest fabric. One in a deep emerald green, the other in the most resplendent shade of violet. As I held the purple dress against me, I twirled like a little girl excited at receiving a new frock. The laugh that surfaced was just surprising as the items that had been selected.

I carefully laid both over the back of a chair, eagerly opening another bag, finding three others that were just as gorgeous. Then there was the lingerie made from the finest silks and satin, panties and bras of a similar design. I shook my head, my fingers stiff as I brushed them across one of the baby-doll gowns. Confusion rushed in replacing the excitement.

Why had he bothered to purchase such beautiful attire? Why? Why not cheap tee shirts and maybe a pair of jeans or two?

The shoes were just as incredible, all but one pair stilettos. The fact he'd figured out my sizes was impressive.

Or had he figured out a way to delve into every aspect of my private life, maybe having one of his goons return to my house and rifle through my things? Bastard. I shoved the shoes aside, backing away from the table, loathing the fact tears had formed in my eyes. Disgusted, I inched toward the island, grabbing the wine and finishing the rest of the glass. There were still a few additional bags.

I poured another full glass, taking another gulp before haphazardly placing the crystal on the counter, advancing like a predator and ripping through the other bags.

Cosmetics.

A dress for a fancy dinner or perhaps going out dancing.

A few pieces of casual but still expensive attire.

And jewelry. Freaking. Gorgeous. Jewelry.

He'd purchased an entire wardrobe.

My God. The audacity of the man was revolting.

Then I opened the last package, gawking at the contents.

An anal plug.

What the hell? Fuck off. If he thought I was going to wear something so… disgusting, he was wrong.

Dead wrong.

A surge of anger and hatred rushed into me. The single purchase stripped everything away that might have been good about the beautiful attire. He only wanted one thing.

My total submission.

Fuck you. Fuck you. Fuck you!

I couldn't think the words enough.

I wanted to rip everything into shreds and almost did. Then my common sense took over. I had nothing to wear but the dress I was in. Whatever was going to happen, I would need shoes in order to flee. The thought gave me another chuckle, visions of attempting to run away from him laughable. He was never going to let me go.

After turning away for a second time, I thought about the expression he'd worn a few seconds ago.

As if he wanted to say something.

As if he wanted to apologize.

Could a man like Cristiano actually do that? No. He would never admit he was wrong. And what about his statement regarding his family? If he was so damn close to them, why the hell didn't he have any photographs? Not one.

If spending a couple thousand dollars on providing clothing was some kind of olive branch, he didn't know me very well. It would take a hell of a lot more than that to get me to like him. My God. What was I thinking? This wasn't a fantasy. This was a sickening reality.

I nursed the wine for a couple of minutes, curiosity getting the better of me. The wine would wait. After moving into the hallway, I listened for any sounds. It was impossible to hear anything over the music. I inched closer to the stairs, looking from one side of the house to the other. He was nowhere in sight.

If a man like Cristiano kept anything personal, he would certainly keep the items where no one else was likely to find them. Near his bed. I took the stairs two at a time, the slight creaks the treads made creating a surge of adrenaline. I quickened my pace, rushing into the bedroom and turning on the lamp on the dresser. After glancing over my shoulder, I opened the drawers, sifting through the contents.

Socks.

Underwear.

Tee shirts.

Everything was normal.

I dropped to the floor, opening the last two drawers. While one held several journals or ledgers, there was nothing personal. I knew my time was running out before he'd come to find me. One more drawer. Just one more drawer. My hands shaking, I opened it, finding a couple of sweaters. There had to be more. I shoved my hand underneath, finding an inch-thick envelope.

After pulling it into the light, I hurriedly untied the string keeping the flap from opening. The contents contained what appeared to be police reports. What? When a picture fell from in between, I was even more confused. The little girl couldn't have been more than twelve or thirteen, although given the way she was dressed, I wasn't certain. She was beautiful; her face serene, her long dark hair flowing over her shoulders. I could see a clear resemblance to Cristiano.

I continued to shake as I turned the photograph over. There was a single word written on the top corner.

Bella.

There was no way of knowing how long I'd been staring at it, but my gut told me too long. I shoved the items back in the envelope, trying to remember exactly where it had been placed, then quietly closed the drawer. I scampered out of the room, almost forgetting to turn off the light. As I raced down the stairs, the creaking sound seemed louder.

Shit. Shit. Shit.

I scampered into the kitchen, almost knocking over the wine in my attempt to grab it. He would certainly burst into the room at any moment.

When a full five minutes passed and he hadn't returned, I became jittery, making my way into the hallway once again. Very slowly I walked down the corridor, finally able to catch the sound of Cristiano's deep voice.

I held my breath and walked closer to the partially open door, listening intently.

"Yeah, well, I have to agree with Joseph, Pops. There doesn't seem to be anything else I can do." Cristiano's tone held an edge. I was also able to hear his deep sigh and then a slight chuckle. "I know. You didn't think your son was ever going to get married. Did you, Pops? And yes, I'm just planning a small wedding. Family, maybe a few friends."

Wedding? What the hell was he talking about? I leaned against the wall, trying to catch my breath.

"Her name?" Cristiano asked. "Emily. I need to come and see you tomorrow. We have some business to discuss. Have a good night."

No. No. No!

Marriage?

This had to be a joke.

There was no fucking way I was going to marry him. None. Unable to stop my reaction, I stormed into the room, stars floating in front of my eyes, moving all the way in front of his desk. I couldn't stop my actions or the hate spewing from my mouth.

Even if he killed me.

I'd rather be dead than to marry a monster.

"How dare you!" I yelled as I tossed the contents of the glass in his face. "I'm not going to ever marry you. I don't care if you chain me or beat me. I don't care if you lock me in a cage. You can't force me to marry someone I don't give a shit about."

He didn't react at first. Finally, he brushed the remnants of wine from his face, shaking his head just once. Then he planted his fists on his desk, leaning over and giving me a hard, cold stare. "I own you, Emily. Now I'm losing my patience with your tirades. The day you went against me was the day your fate was sealed."

"Went against you? I'm not certain anyone ever could because they know you'll kill them."

He laughed, the sound sending chills down my spine. "That is entirely accurate. You have no choice."

Oh, my God. He was serious.

I caught another glimpse of his gun and I couldn't help but wonder if he'd shot anyone during his absence. How could I ever care about a man who I'd question every time he left the house? Own. The word had the sound of an ending, not a beginning.

"No. You will never own me." I wasn't prepared for him to grab my wrists, dragging me over the desk. There was nothing but anger in his eyes, his mouth twisted from his rage.

"Yes, I do. We are getting married. You will be my wife."

I had no idea what to say or think. This was outrageous. This was… He was protecting himself. That's exactly what this was.

"Why? Why?"

"Because it's the only way I can remain out of prison. And it's the only way I can keep you safe. There is a contract out on both our lives."

A contract? This was insane.

The statement was hard to hear, the words ringing in my ears. While he spoke words of protection, I was literally nothing but a possession to him. I struggled, fighting with everything I had, finally able to get out of his firm grip, the force I used tossing me backwards and onto the floor. I crawled away, never taking my eyes off him.

Cristiano took calculated steps around his desk, walking in my direction as I continued to crawl backwards.

"Is that why you had one of your flunkies purchase all those nice things? To bribe me? To get me to agree? Well, that's never going to happen."

"I purchased those beautiful things because I thought you'd like them. I wanted to fucking make you happy." He grabbed me by the wrists again, dragging me to my feet and onto my tiptoes, his fingers digging into my arms.

"You're hurting me," I managed, my voice little more than a whisper. "What are you going to do, spank me again? Maybe pull out your belt?" Somewhere in my mind, I knew what I was doing was the wrong thing, but I was unable to stop, fueled by the horror of what he was suggesting.

No, what he was demanding.

Tears sprang to my eyes again and this time, I was unable to stop them.

"That's exactly what I should do," he said, although his tone had softened. He darted his eyes back and forth. "They will come for you. They will try and hurt you. I can't allow that to happen. I won't allow anyone to touch you. No one."

Shock tore through my system when he crushed his mouth over mine, moving one hand to entangle his fingers in my hair, the other shifting down and cupping my bottom. As he cradled me against him, his throbbing cock digging into my stomach, I could tell he was conflicted. Anger and hate against whatever enemy was threatening his world had stripped him of all rationality.

As he held me, the same desire that I'd felt every time we were close crowded in, trying to push away my resentment and fear, the hatred that I'd convinced myself I had. I no longer knew what to believe, the betrayal of my own body a telling statement. There was something about Cristiano that I couldn't resist. Maybe everything about him.

It was as if the danger and uncertainty, the man's merciless actions and bravado meant nothing. Just the way I felt when I was in his arms. The rush of electricity swam through me like a tidal wave, leaving me hot and wet all over. Before I realized it, I'd snaked my arms around his neck, moaning into the kiss.

He thrust his tongue inside, sweeping his against mine, exploring the wet heat that threatened to consume both of us. I couldn't breathe or think clearly. I no longer knew night from day, love from hate. Everything had meshed together in one entangled web of lies and deceit. How could I want this? How could I stand to be in the same room with him?

As the kiss continued, he squeezed my bottom, continually grinding his hips back and forth in a lurid manner.

When he finally broke the heated intimacy, he took gasping breaths. "God, I want you."

His statement was as close to being endearing as I knew I'd ever hear. I was breathless, struggling to understand what was happening.

Then reality swooped in as it had before, creating another series of reactions. I pushed against him, struggling to get out of his hold. "No. This isn't right. This is pure sin. I don't want to marry you."

Cristiano reared back, letting me go almost instantly, the look of seduction I'd seen all but gone. "That's the way it's going to be, Emily. We will be married in three days."

When he turned away, walking back to his desk, I refused to hold back anything. "Then if we're going to be man and wife, don't you think you need to tell me about your deep dark secret?"

"What are you talking about?"

"Bella. Who the hell is Bella?"

He froze, his entire body tensing, his shoulders heaving for several seconds before he spun around. "You were snooping in my house? You dared to invade my privacy?"

The venom of his tone was shocking, even after everything I'd been through. "Who is she? Your child? Don't you think I at least deserve to know that you have a child? Where is she? Is she hiding somewhere, or do you have her caged up like you plan on doing to me?"

The sadness forming across his face was something that would haunt me for a long time to come. Then I noticed tears in his eyes. He took several deep breaths as he stared at me. I was prepared for him to rush toward me, providing yet another round of discipline. Instead, he remained silent, walking toward a small bar located in the corner of the room.

I watched intently as he pulled two glasses from a shelf, selecting a bottle of some dark liquor and pouring. Every move he made was methodical, labored. When he returned, his complexion was sallow. He remained unblinking as he handed me a glass, moving slowly toward one of the leather chairs and sitting down.

"Bella was my sister."

I was crushed by the way he said the words. 'Was.' My God. I dared to inch closer, sitting on the edge of the seat. "What happened?"

He'd placed his elbows on the armrests and was sliding his index finger back and forth across his mouth. "Bella was killed."

"I'm so sorry," I whispered, wanting nothing more than to reach over, but Cristiano wasn't ready for comfort and I wasn't prepared to provide any. However, I knew this was a story that he needed to share. Whatever had occurred he'd kept bottled up inside.

"Bella was the light of our family. Just a little joy. You should have heard her laughter. It didn't matter what kind of shit I'd been forced to deal with, the moment she laughed, I forgot almost everything." He half snorted, taking several gulps before continuing.

I remained on edge, uncertain of how to react.

"For some reason, I was her favorite. The squeal she'd let off when I came to see her was just so damn special. We had a bond that truly allowed me to understand the power of family. When she became ill at three years old, we had no idea what was wrong. Leukemia. The doctors thought she wouldn't make it. But she did. Somehow her little spirit helped her to survive."

"Cristiano. I…" I couldn't finish my sentence, the pain for him too raw.

He darted a single glance in my direction, attempting to smile. "When she was released from the hospital, we were all surprised how well she did, flourishing more every day. Within a year, you'd never know she'd been sick. She had her whole life ahead of her. My life moved on and I didn't get to see her as much, but when I came to the house, I always brought her something special."

When he stopped talking, I held my breath, several tears sliding down my face. I could tell he was remembering both the joy and the horror.

He took a deep but ragged breath, rubbing his glistening eyes. "Anyway, after I'd been away for almost a month, I went to see her. She wanted to go out for ice cream. Of course, I couldn't resist a single request. The girl managed to wrap me around her little finger." He laughed softly.

"She sounds amazing."

"She really was. Just another angel on this earth. We had our ice cream and were on the way home. Bella had school the next day so Mother made certain I wouldn't keep her out too late. Now, I wish I hadn't taken her out at all. I just..."

Growling, he turned his head away from me.

"What happened, Cristiano?"

"She was killed. Because of me." He jerked out of his chair, walking toward the window and staring out into the darkness.

"What do you mean because of you?"

"When I told you that danger is always surrounding my family, I meant it, Emily. The bullet was meant for me. If she hadn't been in the car, she would still be alive today. I'm the reason for her death."

The last words were devoid of emotion. He was shutting down again. I rose from the chair, second guessing my reasons for walking closer, but I could tell how much he was hurting. "You can't blame yourself."

"Like hell I can't. What's worse it that I had no idea, and still don't know who was behind the shooting, but I will never forget his face. Never. Bastard. No one came forward claiming the kill and there was no evidence, not that the police tried very hard to find her killer." He drained his glass, staring down at his drink. "I assure you that my family made several changes after her murder."

I lifted my arm, hesitating before placing my hand on his, squeezing. "I am so sorry. I wish I knew what to say."

"There's nothing you can say. It was my fault. I'll take that with me to the grave." He took my hand into his, bringing my fingers to his mouth, pressing them against his lips. As he rolled my knuckles back and forth, there wasn't a single inch of my body that wasn't covered in goosebumps, a mixture of anticipation and excitement coursing through me like an uncontrolled blaze.

Easing back, he gave me a smoldering smile, his eyes burning with a deep well of lust.

As well as conviction.

I could tell what he was thinking, his need to possess me bordering on unhinged.

I should remain terrified of him, but the elation from the shared electricity had managed to drag away the tension.

At least for now.

A shiver coursed down my spine, the connection that we'd both felt from the beginning even stronger. But at this moment I was torn between accepting the fact he had another side, a softness that had been crowded out by the tragedy and the fact he was still a ruthless killer. The dichotomy of the two didn't work well in my mind.

When he released my hand, allowing it to drop, his face hardened even more. Yet he gathered me into his arms, his fingers slowly sliding down the back of my head. "Has anyone ever told you just how beautiful you are?"

"I'm not beautiful. I'm just average." The way he was holding me wasn't just possessive. It was as if he was terrified that he'd lose me. I was breathless from his brazen stare, the lust consuming him. I gripped his arms, fearful I would fall if he wasn't holding me.

"You are one of the most incredible women I've ever laid eyes on. And you are all mine." When he pressed his lips against mine, he didn't overwhelm me with his prowess as he usually did. He simply held me, very slowly using his lips to open mine.

I suddenly felt safe in his arms, every cell on fire as he raked his other hand down my back, cupping my buttocks and lifting me onto my toes. The man reeked of passion, an undeniable hunger that ignited the butterflies as well as the rapid beating of my heart. I was intoxicated by his scent, adding fuel to the embers until they burst into flames.

The moment of intimacy remained tender, his tongue barely darting inside, sweeping against mine. This was a different man, one who was attempting to shower me with what little he understood about love. I found myself falling down a spiral of darkness, succumbing to his gentle manner, thirsting to taste all of him. A part of me swooned from his hold, the way he'd crushed his body against mine. The feel of his cock was just as explosive as before, but this time, I wanted him to fill me, fucking me.

Making love to me.

I could envision being with him, learning every nuance of his world, accepting his dangerous tendencies while indulging in every dirty act of sin he demanded.

A growl floated up from the depth of his being, mixing with my strangled moans. I slid my arms around his neck, savoring the moment, praying the world would go away. As the kiss became more forceful, needy, I intertwined my fingers in his hair, every part of me tingling. He thrust his tongue all the way inside, consuming mine as he became dominating, pushing me to the limits of my understanding.

Then as quickly as the beautiful moment had started, it was over, Cristiano pushing me away and turning slightly before issuing the words I would never forget.

"I will find the bastard who killed her. One day. When I do, the man will pay."

The persona that I knew well had returned in full force, his frustration rolling off his body like extreme heat. The menacing expression on his face took my breath away. How could he be so passionate one minute then cold and calculating the next?

"You can't live in the past," I half whispered. "Bella wouldn't want that."

He snorted and returned to the bar, refilling his glass. "That's the only way I know how to live, Emily. Perhaps that will change when we've said our vows."

"You're not going to make me do this. Please."

"I have no choice, Emily. None. I will try and give you a perfect fairytale wedding."

"Fairytales don't come true, Cristiano, and even if they did, they usually have a knight in shining armor, the hero prepared to die for the woman he loves. That's never going to be the case."

"I would die for you. You will be my family."

"That's not love, Cristiano. As a matter of fact, I'm not entirely certain you're even capable of a complex emotion like love. What you've described is nothing more than a responsibility, some sick promise made because of your life-style and the decisions you made in your life. And guilt. I need a man who will love and care for me, not an arranged marriage to a..."

"Monster," he finished for me.

"What if I fight you on the wedding? What then?"

He slowly turned his head, taking a deep breath.

I knew the answer.

I'd disappear permanently.

I didn't bother to say anything. What was there left to be said? He'd determined the course of the rest of my life and at this point, there was nothing I could do. Escape? The possibility seemed slim. Could I earn his trust then contest the marriage at a later time? Maybe that was my only option, but by then, I would definitely have a bigger target on my back as being the former wife of one of the brothers of the New Orleans mafia.

A nervous laugh threatened to bubble up from my chest. I felt giddy, my mind reeling from his demands. I gave him a hard look before leaving the room, moving quickly toward the kitchen. Of course he would follow me, issuing another set of demands, punishing me for whatever additional rules that I'd broken.

I grabbed another wineglass, filling it to the rim, waiting for a full two minutes. When he didn't swagger into the room, I simply took my time, shoving the lingerie and clothing into whatever bag I grabbed. My hands shaking, I selected a few of them then headed for the stairs. That's when I felt his presence, the larger than life man studying me from a distance. I didn't bother looking in his direction. I didn't care any longer what he had to say to me. I was numb, unable to feel my feet as I walked up the stairs.

A part of me wanted to find a way to jump out the window, to end this charade. But there was another portion that continued to crave him, the ache in my tummy increasing with every passing second. He'd managed to slither into my world, claiming a slice of my soul.

And my heart.

How in the hell was that even possible?

He'd been nothing but horrible to me over the last twenty-four hours, acting as if I was a beautiful doll that he could place in a corner, waiting for his arrival and filthy use. Yet there'd been a spark, his emotions disturbing on so many levels. I'd even seen the look in his eyes change as he'd expressed his remorse and guilt.

The kind of love that I'd been searching for my entire life wasn't something he could provide, even if his adoration of his sister, as well as the rest of his family, was captivating.

Special.

Honorable.

What that even possible with a brutal man like Cristiano?

I tossed the bags, took a gulp of wine, and turned to stare at the massive bed. What the hell was I doing? I refused to become emotional, swallowing hard as tears attempted to form all over again. Nope. That wasn't going to happen. I had to develop enough strength to get through this horrible wedding.

Then I would find a way to scream to the world that I was nothing more than a captive.

After taking another swig of wine, I placed the glass on his beloved dresser with enough force that wine sloshed out over the edges. What the hell did I care?

A maniacal smile crossed my face as I tossed the clothes on the beautifully upholstered chair in the corner of the room, pitching the empty bags. Then I grabbed the most incredible baby doll gown, humming as I walked into the bathroom. The tattered dress was the last of my past. I yanked the shoulders, continuing the tear the bastard had already started, finally ripping the seams before dragging it over my head and throwing it against the wall.

While a tantrum meant nothing, likely to invoke another moment of his wrath, it certainly made me feel a hell of a lot better. When I slid into the soft silk, the gown fitting me perfectly, I stared at my reflection. The girl's haunted face glaring back at me was someone I didn't recognize.

Would he actually kill me if I refused to marry him?

I shuddered at the thought, honestly uncertain of the answer. We had an amazing connection, perhaps even a bond, but his business was more important. That was obvious. I tilted my head, allowing my gaze to fall to my shoulders then my breasts. I had to admit that the gorgeous frock was the beginning of a romantic adventure.

At least it was supposed to be.

But we weren't a couple, just plastic soldiers in a war that I couldn't understand.

My feet remained heavy as I turned out the light, heading for the bed and pulling down the covers. When I crawled inside, tugging the covers over my head, I closed my eyes and envisioned the perfect wedding.

A white dress adorned with jewels and beads.

A long veil sweeping a beautiful marble floor.

The most incredible classical music filling a hall full of joyous guests.

Amazing food and drink, the finest wines and champagnes.

Dozens of white and sterling silver roses placed on every table, their scent permeating the air.

And a handsome, loving man prepared to sweep me off my feet, a true knight in shining armor.

I sank further under the crisp cotton sheets, shivering even more than before.

The visions had nothing to do with reality, yet the picturesque images were ones from every little girl's dream.

And revelations from my nightmare.

CHAPTER 13

ristiano

Rage.

As I swept my arm across the desk, I took no comfort in the sound of breaking glass or the hard thudding my laptop made when it smashed against the hardwood floor. I threw my arms behind my head, intertwining my fingers as I paced the floor, trying to wrangle in my emotions. Why had Emily searched through my things?

Because you can't allow her into your world. Because you're the very monster she'd accused you of being. Because she's drawn to you.

Drawn to me. I almost laughed at the thought.

The damn music was still playing, a melodic instrumental that was driving me insane. I took long steps toward the CD player, ready to fist the console. Huffing, I reined in my anger, at least enough to press the off button. She'd gotten all the way under my skin, digging her way into the furthest reaches of my mind. My soul.

Hell, even my heart.

How the hell had I allowed my guard to fall with her?

I took a deep breath, closing my eyes briefly before walking back to my desk, glaring down at the debris. If Joseph was correct, the iron fist my father had used for four decades was coming back to bite him. The list of enemies was far too extensive to easily determine the choice candidates. Whatever the case, Enrique Vendez would need to be found. I would have a more formal discussion with my father in the morning.

However, I'd become convinced there would be another attempt on my life. Right now, I had to push that aside.

Dealing with Emily took precedence at this point.

I slammed my hands on my desk, shoving the last remaining items onto the floor, a bitter smile crossing my face. There was no sense in admonishing my behavior; however, I would be required to get my shit together.

It would also be necessary to face that I actually cared about the woman. My father had told me that I was making a rash decision, relying far too heavily on Joseph's suggestion. However, my father had never spent time behind bars. He also still believed that every enemy we came into contact with could be bought. It had become painfully obvious that wasn't the case. And our Consigliere was absolutely correct about one thing.

Times had changed since the old days, something my father had refused to accept for far too long. That had stymied our growth, even hindered our legitimate businesses. I'd been on the cusp of bringing the King organization into the world of internet business, something that was long overdue, when the attempted assassination had occurred.

I opened one of my desk drawers, retrieving Emily's phone. By just pressing on the screen, I was able to see there were at least two calls, but nothing from her friend. It would seem Julia had believed Emily's story.

However, the other two calls were from in town. I would need to ask her who they were from. Something about her story still didn't add up to me. I slid the phone back in the drawer, thinking about everything she'd told me. There were definitely missing pieces.

I would need Emily by my side in order to flush out Vendez. She would need to learn to trust me, although I'd given her no reason to do so up to this point. Our coveted connection wasn't enough to create the kind of bond needed. That would take time, something we didn't have. With Griffin Williams prepared to announce a new trial date, our marriage was the single factor that could stop the continuation of the case. That could allow for time to find Vendez. The mystery man would certainly be pissed that I'd found a way to thwart the system, which would definitely place her life in further danger.

I took a deep breath, still able to gather her scent. The taste of her had been just as delicious, perhaps even more so. I'd caught a glimpse into her soul after telling her about Bella. I'd sensed her need to comfort me. And I'd felt a portion of the shield that I'd worn since Bella's death falling away. Perhaps I could find a way to give Emily what she needed in order to learn to trust me, at least enough to be able to keep her safe.

My mother would remind me that while powerful men were enticing, those who knew the right moment when to be tender, even romantic were exactly what women needed. Whether or not she'd ever seen that side of my father remained uncertain. All he'd ever portrayed to his children was a firm hand and a gruff demeanor.

Except with his grandchildren.

I laughed softly to myself as I walked toward the kitchen. He doted on Michael's children as if they were the only thing that mattered in his world, showering them with presents. Maybe my father was growing a soft spot after all.

Tonight, I would take my mother's advice for the first time since becoming a man. I'd indulge a woman with exactly what she needed. Well, as much as I could fathom giving to her anyway.

I turned on the security system, double checking that everything was in order before I entered the kitchen. The sight of several bright pink bags scattered across the table was just another reminder that I had a guest in the house. I was surprised given our heated conversation that she'd accepted the gifts, taking at least a few of the pieces of clothing and other things with her.

What she left in the middle of the table was the plug. Still defiant. Still refusing to accept my command. I rolled the plug between my fingers, envisioning her wearing it. One day, I would purchase her one made of stainless steel, the jewel located on the end a stunning ruby, exactly what she deserved. I snagged the lubricant, placing both in my pocket. Tonight, we would begin her training.

Soon, she would get a taste of my darker needs.

I stood staring at the remaining items for a full two minutes before grabbing a second bottle of wine and the opener, taking my time to remove the cork. As I grabbed a platter from the cabinet, I also realized that I'd never shared a meal with anyone in my house. Not once. I treated the location as a landing spot, not as a home. While I could use the excuse that I'd traveled for business, spending a significant amount of time in other cities, even countries, that would be a part of the protection I'd layered around myself.

I'd never wanted to get close to anyone ever again, the pain of losing them too great.

After yanking open the refrigerator, I couldn't help but smile. Dimitri had indeed made certain that everything he knew I liked had been purchased, ready for my return.

And I'd treated him like an inconvenience, a man who'd been with me since my return from college. He'd become more like a friend than a Capo, something I needed to keep in mind.

Hell, I had no other friends.

Smirking, I took my time preparing enough food for both of us, the fruit and cheese barely substantial but at least edible.

As I carried the wine and the plate of food up the stairs, uncertain of what I would find, I couldn't take my thoughts off of her. Emily was certainly resourceful, her determination to fight me continuing. The majority of women would have cracked by now, surrendering to the bad man who held them captive. Not the beautiful blonde with the cornflower blue eyes.

The warm glow of the light filtering into the hallway gave me pause. She was in my house, sleeping in my bed, and I had a moment of awkwardness before walking into the room. Just the sight of a few strands of long hair billowing from under the covers was enough to make my cock ache all over again. While there were still vile, filthy things I hungered to do to her, to share with her, I was forced to remind myself that my sadistic needs would have to wait.

For the time being.

She didn't stir at first, her breathing remaining even as I walked around the bed, forced to remove scattered bags from the small table next to the corner chair. She'd dumped everything she'd brought into the room out of anger, leaving the mess for another time. When I placed the plate on the table, I could hear her slight movements, a rustle of the sheets.

I filled an empty glass, realizing she'd brought her wine with her, although it appeared untouched. As I removed my jacket, I noticed that she'd riffled through every drawer. She was definitely resourceful.

After removing the holster, I placed the gun in the nightstand drawer. While I needed quick and easy access, I also couldn't put it past her that she would attempt to secure it in the middle of the night.

And I had no intention of handcuffing her.

Not unless she was a very bad girl.

I placed the anal plug and tube of lubricant on the nightstand by her glass of wine, unable to keep the smile off my face.

When I was fully undressed, I pushed the bags off the corner chair, easing down and taking the wine into my hand. From where I sat, I was able to catch a glimpse of her face. By the change in her breathing, I knew she was awake, likely waiting until I fell asleep to make another attempt at escape. Given I was wired as fuck, I could stay awake all night if necessary, defying her resolve.

The quiet in the room was oppressive. There was little wind outside, no thunderstorms to interfere in the silence. I took a sip of wine, unable to take my eyes off her. The line in the sand had been drawn, the requirements laid out as if a contract. She would either accept, allowing for a festive event or I'd use the same handcuffs to drag her down the aisle. The thought fueled my sadistic side even as my mother's voice attempted to remind me which I preferred.

Perhaps a little of both.

A gnawing in my stomach was a reminder that I hadn't eaten all day. Food had been the last of my desires, but sustenance would become necessary. I took a strawberry from the platter, holding the juicy piece of fruit into the light, the intense vibrant color indicating just how ripe it was.

The color of hearts.

The color of a perfect rose.

The color of blood.

As I bit into it, a single bead of juice trickled past my lips, cascading down to my jaw. Delicious and perfect. Just like Emily. After taking another bite, I heard another rustle of the sheets, could see her open eyes staring at me, her lips the same hue as the strawberry. I didn't say a word as I consumed the rest, very slowly placing the bright green stalk on the platter and selecting another. I twirled it back and forth several times, cognizant she was watching every move I made.

"Sweet. Ripe. Delectable. You should come join me." I kept my voice low, yet the husky tone refused to be denied. I bit into the second piece, half closing my eyes as the fragrance filled my nostrils.

There was a heightened level of desire in her eyes, but I wasn't certain if it had to do with the plate full of food or her hunger for something more carnal in nature.

"I'm not hungry," she whispered, purposely shifting onto her other side and away from me.

"Come now, Emily. I haven't poisoned the food if that's what you're thinking."

"What I'm thinking? You have no idea," she stated as she finally moved to a sitting position, allowing the covers to fall.

Another surprise hit me hard, my cock standing at full attention from the way the silk lingerie accentuated her breasts. The color, a soft blush, was perfect for her, subtle yet provocative.

Innocent.

She seemed uncomfortable at the way I was looking at her yet she didn't look away nor did she yank the covers over her. She did glare at the plug, making a face of revulsion.

My cock stirred just thinking about placing it between her lovely ass cheeks.

"Then what are you thinking, Emily?'

"I'm thinking that you're crazy if you think I'm going to marry you." She stopped, taking a deep breath before continuing, her tone entirely different. "I'm thinking that I'm really... so sorry about Bella. And I'm thinking that I should apologize for snooping. I didn't mean to hurt you. And I'm thinking I'm still in a nightmare."

The sincerity of her words was surprising. "I've never tried to pretend I was a good man, Emily. You were right from the beginning that I am the kind of monster nightmares are made of, but I am also capable of loving, whether you can believe that or not. And you're right that certain decisions I've made have placed myself and my family in a precarious position, but what you don't understand is that I had no choice to enter into this life."

"We all have choices," she managed as she inched closer to the edge of the bed, easing her feet onto the floor. Her move tentative, she reached out and snatched a strawberry, darting a single look in my direction.

"Perhaps the majority of people, but not a man like me. My father and his father before him and his father before him were all brought up in this lifestyle. It's all I've ever known. Taking over for my father is a requirement, not a choice."

"And what would happen if you would choose to do something else?"

I laughed softly as I grabbed a piece of Gouda, enjoying the way she devoured the strawberry, immediately reaching for a second. "Then my father would have no choice but to end my life."

"Oh, my God. You're kidding?"

"I am not kidding. That is our way."

"That's horrible. Cruel. What does your mother think?"

I thought about her question. "She knew what she was marrying into, the life that she'd be forced to live, but she chose to do so because of her love for my father."

The incredulous look on her face was followed by a shake of her head. "And that would mean our children would be nothing but little soldiers."

Children.

Just hearing the word coming from her mouth stirred something even deeper inside my soul, a craving that I'd never experienced before. A flash of stars rushed across my field of vision, my heart suddenly racing. I took a gulp of wine, fascinated by my body's reaction. I weighed my answer carefully as I had never thought about it before. "If I am lucky enough to become a father, I would want our children to have everything that their heart desired, including choices. The old ways are not necessarily the best ways."

At least a part of her was satisfied from my answer. "I feel so sorry for you."

"Don't feel sorry for me. I've lived a full and rich life, although you're right that I haven't enjoyed a significant portion of it. A part of me died when Bella was taken from my family. I hid behind a mask of steel, a plate of armor to protect what was left of my heart. I hope that's something you can understand."

She nodded her answer, her hand shaking as she tugged a piece of cheese off the plate, bringing it to her mouth slowly.

"Somehow you managed to crack that armor."

A slight tic appeared in the corner of her mouth, a flash occurring in her eyes. She tipped her head, studying me so intently as if she was able to look right through me. "Which is something you don't want."

"I never said that."

"Then what do you want?" She turned her full attention toward me, munching on the cheese, which stirred additional desires from deep within.

"For the first time in my life, I want a home." I smiled, shaking my head. "As difficult as it might be for you might believe, I'm not entirely certain what that means. My childhood was… difficult."

"I can imagine." Her whisper was almost inaudible.

I sat back in the chair, imagining what that would entail.

Emily finished the few bites, reaching for her wine and taking several sips. After putting the glass back on the nightstand, she slowly rose to her feet, walking slowly in my direction. "Are they really going to try the case again?"

"Yes, the prosecuting attorney is determined to make me pay for my crime." Perhaps a part of me was prepared to accept my fate.

Her expression was one of puzzlement as she closed the distance, standing in between my open legs. "I was wrong, Cristiano. You can be loving."

There was no reason for her words to stun me, none at all, but they did and as she selected the largest strawberry, taking a small nibble off the end, I was mesmerized. She removed the stem, every move methodical as she returned it to the plate, then placed the fruit in her mouth. She leaned down until her face was mere inches from mine.

The offer was blatant.

And seductive.

And sinful.

And enticing.

I opened my mouth as I reached for her, caressing her arms. The single bite she was offering was a break in that line she'd drawn. When I bit down on the strawberry, two trickles of juice flowed from my mouth. Only after I'd bitten it in half did she ease away, her eyes glistening. She swallowed her portion then lowered down once more, sliding her tongue through the first trickle of juice then the other, finally capturing my mouth.

Every nerve ending was on fire, every synapse more alive than it had ever been. My grip on her arms became firmer as I pulled her closer to me, my heart thudding.

She palmed my chest, caressing with her fingers as she forced my lips apart, darting her tongue inside. Between the wine and strawberries as well as the taste of her, I was almost instantly drunk on my desire, my cock aching.

I slipped one hand over her shoulder, fingering her long strands of hair. So silky. So damn soft. It was difficult to contain my longing and when she crawled on hand to my cock, wrapping her long fingers around my shaft, it was all I could do not to toss her onto the bed.

She moaned into the kiss as she attempted to dominate my tongue, darting hers back and forth as the kiss became a passionate roar between us. Even the scent of her feminine wiles added to my intoxication. I would never be able to get enough of her. The electricity became a dancing wire, sizzling and crackling as the hungry dance continued.

With every stroke of her hand on my shaft, she twisted her fingers, creating a wave of friction. I found it difficult to breathe, every muscle tense, ripped from excitement. Her moans became more constant even though they remained muted, her body shuddering as she continued teasing me, tormenting the darkness inside.

When she was the one who broke the kiss, she uttered a beautiful and husky growl, the sound permeating my senses. Chuckling softly, she nipped my lower lip before dragging her tongue around my mouth, her hand now concentrating on my cockhead.

"Jesus," I muttered, my eyes finding it difficult to focus as my balls tightened.

"Does that mean you want something?" she asked, purring afterwards.

"Always."

She laughed in a sultry manner before pressing her lips against my chin, sucking for several seconds.

I closed my eyes, letting out an intense growl of my own. Then she purposely tilted my head, brushing her lips down the side of my neck. I wasn't used to her playful side, or the lack of full control, but the way she touched me was chilling. I was more alive than I'd ever been, the jolts of current now slamming into me. My God, the woman had no idea what she was doing to me.

"Mmm..." she muttered as she continued tasting, dragging her tongue from one shoulder blade to the other before concentrating on my chest. As she moved further down, I realized my breathing was rattled, my chest heaving. No woman had touched me in the way she was.

As if she gave a damn.

As if I meant something to her.

She fell onto her knees, continuing to press kisses and licks against my chest, easing ever so slowly to my stomach, even taking her time to swirl the tip of her tongue around my belly button.

I planted my hands on the arms of the chair, determined to allow her to play. The sensations only intensified, pulling me into the most incredible feeling of bliss.

"You're tense," she whispered, removing her hand from my cock and shifting both to one leg. As she kneaded my muscles, her fingers caressing, I gazed down at her, still unable to focus.

"I'm famished," I said before growling, the deep and husky sound floating in the room.

"Good things come to those who wait."

"And I'm not a patient man. You need to keep that in mind."

As if to answer my question, she brought my cock to her lips, rubbing the tip across the seam of her mouth. The back and forth motions only added fuel to the fire, my entire body now aching from the surge of adrenaline.

She kept her eyes on me as she swirled her tongue around my cockhead then across my sensitive slit. Then she resumed her former actions, massaging one calf then the other. Watching her drew the sadistic man from the darkness. I wanted to consume every inch of her body. I longed to strap her to the wooden slats over the canopy bed.

And I hungered to fill every hole with my cum.

She continued caressing me, moving up to my thighs and dangerously close to my cock. Of course she planned on perpetuating her tease, doing everything to push my limits. She only managed to arouse me even more.

After she blew across my cock, she issued another mewing sound. Then she slipped her hand between my legs, taking my balls into her hand, taunting me by sucking on the tip for a few seconds.

"Is that what you want?" she asked, sliding one hand all the way down the length of my cock then pumping up to squeeze my cockhead.

"Hmmm... As a start that will do." As a few drops of pre-cum beaded along the tip, she lowered her head, engulfing the head.

I threw my head back, the sensations more incredible than before. Panting, I realized I'd dug my fingers into the upholstery in an effort to keep from yanking her into my arms.

She began sucking in earnest, her guttural sounds exaggerated.

My heart continued to thud, echoes sounding in my ears as she moved up and down my shaft, the tip hitting the back of her throat. After a full minute, I could take it no longer. Leaning down, I reached under her arms, lifting her into the air.

Her yelps were my reward and when I pulled her down on my lap, the tip of my cock finding her wetness, I let out an intense roar.

"Fuck!"

My bellow seemed to delight her, and she clung to my shoulders as I forced her all the way down, filling her completely. Her muscles clamped around the thick invasion immediately as her entire body shook from the force I used.

This was even more intimate than before and as I gripped her hips, lifting her once again, she closed her eyes.

"Ride me," I commanded as I brought her down, stretching her tight channel. She was so wet, the feel of her incredible.

Emily took a deep breath, staring me in the eyes as she obeyed, using the strength of her thighs to create a perfect rhythm.

Everything about her was beautiful: her skin glistening in the dim lighting, the softness of the slip of a gown accentuating her voluptuous curves, and the way she continued to stare at me.

For a few precious minutes, we were as one, the electricity surging through us. Her lips were pursed, her fingers digging into my shoulders and as she tossed her head back and forth, I made a promise to myself that I would do everything in my power to protect her.

If that was possible.

A cold wave of energy rushed into me, an ugly reminder that she'd been right about a fantasy. What we were sharing was something else entirely. I cupped her breasts, squeezing until she moaned, rolling her fully aroused nipples in my fingers.

"Mmm..." she purred, her body undulating, her actions becoming frenzied as she bucked against me. I could tell she was close to coming.

I eased the straps down her shoulders, exposing her breasts. When I pinched and twisted her hardened buds, she lolled her head, gasping for air.

"Come for me, little flower. I want to feel you erupt around my cock."

A smile crossed her face, her lower lip quivering. When her body stiffened, I took over control, moving her up and down on my cock, bucking my hips and thrusting into her in rapid succession.

"Oh. Oh. Oh..." Her scream was strangled, ultimately becoming silent as she let go, her entire body shaking as the orgasm ripped through her.

I refused to stop, pumping her up and down until the single climax morphed into another. This time, her scream sent vibrations dancing through me.

Only when she stopped shaking did I pull her forward, cupping both sides of her face. "My exquisite flower has awakened."

"Mmm..." she managed, trying to catch her breath.

I gathered her into my arms, cradling her quivering body against my chest. She wrapped her arms around my neck, resting her head on my shoulder. I held her in position for a full minute before walking toward the bed, sitting on the edge.

"You're still a very bad girl," I whispered.

"Hmmm... Not always."

Chuckling, I stroked her hair before easing her onto the bed, immediately turning her onto her stomach.

"What are you doing?" she asked, struggling to push onto her elbows.

I reached for the plug as well as the small tube, holding the red rubber piece so she could see it.

"You're very tight. This will help. You're going to learn to follow my rules, Emily. While I enjoy giving you pleasure, I will not hesitate to punish you if you don't start behaving."

She opened her mouth to protest then obviously thought better of it, looking away, but not before I could see the grimace crossing her face, her body tensing once again.

"Do you understand me?"

Her brow furrowed but she finally nodded.

"When I ask you a question, you will answer."

"Yes. Sir."

Sighing, I rubbed two fingers down her spine. "I'm not trying to hurt you, Emily. Just the opposite. Learning that there are rules within this household and surrounding my life will help ensure your safety." I opened the tube, spreading a dime full on my fingers, watching her processing what I was saying.

"I do understand."

"Good. Now, open your ass cheeks for me."

She seemed insulted by my request but did as she was told, reaching behind her and spreading her luscious cheeks.

"Excellent. You will wear this at all times, removing only when necessary."

"You're kidding… yes. Sir."

The scent of our sex filled my nostrils as I rubbed the lubricant between my fingers before pushing them to her dark hole, taking my time as I eased them inside.

She shuddered visibly, dropping her head as she moaned.

"Breathe," I instructed.

"I'm trying."

After pumping several times, I reached for the plug, rolling my fingers over the tip before placing it at her dark entrance.

As soon as the plug was pressed just inside, she pummeled one hand on the comforter, kicking her legs. "Oh… I hate…"

"You can hate me all you want." I twisted the plug back and forth as I pushed it further inside, caressing her ass with my other hand, the heat from the earlier spanking tingling my skin. When it was firmly seated inside, I patted her bottom. "Are you still hungry?"

"No."

"Then we should get some sleep. The next few days are going to be arduous."

She scrambled to her knees, fighting with the covers until she managed to crawl underneath. When she held up her arm, prepared for me to shackle her, another realization hit me.

I was exactly like my father.

Cold.

Brutal.

Incapable of real love.

And I hated myself because of it.

I gently eased her arm back to the covers, nodding my head. "I trust you, Emily."

Trust.

Trust had never been something I'd been able to do with the exception of my family. We would see if my fears in doing so with someone else were unfounded.

Then again, she'd become a member of our inner circle within days.

After turning off the lights, I stood by the window for a few minutes, peering through the blinds. While the house itself had a significant amount of land, other homes located almost a half mile away, I was able to envision their perfectly manicured lawns and flowering shrubs, pots hanging from the massive front porches. I could even hear the sound of children's laughter.

Although every bit of it was a fantasy.

That would never be a reality because of my bloodline.

Exhaling, I finally crawled into bed, realizing she'd already fallen asleep. Yet when she rolled over, murmuring in her sleep, placing her arm around me, I stiffened.

Another wave of anger swept through me, thoughts of revenge.

But there was also something else.

An ache in my heart.

CHAPTER 14

ristiano

A day of reckoning.

I stood staring out at the pool, my thoughts embroiled in the decisions that would need to be made, discussions that would be required. I had limited patience for excuses, although I knew I had to tread lightly with strong-arming anyone within law enforcement. Today could mean a crowning victory on several levels or the crown of thorns could drip blood.

Although it wasn't clear in my mind whose blood that would be.

Over the course of two hours, I'd made several phone calls, establishing required appointments, but the first two would be the most important.

I'd disarmed the security system and when I heard the front door, I knew who to expect. Still, I placed my hand on my weapon, turning slightly to ensure I wasn't being ambushed.

"Dimitri," I said before relaxing my arm, remaining where I was standing.

"Boss. I brought Nick as requested." Dimitri seemed solemn and with good reason. He was unsure what to expect from here on out.

I gave Nick a onceover, finding his choice in attire interesting. The last time I'd seen him, he'd been in jeans and an older polo, his attempt at fitting in with the various crowds on the streets of New Orleans. Today, he was dressed impeccably, although his suit was ill fitting. Still, I was impressed. He was a man to be watched.

After shifting my gaze toward the passage into the hallway, I motioned them closer. "Nick, I'm placing a significant amount of trust in you. I hope that you're ready to take on additional responsibilities."

Nick beamed, his grin almost too much for my tastes. "Absolutely, sir. I won't let you down."

How many times had I heard that before?

"That's good to hear. I have a job for you that will require your patience. You're taking a very special woman into town to this address," I said as I handed him a note. "You're to make certain that nothing happens to her. I will warn you that she is… feisty and hardheaded. Under no circumstances are you to allow her out of your sight, other than when absolutely necessary. Then you will bring her back here, remaining until I return. Allow no one but our men inside and if you even believe that there is a breach in security, you are to call me. Otherwise, I'll expect you to act accordingly. Is that understood?"

His expression turned somber as he nodded. "Don't worry, boss. I will protect her no matter what I have to do."

"See that you do. I have it on good authority that there could be an attempt made on her life."

Dimitri narrowed his eyes. "Who told you that?"

"It's not important, Dimitri. You and I leave in five minutes. And Nick, the appointment is at eleven. Both of you wait here." I walked around them, heading for the hallway. The sight of Emily gliding down the stairs, wearing one of the dresses I'd selected with matching heels was incredible. The scent of her perfume wafted into my nostrils, exciting every one of my senses.

She locked eyes with mine, taking careful steps as she walked onto the landing. The night before had been incredible, but the early morning had been just as awkward as before, even if I'd gotten the best night's sleep I'd had in years.

When she remained quiet, coming no closer, I inched toward her, slowly placing my hands on her arms. While she didn't flinch, she appeared uncomfortable. "I have significant business to attend to today, which could take me late into the night."

"What about me?" Emily asked, darting her gaze into the room and at the two men.

"Nick will be responsible for your safety today. You have an appointment in town at eleven. I suggest you have some breakfast."

"An appointment?"

I nodded, brushing my fingers up and down gently. "For a wedding dress."

She bristled, her mouth pinched. "Fine."

"I know this isn't what you want, but I promised that I would do everything to make the event special and I intend on honoring that pledge."

"Whatever you want. I'm certain it will be fine. Did you pick the dress you want me to wear, something garish and tight fitting?"

I half laughed, not fighting her as she stepped around me. "You can select anything you'd like. Cost is no objective. I'm certain you will find something you love."

"I'm sure I will." Her look was full of disdain. "And what about the cake or the flowers? The food? Or will this be a civil ceremony?"

"Everything will be taken care of and as I told you, I'm making an attempt to give you a wedding you can remember."

"I'm certain I'll remember it."

She refused to let go of anything beyond sexual in nature. I wasn't entirely certain she ever would, although I'd seen a glimmer of something entirely different in her.

As well as in myself.

"What about my job, Cristiano? Have you thought about that? I also have friends, remember? Well, at least Julia will start to worry about me if I don't call her. What am I supposed to say to her if and when you let me?"

"I'm going to pay your place of business a visit and as far as your friend, unfortunately, you're going to need to stay away from her for now."

"Let me guess. For her safety."

The dark cravings stirred all over again, my cock pushing hard against my trousers. "For one thing, yes." We'd discussed the arrangement, our marriage providing her security as well as keeping me out of prison. Whether or not the second part was true was yet to be seen, but she would at least be under the protection of the King family. However, there was remorse in her eyes, guilt for enjoying what we'd shared the night before.

"My God. This is insane." When she tried to walk away, I dragged her back, sliding my hand under the back of her dress.

Emily's eyes widened, a warm blush creeping up from her jaw from embarrassment. "What are you doing?"

"Checking that you obeyed me." As I eased my fingers into the cleft of her ass, she trembled. When I twisted the plug several times, her body swayed. "Very good girl. I'll have to reward you later." The guttural sound in my voice seemed to give her a smile but it was short-lived, her mouth twisting out of frustration.

I rubbed my thumb across her cheek, savoring the feel of her skin against the rough pad of my fingers. With all the intimacy we'd shared the night before, the continued awkwardness was debilitating.

Without saying anything else, she walked away, stopping long enough to glare at Nick and Dimitri before heading toward the kitchen. The fantasy had been broken.

Exhaling, I moved into the living room, looking from one to the other. "Nick, if this goes well, I will seriously consider placing you on my detail permanently. However, it will all depend on your actions."

"Yes, sir. Thank you, sir," he said far too eagerly.

"Don't thank me yet. The next few days are likely to be dicey." I gave Dimitri a nod before heading toward the front door, Dimitri trailing behind.

Dimitri waited until we were outside before saying anything. "What's going on, Mr. King?"

"The man Ricardo told us about must be found. Whoever he is, there has obviously been a plan in motion long before I was sent to prison. It's time to take out the trash." I said nothing else as I took long strides toward the SUV, easing inside the passenger seat.

When he climbed in, starting the engine, he gave me a single glance. "I don't like the shit I'm hearing." He rolled down the driveway. "Where are we headed, Mr. King?"

"Mario's. I'm certain you know where he lives."

He seemed taken aback. "Yes, of course I do."

A few minutes went by as he drove through the Garden District, taking the highway.

"I will need your thoughts on promoting from within the ranks. I want a small detail surrounding my father's house as well as mine. I will make a threat assessment today in order to determine if other members of the family are in immediate danger."

"This is getting serious."

"This could mean war."

"Then I have the men you'll need, boss."

I nodded as I continued to think about the events of little more than twenty-four hours. I should have paid more attention to the ramblings of various assholes in prison when they'd spewed off their threats. The two halfhearted attempts made on my life behind the concrete walls had been nothing more than a warning. I had the distinct feeling that Vendez actually knew there was a chance I'd be released from prison. If that were the case, the betrayal was far reaching.

And the asshole wanted to handle his selected eliminations himself.

I remained lost in my thoughts as Dimitri continued the drive, heading into a part of town that I loathed going to. When he began to turn on residential streets, my gut started to churn.

Our people were paid a hell of a lot of money.

"Did you have a chance to have any conversations last night?"

Dimitri snorted. "I scoured the damn streets. There's a lot of shit out there, but I found a few assholes who'd talk."

Chuckling, I gave him an appreciative nod. His methods of interrogation were almost as brutal as mine. "Then what did you find out?"

The small building was located in what I would consider a bad part of town, the surrounding houses run down. Dimitri pulled the SUV to the curb, allowing the engine to idle. "I asked around last night. Enrique Vendez has a reputation of being a ballbreaker, but I couldn't find a single person who'd ever spoken with him or even caught a glimpse of him.

However, he is putting pressure on certain businesses to break their loyalty to the King family."

Hissing, I glared out the window, shaking my head. That's exactly what I'd expected to hear. A whole lot of nothing. "Any additional information?"

"Just that he's supposedly from South America. He's got several different businesses, most of them legit. Who is this guy?"

"Someone who must be found. I don't give a shit if you have to turn over every rock. Find him. Enlist Ricardo's help. He needs to begin paying me for allowing him to keep his life."

"I'll find the bastard," Dimitri growled.

"I'm sure you will. Just so you're aware, there's going to be a wedding ceremony at my father's house in two days."

"Who's getting married?"

I simply gave him a look.

"You're marrying that girl?" Dimitri asked, shaking his head as he stepped out of the car. While he wore no expression, I could tell he was surprised. "Are you serious? I mean no disrespect but…"

"None taken. However, it's a necessity."

"Okay, Mr. King. I'll make certain and have the area swept and provide plenty of security."

"Good. One more thing," I hesitated before finishing my statement. "I value everything you've done for me, Dimitri. I trust you more than anyone. There is no need to call me Mr. King. My reaction last night was overblown." He knew that was as close to an apology as he was going to get. Maybe

Emily's goodness was rubbing off on me. I climbed out of the vehicle, adjusting my suit jacket before heading toward the porch. Dimitri trailed behind me, remaining on the small deck, watching for any intruders as I knocked on the door.

When the door opened, Mario frowned. "Mr. King."

"Mario." I wasted no time snapping my hand around his throat and shoving him inside, my schedule filled with ensuring every operation was exactly where it should be. Dimitri closed the door behind me. Witnesses I didn't need. As I slammed him against the wall, he gasped for air but knew better than to fight me. "You fucked up."

Shaking, his mouth twisted as I squeezed, cutting off his air supply.

"When I give you an order, I expect you to follow it. I thought that was clear to you."

"I'm... sorry," he struggled, gasping for air. "I..."

"Sorry means absolutely nothing. You tossed the girl into a cage. Is that the order I gave you?"

"Na... No... sir. That wasn't..."

"That wasn't what? A good idea? You're damn right. She's not an animal but it would appear that you are."

I dug my fingers into his skin. While the brute was large, I could still easily snap his neck if desired. I kept my hold for a full minute, his face turning bright crimson.

Then I let him go, but not without punching him several times, the last hitting him square in the jaw. As he fell to the floor, a gurgling sound erupting from his mouth, I took a step away.

"It's your lucky day, Mario. You get to live. You also get to keep your job; however, you only get one warning in this organization and you've had yours. If you fuck up again, that will be your last time. You're going to get your shit together and at this point, you're reporting to Nick. Call him. Is that clear?" The demotion would either solidify his loyalty or break the ties altogether. I didn't give a shit which.

I didn't bother waiting for his answer. He would never cross another line. That much I knew.

As I walked out of the house, I gazed up and down the street. What the hell was Mario using his money for? It was a question worth finding the answer to.

"Where to, Cristiano?" Dimitri glanced back at the house once. Thank God he had the good insight not to challenge me.

"My father is expecting me."

As I climbed into the vehicle, I noticed Mario was peering out his blinds. A red flag raised, my gut churning. And I had a bad feeling the shit was about to hit the fan.

* * *

"Cristiano," my father said from behind his massive mahogany desk. There was no computer system. He had no email address nor followed any social media. He lived by his old school methods, the ledgers behind his desk notes regarding various punishments and enemies as well as financial information going back several decades. They were likely all up to date and he would be able to find any scrap of information if requested.

At times we sparred, my drive to push us into the future clashing with everything his father had taught him.

"Pops." As I walked in, I could feel the tension in the air. The smoke from his cigar wafted in my direction. "A little early for a cigar, don't you think?"

"Never too early. It would appear that you insisted on teaching Mario a lesson. In case you've forgotten, he was loaned to you as a favor since you've yet to have the time to hire additional soldiers."

"Mario is a pig who can't follow orders. He was lucky I'm in a good mood."

"Because of this woman?" he asked, lifting a single eyebrow.

I laughed softly as I flung myself in the leather chair opposite his desk. "Perhaps."

He shifted in his seat, taking several puffs then blowing the smoke in my direction. That usually indicated he was pissed off. "I understand the reason you're marrying her, but she isn't family."

"She will be. That's something you need to keep in mind, Father."

When he struggled to stand, I started to rise to my feet, but he waved me off.

"I'm not an invalid, Cristiano. I'm also still the head of this family, or is that something you've already forgotten?"

As if I could. He enjoyed reminding me of that fact every chance he got. "I'm aware of that."

"Good. I wanted to make certain you were. You know, I brought Mario up from nothing. He was a street kid. No parents. Refused to live in foster homes. The kid made the mistake of stealing from one of my guys while he was making a pickup. That had never been done before. When the little shit was brought to me, I realized he couldn't be more than eleven, maybe twelve. But I also knew that with that kind of talent, he'd make a damn good soldier. And I was right. Hell, the man took a bullet for me before he was even eighteen."

"I didn't know that." And I wasn't certain I cared.

"There's a lot of shit you don't know, son. What I'm trying to tell you is that you need to pick your battles. Mario was trying to protect you as he's always done for me."

"And I'm certain you pay him well to do just that."

"Hell, yes, I do. You got a problem with that?" my father huffed, daring me to say yes.

"Not at all. I believe in paying our people well. Tell me this, Pops. Why is he living in a shithole on the other side of town?"

He opened his eyes wide, finally sighing. "None of your damn business."

"When I'm attempting to find out who had the balls to issue a hit on your life, everything is my fucking business."

"He has a sister, well, a half-sister. Didn't even know she existed for over twenty years. She's had issues her entire life, the kind that require her to be cared for twenty-four hours a day. He spends the majority of his money keeping her in a nice facility instead of the real shithole he found her in. That's what he spends his money on, not that it's any of your damn business."

"Interesting."

"That's what family does, son. They take care of their own. So, I don't want to hear anything else about where or how he lives. As long as I'm alive, he will remain a respected member of our organization. You got it?"

"Oh, I got it, Pops."

Snuffing, he twirled his cigar. "What about the Azzurris?"

"As I told you before I went to prison, they had nothing to do with the attempt on your life."

"Then who the fuck did?"

I leaned forward, staring him straight in the eyes. "Have you ever heard of the name Enrique Vendez?" At first there was no reaction on my father's face. Then a slight glimmer in his eyes.

"Should I?" he asked, puffing away on his cigar.

"I don't know, Pops. It would appear he's been attempting to either buy off or threaten several owners of our businesses to shift their loyalty. It would also appear that he's managed to put several prominent law enforcement members in his pocket."

"You're saying this person is behind your arrest?"

I'd known my entire life when my father was hiding something. Today was one of those days. Pushing him wouldn't do a damn bit of good. "That's my belief. Joseph believes so as well. He owns a corporation called EV Holdings." I caught a slight return of the same glimmer, although my father remained quiet. "And there's speculation he's working with Carlos Morales."

"Carlos," my father huffed. "Now, there's a real pig for you."

"Have you spoken with Carlos while I was gone?"

"Hell, no. You can ask Lucian, but we made our point clear the last time he attempted a coup with one of our ships."

"Which means he could certainly be working with Vendez."

He gave me a stark look before turning away. "Then do what you need to do in order to get our kingdom under control but be careful in the choices you make."

The choices.

I found his words more disturbing than they should be.

Sighing, I stared at him, expecting something else, perhaps words of encouragement. Hell, I'd settle for his continued admonishment of the way I handled the situation. After a few seconds of silence, it was obvious there was no point in talking with him any further. I rose to a standing position, waiting an additional five seconds before heading for the door.

"Cristiano. I was just like you when I was your age, a fighter. I refused to accept anyone's authority or their pushback, my sadistic retribution feared by enemies and allies alike. I was forced to learn the hard way that my behavior created resentment, which led to acts of betrayal. I don't want that for you. You have what it takes to become a great leader, but you need to temper your anger. You and your brothers and sisters are the greatest accomplishments of my life and I couldn't have done anything without your mother. She was my shining star, the love of my life. That's what's important, son, and something that you need to learn. May this marriage provide you the kind of balance and happiness that you desperately need."

I found myself wanting to challenge him, especially since he'd never shown interest in his children before let alone given any of us reason to believe he adored our mother. If this was his attempt at some kind of an olive branch, a moment of fatherly love, it was far too late. "Noted, Father." As I walked out of the room, I felt a sense of sadness.

Maybe he was right.

Maybe he was wrong.

Only time would tell, and time was one thing I didn't have.

I'd only moved into the entrance foyer before the door burst open, Lucian storming inside.

"What the fuck did you just do?" he demanded, closing the distance until we were only inches apart. The look in his eyes was as riddled with rage as I knew mine must be.

"What had to be done. Mario is a problem."

"Yeah? Well, he's my problem. You had no right."

I shifted even closer, controlling my breathing. "While you are allowed to have your own soldiers, you need to keep in mind that every one of them works for me. I run the organization, Lucian. Not you."

The tension between us was worse than it had ever been, his breathing labored.

"You're nothing but a bully, Cristiano. You think you can rule with the same kind of hatred and anger that's existed for centuries. That way of thinking is going to finally get you killed."

"Maybe so, brother. However, you seem to forget that our enemies are attempting to close in, to eradicate a solid portion of our kingdom. I refuse to allow that to happen. Use any means necessary. I suggest you remember your place in this family."

After a few seconds, he tipped his head and took a step to the side. When I walked past him and toward the door, he laughed. "On the day of your murder, very few people will be upset, Cristiano. Including me."

CHAPTER 15

mily

Prisoner.

A person captured or kept and confined by an enemy.

The definition was clinical but accurate.

But where was an explanation as to why I continued to be attracted to him?

Was Cristiano my enemy or was he merely another victim? That was the question that I hadn't been able to answer. The night of passion had been… incredible. Every touch of his hand, every kiss, let alone the way he'd fucked me twice during the middle of the night had been intense and powerful, leaving me breathless each time. He'd also broken down the thick walls he'd kept himself secured behind enough to allow me to see the man underneath the heavy burden of carved stone.

Yet I remained apprehensive, uncertain of the feelings washing through me, leaving my mind a blur and my heart racing. I wanted to care about him, at least a part of me did. But the nagging in my gut refused to allow me to surrender to my desires.

Or my heart.

He was dangerous, one hell of an angry man. He was also enigmatic and enthralling, sensual and passionate.

And very cold.

I was unable to fathom the life he'd led, the choices he'd been forced to make over the years. He'd given all of himself to a lifestyle not of his choosing. What kind of family did that to their own children? I shuddered at the thought as I gazed at the clock for the fifth time in less than twenty minutes. A wedding dress. I was supposed to pick out some frilly thing in order to stand by his side, reciting vows I had no place saying, ones that held no meaning.

Could they ever?

I'd read about arranged marriages from history books to romance novels. There were still mail-order brides who agreed to marry an unknown man for the chance to live in the United States. Then there were marriages agreed to by members of certain families in an effort to soothe a rivalry or bridge two of them together. In this case, I'd agreed to marrying my captor to keep him out of prison for a crime. I wasn't certain what that made me. An accomplice to a crime?

I fisted one hand, digging my nails into my skin. How the hell could I go through with it? He'd promised me a dowry, a freaking dowry like we lived in the eighteen hundreds. Money. Jewelry. Trips to tropical locations or Swiss chalets.

No, he hadn't promised exactly. He'd stated what I could expect in his usual commanding demeanor.

Then he'd reminded me that there would also be rules to obey and if I didn't, the punishment would be swift. Yep. That was a marriage made in heaven.

As I shifted back and forth from one foot to the other, I was cognizant of the damn plug he'd made me wear. While I'd selected a dress with very soft material, the fabric managed to remind me every time I made a move that I'd been spanked the night before.

Like a bad little girl.

I cringed at the thought, wanting nothing more than to rip out the thick rubber, but I knew at some point I'd be checked for insolence.

The sound of heavy footsteps forced me to close my eyes.

"I'm sorry to interrupt you, miss… I mean we need to go."

The sound of the soldier's voice was at least pleasing. "Porter."

"I'm sorry?"

"Miss Porter, but you can call me Emily." I finally turned to look at him and was surprised that he wasn't a rough as Dimitri. There were no outward scars and his eyes weren't hardened from years of his savage duty. He also couldn't be more than twenty-three. While he wore a suit, I could easily see the outline of a weapon.

He gave a respectful nod. "Miss Porter. I'm Nick. Nick Spice."

A nervous laugh slipped past my lips and immediately I placed my hand over my mouth for a few seconds. "I'm sorry. That wasn't funny."

"You can laugh. Everyone else does about my name." He grinned for a few seconds before regaining a serious expression. "We need to go, Miss Porter. Mr. King doesn't take well to tardiness."

"I don't think he takes well to anything."

There was a slight spark in his eyes although he remained quiet, merely moving so I could walk out the door first. However, when we got to the front door, he stepped in front of me. "I need to go first. Just stay here."

I held back, my pulse racing when he opened the door. Just the thought of living this way every day was horrifying.

Nick kept his hand on his weapon as he walked outside, scanning the surroundings before motioning me into the light, opening the back door of an SUV.

The heat was already oppressive, the bright sun cutting through the thick canopy of trees. I shielded my eyes, turning my attention to the house. The façade was beautiful, a mixture of Victorian with a taste of Georgian plantation. I wasn't certain what to expect, but the gorgeous house wasn't it. As with everything I'd seen inside, the massive double front wraparound porch didn't show signs of tender loving care.

There were no plants or outdoor furniture. There wasn't a lovely decorative flag hanging from a flagpole. And there certainly wasn't a welcoming wreath on the door.

Another moment of sadness washed into my system. I noticed a second car, the engine already running. I shuddered at the realization that Cristiano wasn't taking any chances with regard to my life. Was I really in danger? Would someone attempt to kill me because of my relationship with the mafia?

Breathe, Emily. Breathe.

That wasn't going to be possible.

As I got into the vehicle, I continued looking at the house, imagining for just a few seconds what it would look like with a fresh coat of vibrant paint on the front door, several planters full of flowers adorning the steps, and a swing hanging from the porch ceiling.

Just another fantasy.

When Nick climbed inside, he took a look in the rearview mirror before starting the engine. As soon as he did, the door locks engaged, the slight sound more overpowering than normal. I was jittery as hell, my hands shaking. As he pulled out of the driveway, I realized that I hadn't been made to wear a blindfold. It was another ridiculous thought to make me laugh, the action forcing my stomach to hurt.

I hadn't been able to eat breakfast. The thought of food had been revolting.

"Where are we going, Nick?" I was curious as to what part of town I was being carted away to. I turned around, watching as the other SUV rolled in behind us.

"I don't know the name, Miss Porter, but it's in uptown on Magazine Street."

I knew enough about the area to realize that two of the poshest bridal stores were located there. I still couldn't figure out why Cristiano was bothering with lavishly spending money on an event that was mostly for show.

Unless he planned on publicizing the nuptials in the press. That sounded very much like something he'd do.

"Thank you," I whispered. The windows were tinted and if I had to guess, I'd say the vehicle itself was bulletproof. I watched as all the beautiful houses passed by, the tree-lined streets and sidewalks like something out of a magazine. I could stand watching the world roll by, one that I didn't belong to.

"No problem, Miss Porter."

"You really can call me Emily."

"No can do. Mr. King wouldn't like that. You deserve respect."

"Fuck Mr. King."

I heard a slight noise like he was attempting to hide a chuckle. "He said you were feisty. I'm sorry, Miss Porter. I hope I didn't insult you."

"You can relax, Nick. I have no idea why I'm here or what I'm doing, and I'm certainly not going to bite your head off or turn you in to the great Mr. King. Whatever you say to me is in confidence."

He tipped his head, allowing me to see his grin. "Yes, ma'am."

"Why do you work for him, Nick?"

"Because he and his brothers are good to me."

Good. I wanted to ask him to define what that meant. "But you're always in danger."

"Not always. It's not like we have wars on the streets every day. As a matter of fact, there hasn't been anything like that since I came to work for the King family."

"Then what do you do for them?"

He was obviously choosing his words very carefully. "Until now, keeping the peace. I'm sorry, Miss Porter. I don't think Mr. King would like me to disclose anything about his business."

"Even if I'm going to become his wife?"

There was no doubt about the shock crossing his face or the happiness. I couldn't have been more surprised. "That's fantastic. I'm so happy for the both of you."

For some insane reason, I didn't want to burst his bubble. "I guess we shall see."

"I know he has a reputation of being a hard man, but I could tell by the look in his eyes how much he cares for you. Just sit back and relax. We will be there in a few minutes."

Relax.

The word was likely no longer in my vocabulary.

As I slumped down in the seat, crossing my arms, my thoughts drifted to what Cristiano might do to my poor boss. Then again, was he a part of this attempt to destroy the King family? I thought about everything I'd seen and heard during the course of several months. I'd worked closely with Mr. Dublin, more so than anyone else had. Were there some reports I'd seen that were questionable? Yes. And financials that seemed out of order? Absolutely. But was a dour little man like Mr. Dublin Mr. Vendez's enforcer of some kind?

"We're here, Miss Porter."

As he allowed me outside of the vehicle, hurrying me toward the door, I took several deep breaths.

The moment I walked inside I almost had a panic attack. Every single piece of furniture from the tables to the chairs was frosted in white, flecks of gold embedded into the paint. There were fresh flowers everywhere, the scent of roses assaulting my senses. A sea of white and ivory dresses was hanging on racks on two walls, the most exquisite jewels encrusting glorious veils. There was a scent of vanilla and jasmine coming from carefully positioned candles. And the damn music was Mozart, for God's sake.

"I can't do this," I whispered, backing against Nick's massive frame. A fleeting thought entered my mind. What if I told the store clerk that I was a captive?

I knew the answer. That person would be hurt trying to help me. I was cornered. There were no other choices.

"Yes, you can. You don't want to disappoint Mr. King. Do you?" Nick asked quietly.

I had my answer and the one he needed to hear. As a smiling woman approached, I thought I was going to be sick.

However, her smile was genuine as she held out her hand. "You must be Emily. I'm Sheila. I'm one of the owners of this store. Mr. King speaks of you very highly."

While I allowed her to take my hand, the butterflies remained in my stomach. "Thank you. I'm not certain why I'm here."

"Don't be nervous," she said, barely giving Nick a second glance. It was obvious she knew exactly who Cristiano was. "I know selecting the perfect dress can be scary but I'm here to make this a very special day. Come with me. I have a room set up for you. You have the entire store to yourself today."

A room.

I didn't need to look at single one of the price tags to know just how expensive the dresses were. They weren't me. I was a simple girl with modest needs.

But I allowed her to lead me down a hallway and into a room the size of a freaking house. There was a platform in front of three standing mirrors, plush chairs, and a table full of fruit, cheeses, and chocolates as well as bottles of water and a chilled bottle of Cristal champagne. I'd never felt so out of place anywhere before in my life.

I stood in the middle of the room, trying to catch my breath. When I felt a hand on my arm, I jumped.

"My goodness. You don't have to worry, Emily. You really are going to have a good time. Now, I've taken the liberty of selecting a few dresses for you to look at and try on if you'd like, but you are free to choose any dress within the store."

"And Mr. King? Did he pick out a dress or two as well?" When she didn't answer immediately, I found the courage to look her in the eyes. "He did. Didn't he?"

She was just as uncomfortable as I was, trying to hide the fact behind her kind smile. "He did seem to like two of them very much, but he was insistent that I not try and influence you in any way."

"So you're telling me that he actually came here?"

"Why, yes, he did."

"He doesn't know anything about me, what kind of clothes I prefer or even my favorite color. He merely had one of his flunkies pick out some beautiful clothes for me. I couldn't even do it myself," I insisted as I walked closer to the table of food, staring at the strawberries, allowing one of the few wonderful memories to take over the ugliness in my mind. He'd been playful and sweet, allowing me to enjoy without pressure. He'd even kept me close to him all night, his arm wrapped around me.

So protective.

So… loving.

No. No. This was an arrangement. I was doing him a favor. I'd become a wealthy, influential woman. Wasn't that something?

Sheila walked toward the table, expertly opening the bottle of champagne and pouring a single glass. After making certain I took the flute, she gave me a serious look. "I'm well aware who Mr. King is and about his reputation. I recognized him the moment he walked into my other store."

"Your other store?"

"Yes, my sister and I own this shop as well as a women's clothing store on Bourbon Street. Mr. King followed me here yesterday to ensure that you would be able to find what you were looking for."

The butterflies stirred in my tummy. Did he actually give a damn?

"Sophia's," I said, the beautiful pink bags with white cursive writing floating into my mind.

"Yes." Her eyes lit up. "You look fabulous in that dress by the way."

"How did he know my size?"

She laughed as she walked toward a rack of dresses. "Well, he described you to me and mentioned we were about the same size. He was right. He also said you were extremely beautiful. He wasn't exaggerating."

An involuntary smile crossed my face. "He actually said that?"

Sheila pulled a dress into her hands, turning to face me. "I've spent the majority of my life in retail, so I assure you I'm very observant. I know exactly what the newspapers and television stations say about him and the King family. Maybe it's true, maybe it's not. However, he is also a man first and foremost. You've caught more than just his attention. Enjoy this time, Emily. Whatever the arrangement, it will be your special day. Don't let anyone take that from you."

My special day. I took a sip of champagne as I studied the dress she held out, trying to envision myself wearing a gown of white when I felt tarnished.

Maybe I would be wearing a dress of scarlet.

As I thought about Cristiano, the small pitter-patter in my heart pissed me off. I was falling for the brooding, dark, dangerous, and merciless man.

May God help me.

"That's beautiful. I'd like to try it on."

Sheila lit up even more. "Absolutely. The dressing room is through those swinging doors. I'll be happy to help if you need, but you can take your time. Anything you need, just let me know."

"Just one thing."

"Absolutely."

"Can we change the music to something more modern? I'm sick to death of classical music."

She burst into laughter, rolling her eyes. "Oh, thank God, honey. If I have to hear this loop one more time, I'm going to lose my mind. I'll be right back." After securing the hanger, still allowing me to see just how exquisite the dress really was, she left the room.

Sighing, I took another sip of champagne before placing the glass on the table and moving toward the dress. I held it in front of me, turning to face the mirror. I almost looked like a princess.

Maybe fairytales did come true.

Only my hero wouldn't arrive on a fabulous white steed.

He'd arrive in a bulletproof automobile.

* * *

Cristiano

"Ricardo. It's good to see you again," I stated with no inflection as Dimitri and I sat down at the table the little prick had selected, the coffee shop in the heart of the French Quarter. I was actually surprised that he'd actually made the contact, insisting that he had vital information. He'd selected a table in the back, indicating he was afraid of being seen.

He cradled his bandaged hand against his chest, obviously nervous as hell, his hand shaking as he reached for his coffee. "I'm sorry to bother you, Mr. King, but I thought you'd want to know this."

"What have you found out about Mr. Vendez?" I scanned the window outside the shop, my thoughts drifting to Emily. I didn't necessarily trust that she wouldn't make an attempt to either contact someone or flee. I had to place my faith in Nick's abilities.

"Look," he said as he leaned over. "I don't know if Enrique Vendez is a real person." He took a look around our table, making certain no one was listening in.

"Meaning what?" Dimitri asked.

"Meaning that there hasn't been a single person who's seen him. Not one. That's not normal."

"Granted, his secrecy is troubling," I said in passing, uncertain why I wasted my time coming there. At least I'd been able to find the man Emily was working for by using a contact within the police department that I did trust. Franklin Dublin had no record and seemed to live a quiet life, although he was devoid of any family. I'd assigned two other soldiers to keep tabs on him. He and I would have a discussion at a later time. "Is that why you called me?"

"No. I heard something, and I don't know if it's true." Ricardo was sweating like the pig he was.

I gave him a hard stare, shaking my head. "Tell me."

"There's word on the street that there's a hit planned for you."

Exhaling, I was about ready to lose my patience. "That's old news, Ricardo. You have to give me more."

"Not just you. Some girl. The witness. I don't know who she is. I swear to God."

The information Joseph had learned had been correct. "Still old news."

He narrowed his eyes, obviously confused. "The hit is planned for today, Mr. King. Somebody is hunting you."

The words didn't take long to settle in.

No. No. Fuck, no!

As I jumped out of the chair, I knew there was no time to take the SUV, the bridal shop only a few blocks away. As I began running, Dimitri trailing behind me, all I could think about was saving her life.

The woman who'd nearly destroyed mine.

The woman who'd defied me at every turn.

And the woman I couldn't live without.

CHAPTER 16

Emily

"Mirror, mirror on the wall, who's the fairest of them all?"

As I whispered the words, I turned from side to side, still shocked that every dress Sheila had selected was magical, creating a stunning image of a fairy princess. The thought was ridiculous, but I couldn't keep from feeling elated.

"You look truly beautiful, Emily," Sheila said as she stood behind me, still fluffing out the satin train.

While I wasn't certain I would say beautiful, I did feel special in some odd kind of way. When she moved onto the platform, placing a veil on top of my head, she clapped her hands.

"Amazing. You're truly going to make a gorgeous bride."

Bride.

The word was both chilling and exciting. I had no understanding of what I would face once I exchanged vows, but I knew that it would forever change my life.

"This is the one," I said in such a quiet voice that I wasn't certain she heard me.

"I knew you'd choose this one. And no alterations needed." Very carefully she removed the veil, no longer able to look me in the eyes. She unhooked the two dozen buttons, giving me a maternal smile.

Sighing, I smoothed my hands down the front of the dress, marveling in the number of sequins. After taking another last look, I carefully moved down the platform, heading for the dressing room, stopping just short of going past the set of doors. "How did you know?"

"What do you mean?"

"How did you know I'd select this dress?"

She took her time arranging the veil on the mannequin's head, slowly turning in my direction. "Because Mr. King knew you'd love this one."

All I could do was laugh softly as I walked back into the changing room, carefully easing the dress over my shoulders. I still had no idea what to think or how to feel. Cristiano was surprising in so many ways. Could I ever care for him in the way a wife was supposed to adore the man she was married to? I couldn't be certain.

When I'd finished, I carefully placed the dress on the hanger, brushing my hand down the front one last time before walking back into the room, drinking in the atmosphere. As I handed it to Sheila, I felt a sudden pang in my heart. This just wasn't the way it was supposed to be.

"Thank you for a lovely afternoon."

"You're welcome, dear. I'll have this ready for pickup tomorrow for you."

I moved out of the room, almost regretting that I had to leave. Nick was still in the same location that I'd seen him, only his expression was hard to read. On the phone, he shifted his gaze in my direction.

"Understood," he said in a gruff voice. "Come. We need to leave now."

"What's wrong?"

He grabbed my arm, his fingers with a firm hold, dragging me toward the entrance, his phone in his hand. "We've been compromised." When he spoke into the phone, his tone was full of urgency. "There's a shooter. Stay hidden but cover my back." He ended the call, shoving his phone into his pocket and taking a deep breath.

"What the hell does that mean? A shooter?"

Nick pushed me against the wall of the store at the entrance, pulling his weapon into his hands. "Do not budge from this spot. Do you understand me, Emily?"

The use of my name meant that whatever danger we were in was real. I couldn't stop shaking, my pulse skipping. "No. I won't."

He hunkered down after opening the door, moving just outside, his gun firmly planted in both hands as he scanned the area. When he grabbed me by the arm, I almost froze, my heart racing.

"Stay low and hold onto my jacket." His words were terse, riddled with concern.

This time I followed instructions, trying to keep my footing as he stayed in front of me, crowding the buildings, still keeping the weapon as inconspicuous as possible. I could hear his ragged breathing, could tell by how tense his body was that he was prepared for an attack. As he rounded the corner, the sound of sirens blasted off in the distance, taking his attention away from the immediate area.

"Fuck," he growled, moving quickly until we were at the end of a building, an alley separating us from the SUV only yards ahead. He darted his head into the shadows, huffing the entire time.

"Who's after us?"

"Quiet. Just hold on."

The second he took a giant step forward, a loud bang occurred. Within two seconds, he yanked me against his chest, tumbling to the ground.

Pop! Pop!

The gunfire came from behind us.

An angry cry coming from in front.

As I twisted my head, I was shocked seeing the sight of Cristiano racing toward us.

"Go. Go. Go," Nick barked as he yanked me onto my feet, pummeling us forward, wrapping his body around mine. We were almost to the SUV. Almost.

Pop! Pop! Pop!

Gunfire seemed to come from everywhere.

I was almost dragged to the ground, Nick's heavy body pitching backward.

"No!" I yelled, fighting to stay on my feet, the horror of what was happening creating a fog around the periphery of my vision. I crawled forward, fighting to catch my breath, trying to get to Cristiano. I managed to rise to my feet, my mind a blur, the adrenaline rush forcing me forward.

"No! Get down. Get down!" Cristiano's guttural sound reverberated in the space around me.

Pop! Pop!

Within seconds, he lunged toward me, tossing his body over mine before getting off several shots. I wrenched my head, able to catch a sight of the gunman as his body was pitched backward, falling then scrambling to his feet. He lumbered away, obviously shot. My God, Cristiano had saved my life. I heard thumping footsteps, Dimitri's voice as he shot past us, chasing whoever had been responsible for ambushing us.

"Boss," Nick struggled, struggling to move into a sitting position.

I noticed the key fob in his hand. The *chirp, chirp* as the vehicle was unlocked had the same effect as the gunshots.

Terror raced through me, the horror of what had just occurred sending a series of chills down my spine.

"We're getting the fuck out of here," Cristiano roared, pulling me to my feet and instantly opening the rear door. While his actions were forceful as he placed me into the SUV, he offered a reassuring smile. "Everything is going to be all right."

The door was slammed and I reacted, banging my hands against the window, watching as the man I was supposed to marry yanked Nick to his feet, hurrying him around to the other side.

When he was tossed beside me, Nick let off a ragged growl. "Fuck. Fuck!"

Everything happened so fast. I watched as if in slow motion as Cristiano yanked open the driver's door, jumping inside and immediately starting the engine. He jerked from the curb, rolling toward the last sight of Dimitri.

"Goddamn it!" Cristiano yelled, slamming his hand on the steering wheel.

"You can't leave him," I yelped, shifting toward Nick. A pool of blood had already seeped through his shirt and he was gasping for air. "Oh, my God." This wasn't happening. This couldn't be happening.

I ripped his shirt, eyeing the wound. He'd been shot in the back, the bullet likely going clean through. The bleeding was excessive.

I heard the screech of tires, the passenger door opening and Dimitri yelling in Russian.

Cristiano jammed on the accelerator, the SUV lurching forward.

For the second time in two days, I closed my eyes.

Then I prayed.

Hero.

I wasn't certain the word was appropriate, but Cristiano had been elevated to that level. If he hadn't draped his body over mine, I would likely have been killed. The thought reeled in my mind as the scene played out over and over again.

When an announcement sounded over the intercom, I cringed. Code Blue.

Cristiano snarled, walking closer to the corridor, his hands on his hips.

"It's okay," Dimitri said as he flanked Cristiano's side.

Several medical professionals rushed by, pushing a crash cart. I couldn't help but remember the instance from my past when my mother's heart had failed, the efforts for resuscitation taking almost three full minutes. I swayed in the chair, the cold chill remaining from before.

"Okay? How the fuck could this have happened?" he spewed. "And where the hell is Mario?"

"He's handling the cleanup," Dimitri said, sighing. "Come on. You need to sit down."

"Fuck that," Cristiano roared. "What about Mr. Dublin. Did he move at all?"

My boss? Another cold shiver trickled down my spine. Was Franklin really involved with this? I was sick to my stomach.

Dimitri shook his head. "No. He went out to lunch then purchased a few groceries. From what I was told, he didn't even make or receive a phone call."

"Fuck," Cristiano hissed. "This is getting out of hand."

"We'll figure it out," Dimitri answered. "I'm calling in every fucking favor out there."

Cristiano nodded. "Good. I want his whereabouts by tomorrow. I don't give a shit what we have to do. The man is going down."

I tried to blank out what they were saying, but the surroundings did nothing but fuel the increasing nausea.

Hospitals.

I hated them, my mother spending two months lying in a hospital bed before succumbing to her illness. She'd been my entire world, a woman who'd taken on every challenge of being a single parent, fighting hard to make something of our life. When she'd died, I'd felt lost for a long time. I would never forget the stench of antiseptic or the beeping sounds made by the ventilator she'd been placed on during her last days.

The experience was much the same, although I hadn't gone into Nick's room. I wasn't family. I wasn't anyone important, yet I remained in the waiting room as Cristiano paced back and forth, his anger boiling over. He was so quiet, saying little more than a few words after the horrific incident. I'd seen the look in his eyes, one so dark and bleak that I knew he was planning some kind of retaliation.

I dared not ask questions, not yet. He was far too lost in his own demons to be able to answer. Dimitri had been on the phone for a solid hour, half the time speaking in his native language. Both men were enraged. I'd felt even more terrified when four additional soldiers had shown up, each one of them stoic as they paraded the perimeter, obviously protecting a member of the King family.

I leaned forward, cradling my head in my hands, the bloodstains from Nick's injury remaining, the sounds of the gunshots ringing in my ears. It had all happened so fast. I'd caught a split second of the gunman, the dark hoodie he wore covering the majority of his face. I couldn't think clearly or process what had happened, my entire body continuing to shake.

When I sensed Cristiano's presence and when I felt his hands brushing over my shoulders, a single whimper escaped my mouth.

"Are you certain you're all right?" he asked in an entirely different tone than before.

"Um hm."

"Look at me, little flower. I need to know that you're all right. I promise you that nothing is going to happen to you. You're safe."

Safe. There was no such thing as safety around him. When I didn't respond immediately, he gently lifted my chin with a single finger. His face was so close to mine, his eyes full of concern.

"I'm fine, Cristiano. You should worry about Nick. It's his life you need to be concerned with."

"I do worry about him. He did what he was supposed to do."

His answer pissed me off, but I didn't have the energy to challenge him. I glared at the nurse's station, still remembering how I'd yelled at the nursing staff after my mother's death. I'd been so young, so terrified of being alone. "That's horrible all on its own."

"He's going to be all right, Emily."

"How do you know that? Can you read minds?"

He smoothed stray strands of hair over my ear, stroking me in a tender manner. "Trust me. Can you do that?"

"I don't know, Cristiano. Everything is so horrible."

"Nothing like that is going to occur again."

If only I could believe him.

"Cristiano. Jesus Christ."

The different voice drew my attention. Two men were storming closer. There was no doubt they were relatives. I stiffened, shifting back in my chair, wanting nothing more than to hide.

"Vincenzo. Michael. You didn't have to come," Cristiano said as he approached them.

They had to be brothers. The resemblance was uncanny.

"Like hell we didn't. What the fuck is going on?"

"Slow down, Michael," the one named Vincenzo answered.

"Slow down? Our family is under siege and you want me to slow the fuck down?" Michael retorted. "Did you get the shooter?"

"He was definitely wounded," Dimitri said.

"But not killed? What the fuck is wrong with you, Russian?" Michael snapped. "Did you see who the fuck he was?"

"That's enough," Cristiano demanded. "I caught a glimpse of the asshole's face. Never seen him, but I can guarantee you that he's gone somewhere to lick his wounds."

"I'll make certain the streets are swept," Vincenzo stated.

"Good. Dimitri, follow through with Ricardo. I want to know names of the people who spouted off about the attempt." Cristiano gave me a single glance, a smile curling on his mouth.

Then he pulled the group further into the waiting room. Thank God there wasn't anyone else besides the damn mafia in close proximity. I resisted laughing from the thought. The few people had almost raced away the moment we walked in.

"We need to get a handle on who the fuck is doing this," Cristiano said quietly. "However, the fact the location was discovered means we have a leak in our organization."

I could see Vincenzo's eyes opening wide. "Who the fuck do you think?"

"I have an idea and I need you both to determine whether I'm right." Cristiano darted a glance in my direction before pulling them further away from me. He obviously didn't want me to hear any additional information.

Of course Cristiano couldn't trust me. My guess was he still thought I was working with Mr. Vendez. A few seconds later, I heard footsteps moving closer and froze. When I lifted my head, the sight of all three men staring at me was ominous, the looks on the brothers' faces telling.

Finally, the brothers turned away. There wasn't going to be any introductions, no niceties of family members. I was the woman who'd betrayed their brother. That was all I'd ever be.

As Michael walked away, pulling his phone from his pocket, I could tell that Cristiano was ready to explode.

Thank God, the doctor strode down the hallway, pulling his surgical cap off his head.

I finally stood, my legs shaking.

"Mr. King. I'm Dr. Trebold."

"How is Nick?" Cristiano asked.

"He survived the surgery. Fortunately, the bullet went clean through. One more inch and the bullet would have hit a major artery. He would have bled to death before you got to the hospital," the doctor stated. "We're going to need to keep him for a couple of days, but he will fully recover."

Both Cristiano and Vincenzo breathed a sigh of relief. In truth, so did I.

"That's good to hear. Can I see him?" Cristiano asked.

"Look, he needs his rest. Why don't you wait until tomorrow?"

Cristiano exhaled but nodded. "As you might imagine, I need you to keep this quiet. No police. No reporters. Do you understand?"

There was something about the way Cristiano issued the words that was chilling. While there was no overt threat or even anger in his tone, I could tell the doctor knew exactly what had been mandated. And what would happen if he disobeyed.

"Of course, Mr. King."

I backed against the wall, wringing my hands.

The power of the King.

There were several soldiers positioned outside the house, all with loaded guns. They were prepared for another attack. I couldn't get past the thought. As I took a sip of wine, I stared at the liquid in the glass. Blood red. I'd seen enough blood in one day. My hand shaking, I eased the goblet onto the table before kicking off my shoes. At least I'd scrubbed my hands, removing the awful stain.

I remained on the couch, staring out the French doors, the glistening lights of the pool mesmerizing, only stiffening when Cristiano approached.

He placed his hands around my neck, rubbing gently. "You didn't eat much at dinner."

"I wasn't really hungry." As he continued to caress my skin, the emotional dam almost broke. "Why did that happen?"

"Because as bad as you think I am, there are even more merciless people who will stop at nothing to tear down my family. That includes you."

"I'm not your family."

He chuckled softly, moving to knead my shoulders. I realized the simple act was more intimate than anything we'd experienced. Maybe there was a real person inside, just like Sheila had told me. "You're more than just family, Emily. You're going to be my wife. I hold that more dearly in my heart."

"Yet I don't have a ring." I wasn't entirely certain why I made the stupid statement. Maybe because I was still shaking from what had happened. Or maybe I was still testing him.

"You will have any ring you so desire, but it's only a symbol."

A symbol of commitment. One of love.

When he brushed the tips of his fingers across my cheek, I found myself nuzzling against his hand. Desire remained just below the surface, my body tingling from his touch. I could no longer hate myself because of it. There was far too much electricity between us, a raging connection that refused to be denied.

We'd take a savage vow to become man and wife. I now knew he would protect me with his life, but would he promise to love and honor? That I wasn't certain of. I guess it no longer mattered.

When he took my hand, squeezing and guiding me to my feet, I wasn't certain what to expect.

"Come with me," he said oh-so quietly.

"Where?"

"Just come. Trust me."

Perhaps a tiny part of me actually did trust him. After everything we'd been through, I was no longer positive which one of us was actually the prisoner.

When he led me outside, I couldn't have been more surprised. "Aren't you afraid a sniper remains in the darkness?"

He chuckled as he led me toward one of the tables. I was surprised to see two folded towels as well as a bottle of champagne and two glasses.

The gesture was unexpected, especially after the shooting. I tipped my head, gazing into his eyes. Instead of the anger I'd seen before, there was something else entirely. Not just concern but…

"I realized today that somehow you've managed to yank away all my defenses, Emily. I wasn't expecting to care about you. In fact, I was determined to keep you at a distance, but when that assassin pointed his weapon at your back, I was prepared to do anything to keep you alive. You are very special as well as extremely beautiful." When he lowered his head, pressing his lips against mine, I felt as if the entire world was spinning.

Falling in love with him wasn't something I'd wanted to do, but as he pulled me into his arms, sliding his hands down my back, I was shaken to the core.

The kiss was sweet at first, allowing a gentle side of him to break through the surface. Everything about him was all consuming. He was so powerful, so commanding. Every part of me was aroused, my nipples aching as they slid back and forth against the material of the dress. I could detect my own scent as it floated between us.

He cupped my buttocks, lifting me onto my toes as his actions became more aggressive. Goosebumps popped along my skin as he swept his tongue inside, the kiss just the beginning of his dark cravings. The man was going to devour me.

And this time, I wanted it more than anything.

I continued to shudder as he peeled the dress from my shoulders, tugging until gravity pulled the material to the deck. While there was a distinct possibility that several of his soldiers were watching, I honestly didn't care.

After breaking the kiss, a growl rose from his chest, the sound creating vibrations dancing throughout my body.

He took a step away, slowly unbuttoning his shirt, yanking it off and tossing on one of the chairs. I couldn't take my eyes off him. He was muscular in all the right places, his abs carved out of stone.

"If you don't remove your panties, I will," he said gruffly.

I took a step away, toying with him, sliding my fingers under the thin waistband. "They're mighty expensive."

Another growl permeated the night air. "You won't need to wear panties, not inside this house."

"Hmmm..." A round of butterflies kicked up in my stomach, my hands trembling as I wiggled my hips, slowly lowering the lacy thong. The brisk breeze only added to the shivers, my heart racing as he began to unbuckle his belt.

He noticed my gaze, his breathing even more ragged than before. "Are you looking for a punishment, Emily? Are you ready to repent your filthy little sins?"

"Only if you are."

Laughing earnestly, he tugged on the belt and when it was finally released, he took his time wrapping the thick strap around his hand. "You will be disciplined, just not tonight. Tonight, I plan on ravaging you." He finally placed the belt on the table then removed his shoes, his eyes never leaving me. As he unzipped his linen trousers, my mouth watered, unable to breathe as he rolled the dense material over his chiseled hips.

When he was naked, I couldn't stop my heart from skipping several beats. He was utter perfection in a man.

"Mmm..." I shook my head, giving him a heated look as I continued to back away.

"Where are you going, my little flower?"

After darting a glance at the water, I made a knee-jerk decision. As I dove in, an odd sense of freedom washed over me. I kicked my legs, powering forward, spiraling once before jetting to the surface. Water trickled into my eyes, forcing me to blink several times. Where the hell had he gone?

I should have known he would never let me out of his sight, not even for a few seconds. The splash of water was followed by the savage man dragging me against his chest, his hard cock sliding between my legs.

"As I've told you before, my beautiful but bratty flower, there is no place on earth that you can run or hide from me. I will find you, no matter what it takes."

The words were thrilling, accentuating the fantasy.

And I knew he meant every word.

Cristiano swung me around to face him, our lips almost touching. I eased my arms over his shoulders, fingering his wet hair. He was even sexier, leaving me feeling vulnerable, his eyes more hypnotic than ever.

As he brushed his hand down the back of my head, he swung me around, the water swishing over us.

"What do you want, Emily?" he asked in his deep, husky voice.

"Everything."

"Then that's what you're going to get. Everything you've ever desired. Perhaps even the fairytale."

The words were almost cathartic, chipping away at the insanity that I actually cared for him. There was no such thing as love at first sight, certainly not in this case, but as my heart continued to race, I knew I was lying to myself. He'd awakened the woman locked inside. He'd allowed her to spread her wings, even though nothing made any sense.

I wrapped my legs around his hips as he held me, brushing his fingers up and down my spine. With every shiver, every tingling sensation, the embers sparked more and more.

He lifted me by several inches, sliding the tip of his cock up and down my swollen pussy. A moan skipped past my lips as he continued to tease me.

"Are you wet for me, little flower?"

"Uh-huh."

"Are you hungry for me?"

"Mmm… Yes. Yes, sir."

A smile curled on his lip as he pulled me down, thrusting the entire length of his cock deep inside.

"Oh. Oh!" The ragged whimper was swallowed by the splash of water.

Every sound he made was guttural, the heat of his body searing mine. He was nothing more than a savage beast, one who was ready to consume me. I couldn't stop trembling as he lifted me again, yanking down with enough force I couldn't hold back a series of cries.

"Tight and so wet," he muttered before entangling his fingers about my arms, turning in circle after circle.

The feel of the plug as well as his thick cock was enthralling.

As he took control, pounding into me, I clung to his shoulders, taking gasping breaths. The electric surge was almost dangerous, the live wire skittering to the edge of all rationality. This shouldn't be happening. I shouldn't want him.

But I did.

Whatever the reason, I never wanted this to end.

As he thrust brutally, my muscles clamped around the thick invasion, pulling him in even deeper.

He cupped my breasts, kneading my aching nipples between his fingers, pinching then releasing. The flash of pain was exquisite, pulling me closer to nirvana.

I bucked against him, the friction adding gasoline to the heated flames. I was breathless, my pussy clenching then releasing. He refused to stop, taking me to new heights of pleasure. As a climax trickled up from my toes, he yanked me even closer, crushing his mouth over mine.

The orgasm was just as powerful as the man, driving into me with such ferocity that I could no longer feel my legs. The kiss was just as savage, his tongue dominating mine, growls slipping past his lips.

I was lightheaded, unable to stop shaking, the beautiful wave of pleasure sweeping over me, keeping my heart racing.

After ending the kiss, he continued to hold me close, dragging his tongue around the edge of my mouth. Every sweep of his tongue, every thrust of his cock yanked me closer to another raging orgasm. I wanted to hold back, to make the moment last.

His breathing even more labored, he dug his fingers into me, continuing to pump hard and fast. Within seconds, I couldn't stop another climax from building. When I clamped down on my muscles, his body began to shake violently as he erupted inside, filling me with his seed.

The second he threw his head back and roared, I finally let go, the beautiful wave of ecstasy blanketing every inch. I was unable to breathe, my eyes no longer focusing. And at this moment, the rest of the world didn't matter.

Not the danger.

Not the horrors of the day.

Not the jaded future.

When he eased away, I lolled my head on his shoulder, cognizant he was moving through the water. The moment was soft and sweet, his fingers rubbing my neck. I closed my eyes, more satisfied than I'd ever been. He walked out of the pool still holding me. I'd never felt so safe in my life.

With careful motions, he lowered me down onto a lounge chair, immediately leaning over.

"You've become my life, Emily Porter. Very soon, no one will be able to take you away from me. You are mine. Mine to care for. Mine to protect. Mine to discipline. And mine to love."

Love.

Was the four-letter word even possible?

As he walked away and toward the champagne, I studied the man who would become my husband, a man riddled with sadness.

Then I thought about my favorite quote.

"In all the world, there is no heart for me like yours. In all the world, there is no love for you like mine."

Maya Angelou

CHAPTER 17

ristiano

Kings.

Perhaps they were more like fools, men aching to be something that they could never understand. I'd come to realize I'd fallen into that category.

There had been several revelations that had come to light during the late hours of the night, the first being that the treachery of betrayal was never easy. The second was that every family held secrets, some more damning than others, the lies and deceit surrounding them allowing enemies a foot into the kingdom.

And third…

That I was a man capable of love.

While it was difficult to express, the swell of emotions inside could no longer be denied. The moment of horror from the day before had represented all the evil in the world, so much of it based on decisions the family had made in our attempt to maintain control. It had also represented the very reason for living.

Love.

The thought was one I tried to hold onto as I stormed into my father's house and into his office, finding him sitting in the same chair as the day before. There was an aura around him, the news of the previous day weighing heavily on him. He looked haggard, as if the secrets he'd been keeping had finally reached a necessary end, a requirement to confess his sins.

Only I wasn't certain he had the capability.

He'd never been a man to admit when he was wrong, his brutality often covering up for his mistakes. He should be proud. I'd turned out just like him.

I wasn't there to coddle the man. The earlier attempt was just the beginning.

As I approached, he barely glanced in my direction, at least not until I slammed my palms onto his precious wooden desk. "You lied to me."

He took his time answering, further fueling my anger.

"About what, son?"

"About knowing who Enrique Vendez really is. Didn't you? Does the man even exist or only in some variation that you alone understand?"

A wry smile crossed his face. "When you were a little boy, I had doubts that you'd ever be able to take over the kingdom."

"Stop the bullshit, Pops. We don't have a kingdom. We have a fucked-up family who are required to sleep with weapons under our pillows. We have unbelievable wealth, but we can't enjoy our spoils of war."

"Our life isn't about a war!" he exclaimed with all the attitude I'd grown used to.

"Oh? It isn't? Then why do we employ seventy soldiers? Why do we all live in secure fortresses? And why do we have a number of enemies who refuse to back down if we aren't in a war?"

His face seemed to crumble, his body slumping in his thick leather chair. "I did my best, son. I wanted to leave my children a legacy."

I laughed bitterly. "Well, if you mean a trail of blood, you did a damn good job. I'm not here to debate whether or not you were a good father. I'm here to find out who's behind an attempt to destroy us."

"I... I'm not certain."

I stared at him incredulously. "I think you know exactly who has the balls to attempt something like this."

Very slowly he rose to his feet, moving to the small safe hidden amongst his library of books. I watched him curiously, wondering if he had any understanding of the urgency. The scuttlebutt on the street was getting worse, other members of our family in the crosshairs. It would appear that additional hits had been taken out, the information leaked as if a master game player's warning. The asshole wanted us on edge, which would mean any one of us could make a mistake.

"You might not believe me, but I'm proud of you, son. You've turned out to be a fine man. You will make a very good leader one day. I'm very happy you're getting married. I hope you will enjoy a long and happy life together. It doesn't matter the circumstances regarding how your marriage began."

I shook my head, managing to remain patient. "Does this have some kind of a meaning or are you trying to be my father for once?"

"You owe me some respect, Cristiano. I am your father." He pulled an envelope from his safe, holding onto it with a shaking hand. "What I'm telling you is that the marriage with your mother was arranged and while it took a long time, we eventually fell in love."

"What?" The news wasn't anything that I would have expected. "Why? How?"

"There will always be rival crime syndicates, mob families who attempt to take over. There will always be wars on the street, lives lost. The Vendettis were insufferable bastards, Italians from the old country who refused to surrender to the ways of America. They were brutal, even though they were not nearly as powerful as the King family. However, the blood that was spilled in the streets because of the battles was becoming an issue. My father confronted the Vendetti Don, determined to come to some form of peace."

As I listened to the story, a powerful sense of knowing settled in.

"A deal was proposed. Vendetti's daughter would be betrothed to the eldest son of the King family." He laughed, finally able to look me in the eyes. "As you might imagine, I was not happy with my father's decision. I even refused to accept the deal made. I learned the hard way that daring to defy my father was not in my best interest. So, we were married and an all-out war was prevented."

"No wonder you tried to force me into an arranged marriage."

He exhaled, the sound rattled. "I was wrong, very wrong."

"Why are you telling me this now?"

"Because I do not believe in coincidences, but I do believe in karma."

"Riddles, Pops. What the fuck are you talking about?"

He took a deep breath before continuing, the rattled sound more troubling than it had been just the day before. "The patriarch of the Vendetti family was Endrigo. Endrigo Vendetti. Enrique Vendez."

I took a step back, sucking in my breath. "Why would a member of the Vendetti family be coming after us?" When he didn't answer, I smashed my hand on his desk again. "Why?"

"Because my father didn't keep the end of the bargain and neither did I. That period of time was difficult. The economy was horrible, the recent hurricanes making life in New Orleans demanding. Tensions were high, tempers even more so. When my father believed the Vendettis had moved into our turf, taking what few profits we had, he reacted, killing two of Teresa's brothers. In turn, your grandfather was murdered in cold blood in the middle of a restaurant, several of his Capos as well. I was thrust into becoming the leader of this family when I was only twenty-three."

As everything started to come together, I felt an odd calm settling into my system.

"There was so much blood in the streets, so many deaths. I had a wife and a baby to take care of, another on the way. I had no sense of the loyalty within our ranks and so I reacted badly, assigning hits to every important member of the Vendetti family. And yes, your mother was horrified, even catatonic as one by one members of her family were murdered. If it hadn't been for you, then your brother, I don't think she would have survived." He continued to shake, his face paling.

And for the first time that I could remember seeing, there were tears in his eyes.

"I killed them all, with one exception. One. The youngest son. He fled New Orleans before my men had a chance to find him."

Joseph had suspected and he'd kept my father's secret.

"His name?"

He handed me the envelope, locking eyes with mine. "Enrico. This is the last picture I have of him. I have no doubt he is capable of retaliation. I tracked him for years. I knew he'd at least made contact with the Morales Cartel, but then he disappeared."

"And Enrique Vendez suddenly appeared."

"Yes, but I didn't hear that name until recently. The last thing he said to me all those years ago was that revenge would be sweet." He inched closer, now appearing to be a weak man.

As the damning news settled in, I could no longer think clearly. I tore open the envelope, staring at the black and white photo of a young man, a man who would be my father's age now. There was something about the face that I recognized. Then I realized that Enrico's reign of terror on my family had begun with Bella all those years ago. My body began to shake. "You allowed Bella to be killed for something you did. You allowed my baby sister to be murdered because of your anger." I reached across the desk, wrapping my hand around his throat.

He made a choking noise, but not from my actions. From the tears flowing down his face.

At that moment, I realized that I could no longer remain the monster I'd allowed myself to become. Slowly, I dropped my hand, retreating with the picture still in my fingers. "You should have told me. You almost cost me everything, old man. For that, I will never forgive you."

As I stormed toward the door, I stopped long enough to take a deep breath and issue one last statement. "I am well aware of Mario's gambling problem, Pops. Now I know what I have to do."

Once again, blood would be shed in the streets of New Orleans.

Like father. Like son.

* * *

Enrico Vendetti. As soon as the name was released, several of our informants disappeared, likely sequestering themselves from the violence about to occur. It was only a matter of time before the man would be found.

And I would be the one ending the vendetta that had gone on for far too long.

I stood in my office, staring out the window as I'd done so many times during the years. My father had called me a wanderer, a dreamer, and a man incapable of putting down roots. Maybe that had been the case before, but the thought of a quiet life, a house filled with laughter was forefront in my mind.

Although I wasn't certain that would ever happen.

I heard the footsteps and didn't bother turning around, merely taking a deep breath. While I'd never brought a lowlife into my house nor had I ever attempted to dole out any form of punishment, I felt a strange need to have the asshole fully comprehend why he would face the devil himself.

"Mr. King?" Dimitri asked, the formality almost giving me a smile. As I turned, the sight of Mario almost pushed me over the edge. He'd been roughed up, Dimitri no doubt enjoying taking out his own sense of anger on the man who'd betrayed us.

"Leave us, Dimitri. And if you will, bring Ms. Porter to my office."

Dimitri gave me a strange look before nodding and walking out.

Mario stumbled forward, his mouth sagging. One eye was swollen shut, his mouth bloodied from the recent beating. Sighing, the distaste in my mouth was another oddity.

"As I told you before, Mario, fucking with me isn't in anyone's best interest, especially from someone trusted by my family for years. Years." My voice rumbled in the room.

"I didn't betray you, Mr. King. I would never do that."

"Interesting. So you're trying to tell me that you didn't provide certain details of our organization to Enrico Vendetti, otherwise known as Enrique Vendez?"

He seemed genuinely confused, his good eye darting back and forth. "I swear on my sister's life that I didn't do that. I don't even know who he is."

"You expect me to believe that given the fact you owe almost two hundred thousand dollars in gambling loans?"

Mario coughed, taking gasping breaths. "I swear that I never sold any secrets. You don't know how good your father has been to me over the years. He's been like a father to me. I owe a lot of money but I'm paying it back. I sold my house in order to do so."

What a crock of shit.

"I should have known when you tossed Ms. Porter into that cage that I couldn't trust you."

Once again, he shook his head, walking even closer. "No. I tried to tell you that I didn't do that. I didn't toss her into that cage."

"He's not lying."

The sound of Emily's voice wasn't surprising, but her words certainly were. "You were blindfolded. You wouldn't know."

"Yes, I would. I heard their voices, Cristiano. The other asshole was horrible, groping me then hitting me when I fought back. This man refused to even come down into the basement." She was insistent, her face pinched.

I thought about what she was saying, turning my attention to my Capo. "When did Darren come to work for us?"

Dimitri narrowed his eyes. "Two years ago."

Two years. The timing was interesting.

"From where?" I asked, my tone more demanding.

"I don't know." Dimitri shook his head. "He volunteered to be on your temporary detail."

"I'm sure he did." I took a deep breath as I walked toward Mario. "If I'm made aware you had anything to do with betraying this family…" I allowed the words to linger.

"I swear, Mr. King," he said quietly. "Your family is very important to me."

And damn it if I didn't believe him.

"Find Darren."

Dimitri nodded.

When I heard the sound of my phone, I grimaced. Seeing my father's name appear on the screen did nothing but fuel the anger boiling inside of me.

"Now is *not* the time, Father."

There was nothing but silence on the other end of the phone for a full five seconds. Instantly, my hackles were raised. "Who the fuck is this?"

The laugh would have curdled the majority of men's blood. For me, it brought the need for vengeance into my soul.

"From what your father has told me, you've already figured it out."

"Enrico."

"Very good. At least your father confessed the truth. I'm certain his guilt has been weighing on him." Enrico laughed again.

"What do you want and what have you done with my father?"

"Nothing yet, which is why I suggest that you and I have a meeting."

I turned my attention to Dimitri, giving him a hard stare. "That's fine with me. I think we have a score to settle."

"Don't take too long, Cristiano. My patience is wearing thin."

I ended the call, throwing back my head and roaring. My patience was now gone. "Dimitri. Stay with Emily. Do not let her out of your sight."

"What the hell is going on, boss?" he asked, moving to flank Emily's side.

Her face was pinched, her eyes imploring. I gave her a loving look, longing to end this nightmare. "Enrico Vendetti has been found. He's threatening to kill my father."

"Jesus fucking Christ." As the Russian spewed hatred in his native tongue, I moved behind my desk, grabbing a second clip of ammunition. All the while, Emily watched my every move. I was surprised there was no horror in her eyes, only a concept of resignation as to the life she was prepared to live.

"Let me go with you, Mr. King," Mario implored. "Please."

I moved to Emily, cupping her face. "Everything will be all right." As I kissed her forehead, I heard her whisper words that would haunt me.

"Don't kill anyone, Cristiano. You aren't that man any longer."

But I was that man.

A monster.

A murderer.

I was also a son.

Sighing, I nodded. "Then you're going to need a weapon." Walking back to my desk, I pulled a second gun from a drawer, slapping in a round of ammunition. "But don't fuck with me."

"I won't, sir. That I promise you."

A promise.

An act of revenge.

An arranged marriage to save the peace.

Only one of which made any sense.

* * *

The house was quiet, not a sound to be heard. With Mario remaining behind, I walked toward the partially cracked door to my father's office, pushing it open with a single finger, waiting before walking inside.

The face was exactly as I remembered from all those years ago, the horrible day Bella was murdered.

Enrico had his arm around my father's neck, the barrel of his gun placed at my father's temple. I was able to recognize the face from the boy smiling in the picture. Age had been difficult for him, his once good-looking features morphing in a man hell bent on revenge.

"You're so much like your father," he said casually, his gaze ripping a hole through me.

"What do you want, Enrico? More blood?"

"You handle your business just like your father as well. That's good to know. What do I want? Peace. You see, your family murdered mine. I have no beautiful sister or loving brothers. I have no father to talk to. I also have no legacy to depend on."

Legacy.

I hated the word.

I walked closer, my Beretta firmly placed in both hands. "We can either end this peacefully or one of us is going to die."

He laughed, the sound full of bitterness. "I assure you that there will be blood spilled today, but it won't be mine."

"I'm curious. What did you think you were going to accomplish?" I was able to dart a quick glance out the window, able to see movement. My gut had told me that he wouldn't come alone.

"What did I hope to accomplish. Let me see," he said, pushing the barrel against my father with enough force my father moaned. His eyes held the kind of fear I'd never seen in them. "Oh, yes. Ruining your business. Taking back what your family stole from me. Returning to the city I loved."

"Through your connection with Carlos Morales."

Enrico's eyes opened wide. "You've been doing your homework. Good boy. I learned a lot from the fascist pig. I also gained enough connections to allow me to fund my love of business."

"And the woman? Was she a plant in your organization?" I had to know the truth about Emily.

He huffed, shaking his head. "The lovely blonde was merely a coincidence, but she proved to be very useful. Too bad your attorney managed to get you out of prison. I admit that I enjoyed watching you suffer on a daily basis." His laugh filled the space, adding another layer to my rage.

"You seem to underestimate my family," I said quietly, inching even closer, the action forcing Enrico to yank my father back another two feet.

"You shouldn't threaten me, Cristiano. You have no idea what I'm capable of."

"Oh," I said, chuckling under my breath. "I think I do. First, you started with my sister, then you murdered my brother's wife."

He laughed, the sound sending a chill down my spine.

I'd learned through my years that when business became personal, mistakes were always made. The second the sun was shadowed by movement, I ducked, my aim concentrated on Enrico's head.

As the explosion of glass permeated the room, I reacted, but not as quickly as Mario. When he bolted forward, everything seemed to go into slow motion, several shots shattering the windows. Everything moved into slow motion, the sight of the soldier who'd betrayed us something I would never forget.

Mario threw himself in front of the window, managing to get off several rounds as I rushed forward, taking aim while Enrico laughed and laughed.

Pop!

Blood spewed from Mario's chest and he was pitched backwards, but his spray of bullets had taken out the man who'd betrayed us. I turned my attention to Enrico, my father's eyes watching everything I did. When I gave a slight nod, my father jammed his elbow in Enrico's chest, managing to break free of the man's hold.

Pop! Pop!

Boom!

CHAPTER 18

Emily

Love.

Family.

Friends.

For most people, these were the three things that mattered the most. While wealth and power were certainly desirable for many, they meant nothing without a sense of joy, which only relationships could bring.

The last few days had been difficult, Cristiano remaining distant for the most part, although he'd held me tightly every night. While there were still soldiers surrounding the house, Cristiano had allowed me additional freedoms. In turn, he'd been forced to clean up the remainder of the mess created by a true monster.

Then again, everyone was capable of violence if it meant protecting their loved ones.

While I couldn't understand every aspect of the revenge Enrico Vendetti had inflicted, it was clear that his years of planning had almost destroyed the entire family.

Secrets and lies.

Everyone had them.

The day was beautiful; bright sun in the sky, wispy clouds and even a light breeze to squelch part of the humidity. I'd ventured to the small garden near the pool, a place I'd visited several times, weeding the bed until the flowers were allowed to breathe. I felt a sense of accomplishment, a moment of pride as I eased back onto my knees.

"Grow and thrive," I said in passing, my heart still heavy. I had no idea what to expect any longer. I'd caught several news reports, the prosecuting attorney more interested in Enrico Vendetti's criminal activities, the drugs he'd brought into the city. Griffin Williams beamed in front of the cameras, taking credit for capturing a notorious criminal when Enrico had been delivered to the man's doorstep by Cristiano.

The irony was amusing.

One of his former soldiers had been killed during the attack on Cristiano's father, the very man who'd been betraying the entire family for two years. At least I hadn't been told about any of the gruesome details. Things were much quieter.

Except that Cristiano's fate still hung in the balance because I was still alive.

The thought was never far from my mind.

I smiled when I sensed him, my heart palpitating. When Cristiano hunkered down beside me, staring at the flowers, another moment of longing crept into my system. He'd spared Enrico's life. Maybe because I'd asked him to or maybe because he was trying to become a better man.

"Beautiful," he said softly.

"Yes, they are."

"I was talking about you."

I felt a blush creeping up from my neck, the same as always when he complimented me. "I didn't expect to see you."

"I wanted to talk to you."

I turned to face him and as he took my hand into his, pulling me to a standing position, I could see a pained look in his eyes. "What's wrong?"

He took his time rubbing my fingers before pulling my hand to his lips, kissing my knuckles. "Nothing is wrong."

"How is Mario?"

"He's a tough man. While his road to recovery will take some time, he should make a full one."

"And Nick?"

When he pointed behind him, I tipped my head, happy to see the grinning blond standing near the door. "He's earned his promotion in spades."

"I'm so glad."

"You are such an amazing woman."

"I'm just me, Cristiano."

He was silent for a few seconds, returning his attention to the flowers, whatever burden was on his mind weighing heavily.

"I'm not a good man, Emily. I'm not certain I ever will be, but I intend on changing some things. Maybe too little too late, but it's important to me."

"I can tell you're already changing."

After taking a deep breath, he lowered our hands, still keeping his grip. "I was wrong in taking you from your life. I know my apology can't mean very much, but it wasn't fair to you. You did nothing wrong. I'm the monster and I certainly will understand if you call the authorities."

"I was wrong for calling you a monster. There's no reason to talk to the authorities. I've learned a lot about you as well as myself over the last week. Sometimes, you have to look beyond the obvious, peeling away the layers in order to find the diamond inside. You're a kind, decent man who lost his way. You've suffered in order to protect your family and those you care about, and you do care about them tremendously, including the men who work for you."

I knew he'd never completely change, but I couldn't stand the thought of living without him.

"Well, you helped me discover what's important, the joys that exist, things I never knew were possible."

"What are you trying to tell me, Cristiano?"

"I'm trying to say that I'm releasing you from my insane obligation and demands. While you may be called to testify at the new trial, I refuse to alter your life any longer. You allowed me a chance to experience life. For that, I'll always be grateful."

"I don't understand."

"I think you do. You're free to go. I don't believe you'll be in any danger since Enrico and the men working for him have been arrested. However, I'll make sure that no one bothers you."

"Why are you doing this?"

"Why?" he repeated, a thoughtful look crossing his face. "Because I love you. I think I loved you from the first moment I laid eyes on your picture. But sometimes love isn't enough." He leaned forward, kissing my forehead. "I will make good on my promise to provide some money. It would seem your boss was in on Enrico's plan all along. I don't think you're going to have a job any longer. You can stay as long as you like, but Dimitri is prepared to take you home whenever you are ready. Just know you will always be in my heart."

The shock of his words kept me from finding anything to say, but when he walked away, his shoulders slumped, there was no doubt how I felt any longer.

"Wait. Please wait. I love you, Cristiano. I would be happy to become your wife." As I walked toward him, he slowly turned to face me. No longer was there coldness in his eyes.

They glimmered from happiness as well as love.

* * *

The knock on the door was sharp and unexpected.

Angelique lifted her eyebrows, waving her hand to force me into another part of the room. Cristiano's sister had been a godsend the last few days of preparations, becoming another friend as well as a bridesmaid.

Julia shook her head and moved in front of me in her usual protective mode.

"Stop," I hissed, although I had to admit that I loved their attention.

When Angelique opened the door, she growled in exactly the same way as her brother. "You can't come in."

"Like hell I can't." Cristiano's booming voice gave me a smile, my entire body trembling. "She is going to be my wife, which give me certain privileges. Now, give us a few minutes."

"Thank God she's not in her dress yet," Angelique admonished. "That's bad luck, dear brother of mine. Come on, Julia. I think the three of us are going to need some champagne."

I laughed as they left the room, my heart fluttering. The sight of him in a tuxedo took my breath away while I remained in a white slip, the beautiful silk just another present from the man I adored.

"What are you doing here?" I asked coyly.

He locked the door before advancing, taking me into his arms. "There is a family tradition that must be adhered to."

"A family tradition, huh? I wonder what that is?"

The grin on his face reminded me of a little boy, full of joy.

As well as love.

"Absolutely. And you know how traditions go." He pulled me toward the vanity, standing behind me as we gazed at our reflection. "We make a nice-looking couple."

"Imagine what our children will look like."

For the first time, I noticed a slight blush on his face, which brought me a smile.

"Now, down to business."

When he leaned me over the vanity, yanking my gown around my waist, I groaned. "What are you doing?"

"First, I'm checking to see if you've remained obedient."

When he twisted the plug back and forth, my legs trembled.

"Good girl." He hummed as he picked up the wooden brush, twirling it several times. "A pre-wedding spanking. All bad girls need that."

"That's not a tradition!" I yelped as he brought the brush down several times, moving from side to side. The pain was biting, my legs quivering instantly. "Ouch!"

"Long overdue and needed," he commented, issuing several more swats in rapid succession.

"This isn't fair."

"All if fair in love and… war." Laughing, he rubbed his hand over my already aching bottom before starting again, the thudding sound as difficult to bear as the anguish that continued to build.

I kept my eyes on the mirror, still able to smile as the hard spanking continued. I knew this was only the start of a routine. He was even more dominating, reminding me that there would be rules.

But I also knew there would be love in our household, even if we faced danger on a regular basis.

Cristiano continued humming as he swatted me several more times, making certain he smacked my sit spot repeatedly. I would have trouble sitting comfortably at the reception.

"Five more. Why don't you count them off for me? Oh, and remember to provide that level of respect we've been talking about."

I gritted my teeth as he cracked the brush on my buttocks even harder, waiting for my response.

"One, sir," I moaned, resisting giving him a nasty look.

He gave another.

"Two. Sir."

Whistling, he delivered a third.

"Three. Sir!"

"You're doing very well," he whispered then brought the brush down again.

"Four… sir."

"And one more."

The last smack was the worst, forcing me to lean over the vanity, taking several deep breaths. "Five. *Sir*." The defiance in my voice was unstoppable.

"Such a little brat. I adore that about you." His grin was even wider. He was enjoying the hell out of this. Damn him.

He pulled me into his arms, turning me around to face him. "I have two more presents for you."

I rubbed my behind, wrinkling my nose.

His laugh sent a series of vibrations dancing through me. The white box had a simple red bow around it. I eagerly pulled the string and yanked off the lid, smiling at the sight of pink tissue paper. After moving it aside, I groaned, pulling the sterling silver anal plug into my fingers.

"Do you see the jeweled end?" he asked, his tone full of mischief.

"Uh-huh. I mean, yes, sir."

"That's a real ruby. I had it crafted for you."

I wasn't certain how I felt about it. All I could do was giggle.

When he eased a small velvet box into the light, a shiver trickled down my spine. "I almost forgot this."

My hand shaking, I struggled to open the little box.

The ring was the most beautiful thing I'd ever seen, the diamond spectacular.

Gasping, tears formed in my eyes.

He took my hand, his eyes twinkling. As he placed the ring on my finger, I heard him say the words that would always make me swoon.

"I love you, little flower. You are my life."

* * *

While every little girl dreamt of their perfect wedding, I'd never expected that I'd have such joy in my heart as I walked down the aisle. The day was perfect, much like the one I'd shared with him in the garden.

Bright blue skies.

A light breeze.

Amazing music.

Exquisite white and sterling silver roses in my arms.

The most gorgeous dress.

And the love of a dangerous yet amazing man.

While life would never be easy or perfect, I was determined that my knight in shining armor would keep the joy in his heart.

And I knew that sweet Bella was watching from heaven, her love imbedded in his heart.

The End

AFTERWORD

Stormy Night Publications would like to thank you for your interest in our books.

If you liked this book (or even if you didn't), we would really appreciate you leaving a review on the site where you purchased it. Reviews provide useful feedback for us and our authors, and this feedback (both positive comments and constructive criticism) allows us to work even harder to make sure we provide the content our customers want to read.

If you would like to check out more books from Stormy Night Publications, if you want to learn more about our company, or if you would like to join our mailing list, please visit our website at:

http://www.stormynightpublications.com

BOOKS OF THE MAFIA MASTERS SERIES

His as Payment

Caroline Hargrove thinks she is mine because her father owed me a debt, but that isn't why she is sitting in my car beside me with her bottom sore inside and out. She's wet, well-used, and coming with me whether she likes it or not because I decided I want her, and I take what I want.

As a senator's daughter, she probably thought no man would dare lay a hand on her, let alone spank her thoroughly and then claim her beautiful body in the most shameful ways possible.

She was wrong. Very, very wrong. She's going to be mastered, and I won't be gentle about it.

Taken as Collateral

Francesca Alessandro was just meant to be collateral, held captive as a warning to her father, but then she tried to fight me. She ended up sore and soaked as I taught her a lesson with my belt and then screaming with every savage climax as I taught her to obey in a much more shameful way.

She's mine now. Mine to keep. Mine to protect. Mine to use as hard and as often as I please.

Forced to Cooperate

Willow Church is not the first person who tried to put a bullet in me. She's just the first I let live. Now she will pay the price in the most shameful way imaginable. The stripes from my belt will teach her to obey, but what happens to her sore, red bottom after that will teach the real lesson.

She will be used mercilessly, over and over, and every brutal climax will remind her of the humiliating truth: she never even had a chance against me. Her body always knew its master.

Claimed as Revenge

Valencia Rivera became mine the moment her father broke the agreement he made with me. She thought she had a say in the matter, but my belt across her beautiful bottom taught her otherwise and a night spent screaming her surrender into the sheets left her in no doubt she belongs to me.

Using her hard and often will not be all it takes to tame her properly, but it will be a good start…

Made to Beg

Sierra Fox showed up at my door to ask for my protection, and I gave it to her… for a price. She belongs to me now, and I'm going to use her beautiful body as thoroughly as I please. The only thing for her to decide is how sore her cute little bottom will be when I'm through claiming her.

She came to me begging for help, but as her moans and screams grow louder with every brutal climax, we both know it won't be long before she begs me for something far more shameful.

MORE MAFIA ROMANCES BY PIPER STONE

Caught

If you're forced to come to an arrangement with someone as dangerous as Jagger Calduchi, it means he's about to take what he wants, and you'll give it to him… even if it's your body.

I got caught snooping where I didn't belong, and Jagger made me an offer I couldn't refuse. A week with him where his rules are the only rules, or his bought and paid for cops take me to jail.

He's going to punish me, train me, and master me completely. When he's used me so shamefully I blush just to think about it, maybe he'll let me go home… or maybe he'll decide to keep me.

Ruthless

Treating a mobster shot by a rival's goons isn't really my forte, but when a man is powerful enough to have a whole wing of a hospital cleared out for his protection, you do as you're told.

To make matters worse, this isn't first time I've met Giovanni Calduchi. It turns out my newest patient is the stern, sexy brute who all but dragged me back to his hotel room a couple of nights ago so he could use my body as he pleased, then showed up at my house the next day, stripped me bare, and spanked me until I was begging him to take me even more roughly and shamefully.

Now, with his enemies likely to be coming after me in order to get to him, all I can do is hope he's as good at keeping me safe as he is at keeping me blushing, sore, and thoroughly satisfied.

Dangerous

I knew Erik Chenault was dangerous the moment I saw him. Everything about him should have warned me away, from the scar on his face to the fact that mobsters call him Blade. But I was drawn like a moth to a flame, and I ended up burnt… and blushing, sore, and thoroughly used.

Now he's taken it upon himself to protect me from men like the ones we both tried to leave in our past. He's going to make me his whether I like it or not… but I think I'm going to like it.

Prey

Within moments of setting eyes on Sophia Waters, I was certain of two things. She was going to learn what happens to bad girls who cheat at cards, and I was going to be the one to teach her.

But there was one thing I didn't know as I reddened that cute little bottom and then took her long and hard and oh so shamefully: I wasn't the only one who didn't come here for a game of cards.

I came to kill a man. It turns out she came to protect him.

Nobody keeps me from my target, but I'm in no rush. Not when I'm enjoying this game of cat and mouse so much. I'll even let her catch me one day, and as she screams my name with each brutal climax she'll finally realize the truth. She was never the hunter. She was always the prey.

Given

Stephanie Michaelson was given to me, and she is mine. The sooner she learns that, the less often her cute little bottom will end up well-punished and sore as she is reminded of her place.

But even as she promises obedience with tears running down her cheeks, I know it isn't the sting of my belt that will truly tame her. It is what comes next that will leave her in no doubt she belongs to me. That part will be long, hard, and shameful… and I will make her beg for all of it.

Dangerous Stranger

I came to Spain hoping to start a new life away from dangerous men, but then I met Rafael Santiago. Now I'm not just caught up in the affairs of a mafia boss, I'm being forced into his car.

When I saw something I shouldn't have, Rafael took me captive, stripped me bare, and punished me until he felt certain I'd told him everything I knew about his organization… which was nothing at all. Then he offered me his protection in return for the right to use me as he pleases.

Now that I belong to him, his plans for me are more shameful than I could have ever imagined.

Indebted

After her father stole from me, I could have left Alessandra Toro in jail for a crime she didn't commit. But I have plans for her. A deal with the judge—the kind only a man like me can arrange—made her my captive, and she will pay her father's debt with her beautiful body.

She will try to run, of course, but it won't be the law that comes after her. It will be me.

The sting of my belt across her quivering bare bottom will teach Alessandra the price of defiance, but it is the far more shameful penance that follows which will truly tame her.

Taken

When Winter O'Brien was given to me, she thought she had a say in the matter. She was wrong.

She is my bride. Mine to claim, mine to punish, and mine to use as shamefully as I please. The sting of my belt on her bare bottom will teach her to obey, but obedience is just the beginning.

I will demand so much more.

BOOKS OF THE CLUB DARKNESS SERIES

Bent to His Will

Even the most powerful men in the world know better than to cross me, but Autumn Sutherland thought she could spy on me in my own club and get away with it. Now she must be punished.

She tried to expose me, so she will be exposed. Bare, bound, and helplessly on display, she'll beg for mercy as my strap lashes her quivering bottom and my crop leaves its burning welts on her most intimate spots. Then she'll scream my name as she takes every inch of me, long and hard.

When I am done with her, she won't just be sore and shamefully broken. She will be mine.

Broken by His Hand

Sophia Russo tried to keep away from me, but just thinking about what I would do to her left her panties drenched. She tried to hide it, but I didn't let her. I tore those soaked panties off, spanked her bare little bottom until she had no doubt who owns her, and then took her long and hard.

She begged and screamed as she came for me over and over, but she didn't learn her lesson...

She didn't just come back for more. She thought she could disobey me and get away with it.

This time I'm not just going to punish her. I'm going to break her.

Bound by His Command

Willow danced for the rich and powerful at the world's most exclusive club... until tonight.

Tonight I told her she belongs to me now, and no other man will touch her again.

Tonight I ripped her soaked panties from her beautiful body and taught her to obey with my belt.

Tonight I took her as mine, and I won't be giving her up.

BOOKS OF THE DANGEROUS BUSINESS SERIES

Persuasion

Her father stole something from the mob and they hired me to get it back, but that's not the real reason Giliana Worthington is locked naked in a cage with her bottom well-used and sore.

I brought her here so I could take my time punishing her, mastering her, and ravaging her helpless, quivering body over and over again as she screams and moans and begs for more.

I didn't take her as a hostage. I took her because she is mine.

Bad Men

I thought I could run away from the marriage the mafia arranged for me, but I ended up held prisoner in a foreign country by someone far more dangerous than the man I tried to escape.

Then Jack and Diego came for me.

They didn't ask if I wanted to be theirs. They just took me.

I ran, but they caught me, stripped me bare, and punished me in the most shameful way possible.

Now they're going to share me, and they're not going to be gentle about it.

BOOKS OF THE MONTANA BAD BOYS SERIES

Hawk

He's a big, angry Marine, and I'm going to be sore when he's done with me.

Hawk Travers is not a man to be trifled with. I learned that lesson in the hardest way possible, first with a painful, humiliating public spanking and then much more shamefully in private.

She came looking for trouble. She got a taste of my belt instead.

Bryce Myers pushed me too far and she ended up with her bottom welted. But as satisfying as it is to hear this feisty little reporter scream my name as I put her in her place, I get the feeling she isn't going to stop snooping around no matter how well-used and sore I leave her cute backside.

She's gotten herself in way over her head, but she's mine now, and I protect what's mine.

Scorpion

He didn't ask if I like it rough. It wasn't up to me.

I thought I could get away with pissing off a big, tough Marine. I ended up with my face planted in the sheets, my burning bottom raised high, and my hair held tightly in his fist as he took me long and hard and taught me the kind of shameful lesson only a man like Scorpion could teach.

She was begging for a taste of my belt. She got much more than that.

Getting so tipsy she thought she could be sassy with me in my own bar earned Caroline a spanking, but it was trying to make off with my truck that sealed the deal. She'll feel my belt across her bare backside, then she'll scream my name as she takes every single inch of me.

This naughty girl needs to be put in her place, and I'm going to enjoy every moment of it.

Mustang

I tried to tell him how to run his ranch. Then he took off his belt.

When I heard a rumor about his ranch, I confronted Mustang about it. I thought I could go toe to toe with the big, tough former Marine, but I ended up blushing, sore, and very thoroughly used.

I told her it was going to hurt. I meant it.

Danni Brexton is a hot little number with a sharp tongue and a chip on her shoulder. She's the kind of trouble that needs to be ridden hard and put away wet, but only after a taste of my belt.

It will take more than just a firm hand and a burning bottom to tame this sassy spitfire, but I plan to keep her safe, sound, and screaming my name in bed whether she likes it or not. By the time I'm through with her, there won't be a shadow of a doubt in her mind that she belongs to me.

Nash

When he caught me on his property, he didn't call the police. He just took off his belt.

Nash caught me breaking into his shed while on the run from the mob, and when he demanded answers and obedience I gave him neither. Then he took off his belt and taught me in the most shameful way possible what happens to naughty girls who play games with a big, rough Marine.

She's mine to protect. That doesn't mean I'm going to be gentle with her.

Michelle doesn't just need a place to hide out. She needs a man who will bare her bottom and spank her until she is sore and sobbing whenever she puts herself at risk with reckless defiance, then shove her face into the sheets and make her scream his name with every savage climax.

She'll get all of that from me, and much, much more.

BOOKS OF THE ALPHA BEASTS SERIES

King's Mate

Her scent drew me to her, but something deeper and more powerful told me she was mine. Something that would not be denied. Something that demanded I claim her then and there.

I took her the way a beast takes his mate. Roughly. Savagely. Without mercy or remorse.

She will run, and when she does she will be punished, but it is not me that she fears. Every quivering, desperate climax reminds her that her body knows its master, and that terrifies her.

She knows I am not a gentle king, and she will scream for me as she learns her place.

Beast's Claim

Raven is not one of my kind, but the moment I caught her scent I knew she belonged to me.

She is my mate, and when I claim her it will not be gentle. She can fight me, but her pleas for mercy as she is punished will soon give way to screams of climax as she is mounted and rutted.

By the time I am finished with her, the evidence of her body's surrender will be mingled with my seed as it drips down her bare thighs. But she will be more than just sore and utterly spent.

She will be mine.

Alpha's Mate

I didn't ask Nicolina to be my mate. It was not up to her. An alpha takes what belongs to him.

She will plead for mercy as she is bared and punished for daring to run from me, but her screams as she is claimed and rutted will be those of helpless climax as her body surrenders to its master.

She is mine, and I'm going to make sure she knows it.

MORE STORMY NIGHT BOOKS BY PIPER STONE

Claimed by the Beasts

Though she has done her best to run from it, Scarlet Dumane cannot escape what is in store for her. She has known for years that she is destined to belong not just to one savage beast, but to three, and now the time has come for her to be claimed. Soon her mates will own every inch of her beautiful body, and she will be shared and used as roughly and as often as they please.

Scarlet hid from the disturbing truth about herself, her family, and her town for as long as she could, but now her grandmother's death has finally brought her back home to the bayous of Louisiana and at last she must face her fate, no matter how shameful and terrifying.

She will be a queen, but her mates will be her masters, and defiance will be thoroughly punished. Yet even when she is stripped bare and spanked until she is sobbing, her need for them only grows, and every blush, moan, and quivering climax binds her to them more tightly. But with enemies lurking in the shadows, can she trust her mates to protect her from both man and beast?

Millionaire Daddy

Dominick Asbury is not just a handsome millionaire whose deep voice makes Jenna's tummy flutter whenever they are together, nor is he merely the first man bold enough to strip her bare and spank her hard and thoroughly whenever she has been naughty. He is much more than that.

He is her daddy.

He is the one who punishes her when she's been a bad girl, and he is the one who takes her in his arms afterwards and brings her to one climax after another until she is utterly spent and satisfied.

But something shady is going on behind the scenes at Dominick's company, and when Jenna draws the wrong conclusion from a poorly written article about him and creates an embarrassing public scene, will she end up not only costing them both their jobs but losing her daddy as well?

Conquering Their Mate

For years the Cenzans have cast a menacing eye on Earth, but it still came as a shock to be captured, stripped bare, and claimed as a mate by their leader and his most trusted warriors.

It infuriates me to be punished for the slightest defiance and forced to submit to these alien brutes, but as I'm led naked through the corridors of their ship, my well-punished bare bottom and my helpless arousal both fully on display, I cannot help wondering how long it will be until I'm kneeling at the feet of my mates and begging them take me as shamefully as they please.

Captured and Kept

Since her career was knocked off track in retaliation for her efforts to expose a sinister plot by high-ranking government officials, reporter Danielle Carver has been stuck writing puff pieces in a small town in Oregon. Desperate for a serious story, she sets out to investigate the rumors she's been hearing about mysterious men living in the mountains nearby. But when she secretly follows them back to their remote cabin, the ruggedly handsome beasts don't take kindly to her snooping around, and Dani soon finds herself stripped bare for a painful, humiliating spanking.

Their rough dominance arouses her deeply, and before long she is blushing crimson as they take turns using her beautiful body as thoroughly and shamefully as they please. But when Dani uncovers the true reason for their presence in the area, will more than just her career be at risk?

Taming His Brat

It's been years since Cooper Dawson left her small Texas hometown, but after her stubborn defiance gets her fired from two jobs in a row, she knows something definitely needs to change. What she doesn't expect, however, is for her sharp tongue and arrogant attitude to land her over the knee of a stern, ruggedly sexy cowboy for a painful, embarrassing, and very public spanking.

Rex Sullivan cannot deny being smitten by Cooper, and the fact that she is in desperate need of his belt across her bare backside only makes the war-hardened ex-Marine more determined to tame the beautiful, fiery redhead. It isn't long before she's screaming his name as he shows her just how hard and roughly a cowboy can ride a headstrong filly. But Rex and Cooper both have secrets, and when the demons of their past rear their ugly heads, will their romance be torn apart?

Capturing Their Mate

I thought the Cenzan invaders could never find me here, but I was wrong. Three of the alien brutes came to take me, and before I ever set foot aboard their ship I had already been stripped bare, spanked thoroughly, and claimed more shamefully then I would have ever thought possible.

They have decided that a public example must be made of me, and I will be punished and used in the most humiliating ways imaginable as a warning to anyone who might dare to defy them. But I am no ordinary breeder, and the secrets hidden in my past could change their world… or end it.

Rogue

Tracking down cyborgs is my job, but this time I'm the one being hunted. This rogue machine has spent most of his life locked up, and now that he's on the loose he has plans for me…

He isn't just going to strip me, punish me, and use me. He will take me longer and harder than any human ever could, claiming me so thoroughly that I will be left in no doubt who owns me.

No matter how shamefully I beg and plead, my body will be ravaged again and again with pleasure so intense it terrifies me to even imagine, because that is what he was built to do.

Roughneck

When I took a job on an oil rig to escape my scheming stepfather's efforts to set me up with one of his business cronies, I knew I'd be working with rugged men. What I didn't expect is to find myself bent over a desk, my cheeks soaked with tears and my bare thighs wet for a very different reason, as my well-punished bottom is thoroughly used by a stern, infuriatingly sexy roughneck.

Even though I should have known better than to get sassy with a firm-handed cowboy, let alone a tough-as-nails former Marine, there's no denying that learning the hard way was every bit as hot as it was shameful. But a sore, welted backside is just the start of his plans for me, and no matter how much I blush to admit it, I know I'm going to take everything he gives me and beg for more.

Hunting Their Mate

As far as I'm concerned, the Cenzans will always be the enemy, and there can be no peace while they remain on our planet. I planned to make them pay for invading our world, but I was hunted down and captured by two of their warriors with the help of a battle-hardened former Marine. Now I'm the one who is going to pay, as the three of them punish me, shame me, and share me.

Though the thought of a fellow human taking the side of these alien brutes enrages me, that is far from the worst of it. With every searing stroke of the strap that lands across my bare bottom, with every savage thrust as I am claimed over and over, and with every screaming climax, it is made more clear that it is my own quivering, thoroughly used body which has truly betrayed me.

Primitive

I was sent to this world to help build a new Earth, but I was shocked by what I found here. The men of this planet are not just primitive savages. They are predators, and I am now their prey…

The government lied to all of us. Not all of the creatures who hunted and captured me are aliens. Some of them were human once, specimens transformed in labs into little more than feral beasts.

I fought, but I was thrown over a shoulder and carried off. I ran, but I was caught and punished. Now they are going to claim me, share me, and use me so roughly that when the last screaming climax has been wrung from my naked, helpless body, I wonder if I'll still know my own name.

Harvest

The Centurions conquered Earth long before I was born, but they did not come for our land or our resources. They came for mates, women deemed suitable for breeding. Women like me.

Three of the alien brutes decided to claim me, and when I defied them, they made a public example of me, punishing me so thoroughly and shamefully I might never stop blushing.

But now, as my virgin body is used in every way possible, I'm not sure I want them to stop…

Torched

I work alongside firefighters, so I know how to handle musclebound roughnecks, but Blaise Tompkins is in a league of his own. The night we met, I threw a glass of wine in his face, then ended up shoved against the wall with my panties on the floor and my arousal dripping down my thighs, screaming out climax after shameful climax with my well-punished bottom still burning.

I've got a series of arsons to get to the bottom of, and finding out that the infuriatingly sexy brute who spanked me like a naughty little girl will be helping me with the investigation seemed like the last thing I needed, until somebody hurled a rock through my window in an effort to scare me away from the case. Now having a big, strong man around doesn't seem like such a bad idea…

Fertile

The men who hunt me were always brutes, but now lust makes them barely more than beasts.

When they catch me, I know what comes next.

I will fight, but my need to be bred is just as strong as theirs is to breed. When they strip me, punish me, and use me the way I'm meant to be used, my screams will be the screams of climax.

Hostage

I knew going after one of the most powerful mafia bosses in the world would be dangerous, but I didn't anticipate being dragged from my apartment already sore, sorry, and shamefully used.

My captors don't just plan to teach me a lesson and then let me go. They plan to share me, punish me, and claim me so ruthlessly I'll be screaming my submission into the sheets long before they're through with me. They took me as a hostage, but they'll keep me as theirs.

Defiled

I was born to rule, but for her sake I am banished, forced to wander the Earth among mortals. Her virgin body will pay the price for my protection, and it will be a shameful price indeed.

Stripped, punished, and ravaged over and over, she will scream with every savage climax.

She will be defiled, but before I am done with her she will beg to be mine.

Kept

On the run from corrupt men determined to silence me, I sought refuge in his cabin. I ate his food, drank his whiskey, and slept in his bed. But then the big bad bear came home and I learned the hard way that sometimes Goldilocks ends up with her cute little bottom well-used and sore.

He stripped me, spanked me, and ravaged me in the most shameful way possible, but then this rugged brute did something no one else ever has before. He made it clear he plans to keep me…

Auctioned

Twenty years ago the Malzeons saved us when we were at the brink of self-annihilation, but there was a price for their intervention. They demanded humans as servants… and as pets.

Only criminals were supposed to be offered to the aliens for their use, but when I defied Earth's government, asking questions that no one else would dare to ask, I was sold to them at auction.

I was bought by two of their most powerful commanders, rivals who nonetheless plan to share me. I am their property now, and they intend to tame me, train me, and enjoy me thoroughly.

But I have information they need, a secret guarded so zealously that discovering it cost me my freedom, and if they do not act quickly enough both of our worlds will soon be in grave danger.

Hard Ride

When I snuck into Montana Cobalt's house, I was looking for help learning to ride like him, but what I got was his belt across my bare backside. Then with tears still running down my cheeks and arousal dripping onto my thighs, the big brute taught me a much more shameful lesson.

Montana has agreed to train me, but not just for the rodeo. He's going to break me in and put me through my paces, and then he's going to show me what it means to be ridden rough and dirty.

Carnal

For centuries my kind have hidden our feral nature, our brute strength, and our carnal instincts. But this human female is my mate, and nothing will keep me from claiming and ravaging her.

She is mine to tame and protect, and if my belt doesn't teach her to obey then she'll learn in a much more shameful fashion. Either way, her surrender will be as complete as it is inevitable.

Bounty

After I went undercover to take down a mob boss and ended up betrayed, framed, and on the run, Harper Rollins tried to bring me in. But instead of collecting a bounty, she earned herself a hard spanking and then an even rougher lesson that left her cute bottom sore in a very different way.

She's not one to give up without a fight, but that's fine by me. It just means I'll have plenty more chances to welt her beautiful backside and then make her scream her surrender into the sheets.

Beast

Primitive, irresistible need compelled him to claim me, but it was more than mere instinct that drove this alien beast to punish me for my defiance and then ravage me thoroughly and savagely. Every screaming climax was a brand marking me as his, ensuring I never forget who I belong to.

He's strong enough to take what he wants from me, but that's not why I surrendered so easily as he stripped me bare, pushed me up against the wall, and made me his so roughly and shamefully.

It wasn't fear that forced me to submit. It was need.

Gladiator

Xander didn't just win me in the arena. The alien brute claimed me there too, with my punished bottom still burning and my screams of climax almost drowned out by the roar of the crowd.

Almost…

Victory earned him freedom and the right to take me as his mate, but making me truly his will mean more than just spanking me into shameful surrender and then rutting me like a wild beast. Before he carries me off as his prize, the dark truth that brought me here must be exposed at last.

Big Rig

Alexis Harding is used to telling men exactly what she thinks, but she's never had a roughneck like me as a boss before. On my rig, I make the rules and sassy little girls get stripped bare, bent over my desk, and taught their place, first with my belt and then in a much more shameful way.

She'll be sore and sorry long before I'm done with her, but the arousal glistening on her thighs reveals the truth she would rather keep hidden. She needs it rough, and that's how she'll get it.

Warriors

I knew this was a primitive planet when I landed, but nothing could have prepared me for the rough beasts who inhabit it. The sting of their prince's firm hand on my bare bottom taught me my place in his world, but it was what came after that truly demonstrated his mastery over me.

This alien brute has granted me his protection and his help with my mission, but the price was my total submission to both his shameful demands and those of his second in command as well.

But it isn't the savage way they make use of my quivering body that terrifies me the most. What leaves me trembling is the thought that I may never leave this place… because I won't want to.

Owned

With a ruthless, corrupt billionaire after me, Crockett, Dylan, and Wade are just the men I need. Rough men who know how to keep a woman safe… and how to make her scream their names.

But the Hell's Fury MC doesn't do charity work, and their help will come at a price.

A shameful price…

They aren't just going to bare me, punish me, and then do whatever they want with me.

They're going to make me beg for it.

Seized

Delaney Archer got herself mixed up with someone who crossed us, and now she's going to find out just how roughly and shamefully three bad men like us can make use of her beautiful body.

She can plead for mercy, but it won't stop us from stripping her bare and spanking her until she's sore, sobbing, and soaking wet. Our feisty little captive is going to take everything we give her, and she'll be screaming our names with every savage climax long before we're done with her.

PIPER STONE LINKS

You can keep up with Piper Stone via her newsletter, her website, her Twitter account, her Facebook page, and her Goodreads profile, using the following links:

http://eepurl.com/c2QvLz

https://darkdangerousdelicious.wordpress.com/

https://twitter.com/piperstone01

https://www.facebook.com/Piper-Stone-573573166169730/

https://www.goodreads.com/author/show/15754494.Piper_Stone

Printed in Great Britain
by Amazon